WHITE SUMMER

LUKE BITMEAD

Independent Book Publisher

Legend Press Ltd
13a Northwold Road, London, N16 7HL
info@legendpress.co.uk
www.legendpress.co.uk

Contents © Luke Bitmead 2006

First edition published May 2006.
This edition published June 2008

British Library Cataloguing in Publication Data available.

ISBN 978-1-9065580-2-4

Set in Times
Printed by J. H. Haynes and Co. Ltd., Sparkford.

Cover designed by Gudrun Jobst
www.yellowoftheegg.co.uk

Legend Press

Independent Book Publisher

FOR MY MOTHER...

OTHER WORKS BY LUKE BITMEAD:

HEADING SOUTH BY LUKE BITMEAD
AND CATHERINE RICHARDS
PUBLISHED MAY 2007

VISIT LUKE BITMEAD'S WEBSITE:
WWW.LUKEBITMEAD.COM

Chapter One

Okay, I thought. Okay. She's aiming for fashionably late. On a first date, girls do. It's accepted practice. Expected almost, like the spot on the side of your nose that arrives the day before, so large that it's in danger of closing the eye above it. I didn't have one of these. This made me nervous. Something else would go wrong then...

No... I shut this thought out. I pinned myself to the mental door marked 'upbeat' and tried to pick the lock.

I lit another cigarette and glanced at my watch. It was only nine-twenty-three. She'd got held up that was all, or was re-touching her nails, changing her outfit, checking her bum in the mirror – doing things only girls do.

To get my nerve up, I drank. First dates... they're not easy, are they? They're like learning to swim. You dive in and get on with it, splash about for the first couple of minutes, then break into a tentative doggy-paddle. Months later you hope to be doing a fluent crawl, or better yet a gentle breaststroke. If not, you sink without trace.

I refused to go under this time. The booze was going to doggy-paddle me through.

The waitress clip-clopped over. She was cute, chubby and heavily made-up. She looked like she worked behind the counter at The Perfume Palace.

"Do you want to order?" she said brightly. Her voice was clipped. She was destined for better than this. She could already have been dating a Coxwell Rogers, Peters-Farquhar or Slight Campbell. She was probably driving home in a Range Rover.

I asked for a pint.

"Your friend hasn't showed up then."

"Unless she's hiding under another table," I said, immediately regretting it. It was *so* hard to be funny when the nerves were jangling like sleigh-bells. It was taking all my concentration to make sure my voice didn't warble.

The girl laughed, presumably out of politeness.

"She'd be silly to stand you up."

"Why?" I was intrigued. This wasn't the common consensus.

"It's silly to stand anyone up. If you don't want to go out with someone, you should just say no when they ask."

I nodded without looking up. This was cold comfort. A frozen Hessian rug of it, brittle against my soft skin.

"I'm sure she'll come," she said, walking away. "She's just making you wait. Doesn't want to appear too keen."

"Yeah. Don't bet on it."

She'd stood me up once already. This was the second time of asking. Her way of making it up to me.

So, a first date, second time of asking. Was this therefore a second date? Had all the romance gone with the first no-show? Perhaps for her, but for me the stubble-field fire of passion was raging all the stronger, almost out of control.

I lent back in my chair. Blimey, I thought (I'd recently given up the word 'fuck'). Not content with blowing me out once, she was going for the double. And this time it was going to hurt twice as much, the inverse of the second stamp on the bollocks (which, if you're a girl, by the way, doesn't hurt nearly as much as the first).

I looked around the restaurant. Every table was full. Couples chatted and tasted each other's food. Parents guided their dribbling children through the menus. Waitresses went about their work with bored efficiency. And then there was me, the figure depicted in popular fiction as the saddest of all social 'groups': the lone drinker.

Only one table caused concern. The one behind me. Take a quiet night out, invert and magnify, and this was it. Behind me were kids who your mother might call 'trouble'. In short: a table of rugger lads.

I was doing my best to appear invisible but they were bound to spot me.

"Hey mate," a voice sounded over my shoulder.

I lit a cigarette from the one I'd only half-smoked. I kept my cool. The light was dim but I wished it was dimmer.

"Hey mate." The voice was deep, confident, no stranger to calling line outs and scrum tactics.

Reluctantly, I turned.

"How good looking is she?" said the voice. The face it came from was broad with a heavy chin and blue eyes.

I drew on my cigarette, acting casual.

"She's better looking than you."

The table rippled with laughter. Seven or eight throaty, super-masculine guffaws.

"Wouldn't be difficult. What's her name? Maybe we know her."

I pulled on my cigarette.

"Come on. You can tell us her name."

"Why do you want to know?"

"I told you. Maybe I know her."

"He's shagged most of the talent round here," said a fat, drunk friend. The flesh of his neck hung over the collar of his rugby shirt like a series of miniature beer bellies hanging over jeans. The table laughed again. "He might be able to give you some advice."

"Oh cool," I said, sitting back. "Has he ever given you any? I mean, has he? Given you advice on chicks?" (I wasn't sure if this is what rugger lads called girls these days, but no one raised

7

an eyebrow.) "Have you got lucky this year? This decade? This century?"

"Yeah, you drunk virgin," said a voice from the end of the table, appropriately Northern accented. "Poof!"

The following happened in slo-mo: the fat one, lunging forward to grab the guy's throat, missed and cartwheeled his pint. It bucked and sprayed like a kicked cat. The friend sitting opposite gaped at the advancing tidal wave for a second before scooting back on his chair, torpedoing into me. I went down (like many a political career) without dignity.

As I writhed and wept on the beer-wet wood, all I could hear was laughter and swearing. I grabbed my chair with unsteady hands and clenched my teeth. Pulling myself up, I came face to face with her. The girl of my dreams.

"Hi, Guy," she said, with an amused smile. "Don't get up."

The sport monkeys roared as one.

"Hi," I croaked, slumping back. "Pleased you could make it, finally…"

*****

"Ben," I'd said, some months previously. "Ben. I'm not joking. I've met the girl of my dreams."

Ben shrugged nonchalantly, something he often does in my company. I don't know if he does it in the company of others, but with me he does it plenty.

"Again?"

"Forget the others. This is it. This is... the one."

He put his head down and laughed into his pint. His double chin had turned into a tripler that year. Too many burgers. Too much take-out. He says he goes to the gym. He probably does and lies on the mats for an hour-long snooze, rousing only to view an attractive newcomer, her gym kit as yet unstained by sweaty workouts.

"I know I've said it before. But I was younger then. It was all about libido."

"And now?" he said, arching an eyebrow. "And now you're all grown up. You're looking for commitment, right?"

His tone was laced with sarcasm.

"You said it," I replied. And meant it. I wanted my days of bouncing Tiggerish from bed to bed to be over. They'd practically stopped as it was.

"So where is she?" he asked, looking around the pub. We were in The Old Bell. A lifeless, smoke-filled boozer. Always devoid of talent. Average age: sixty in the shade.

But it was my local. Like a nervous tick, or an odour problem – *it was mine*. It had a dart-board and a pool table and... it was the kind of pub where you could have a drink with a mate without the other punters conjecturing if you were queer.

"You're kidding, aren't you?" I said. "I don't move that quickly."

"If at all."

"What docs that mean?"

Ben sighed. He's known me since school and therefore he knows me.

"Half the time I come down here, you've got some girl lined up. It's always, 'next time you'll meet her, next time'. And she never shows up."

I lit a cigarette and offered Ben one. He refused. Currently given up. It won't last. It never does.

"Once or twice," I said, getting back to the conversation. "That may have happened once or twice."

Ben laughed. His big, friendly face creased, his eyes crinkled. "I can't remember the last time I came down here and you had a date."

"I've had dates in-between. You don't have to meet every girl I go out with."

But Ben was right. I'd been in Cirencester two years and never had a girlfriend. Oh.

Three or four times, I'd woken dry-mouthed and dazed to

find someone in bed next to me. Someone I'd had to rush out the back door without breakfast, very early, to avoid panicking the jumpy milkman. But I hadn't had a girlfriend. I hadn't related to anyone. I hadn't committed. Not for a long time.

"Go on then," Ben said. "Tell me."

So I told him. I found it difficult to describe her impressively enough. But I tried.

Ben sat back in his chair.

"So let me get this straight. The times you've seen her, she's had her hair tied back, she's been wearing jeans covered in paint..."

"Yeah."

"She's a bit Sloaney. Slim, but she's got boobs. You think. And her mouth might be dodgy."

"No, she's got big lips."

"What colour are her eyes?"

"Don't know."

"Hair?"

"Brown...ish. Mousy. Streaky. I don't know. Look, it's not all this that matters. It's the feeling I get when she walks in the door."

"Which is like what? A hard-on?"

"Like I'm going to pass out."

"That big a hard-on?"

"No. She takes my breath away. My heart hammers. You know what I mean, don't you? I feel sweaty."

Ben shook his head. "Sounds like flu. Or badly cut Speed. Do you think she fancies you?"

"Who can say? I think so."

"Why would she fancy you?"

"Why not?"

"Err...you work in a travel agent's."

"I'm practically the boss."

"You work in a travel agent's. You drive a piece of shit. You earn less than a student."

"I've just had a pay rise."

"You earn the same as a student. Are you a catch?"

"I'm not fat."

"Girls like fat. Makes them feel thin."

"I'm in trouble then. Unless she likes my personality."

"What – gibbering, obsessive wreck with no mates?"

"One mate. One fat mate who sells computers in London, supposedly earns a fortune, and has loads of sex."

"I *do* earn a fortune," he said, "and I do have loads of sex. Talking of which, how's that Filipino hooker?"

"Filipina," I said, stressing the 'a'. "She was a girl."

"What do you mean 'was'?"

"I mean she's moved out."

"So what happened to her?"

"How should I know? She moved out, okay. I never even spoke to her. Her life story as far as I know is: she lived in the flat below mine, she got shagged out and left."

"So who's moved in?"

"A weirdo who looks just like a goblin."

"A goblin?"

"Well," I said, feeling the doubt in his gaze, "yeah. He does."

"So where did he come from?"

"Somewhere else. I have no idea. He only moved in yesterday."

"What does he look like? I mean, what does a goblin look like?"

"Like this bloke. Small, crazy looking."

Ben smiled.

"You're so full of shit," he said. "Come on. Let's go to the Crown. There'll be some talent in there tonight. Maybe we'll pull."

"Maybe *I'll* pull."

I stubbed out my cigarette and we left.

At the Crown we got very, very drunk. Ben smoked. We didn't pull.

And when we got home, I swear my neighbour was prancing around a roaring bonfire, poking and waving a stick at the lawn.

"Yikes," said Ben, who was also attempting to launder his language. "He does look like a goblin. It's *Lord of the Rings*."

"Good versus evil," I replied wistfully, "it surrounds our lives."

"Yeah, like debt and death."

I shrugged and watched the man dance. He wasn't bad. I wondered idly if he was a heavy drinker.

Chapter Two

I'd worked at the Go Away Travel Centre for two years. It doesn't fulfil a life-long dream. We workers in the service industry don't choose these jobs. They choose us. We slide down the greased vine of ambition. We start at Prime Minister or pub landlord and free-fall until we find our level. This is my level. Flights and hotels.

I don't mind. I have the odd day off (just me and the hangover). I take holidays, but don't go anywhere interesting (I'm scared of flying; no, I'm not joking). I pretend to read intellectual novels (but they simply gather dust and pubes by the bed).

I'm not wild about my place of work, but it did me one big favour. For it was here, at the Go Away, that I met Daisy.

I remember I was flicking rubber bands at my co-worker Kate's cleavage (attractive and together, and that's just her breasts) when I heard a polite cough come from the other side of my desk. I hadn't even heard her come in.

I relinquished my stash of rubber bands and attempted a professional look. I found myself staring at a beautiful, if untamed, face; the dark eyes, the perky nose, the fine cheekbones and the sultry lips. I was immediately smitten. No, more than smitten. This was love, or at least mega-watt lust, at first sight. My heart stopped beating and then resumed, a little quicker. I looked down at my desk, as if kowtowing, then up again.

Raising my eyebrows in what I hoped was a cool and controlled way, I said, "And what can I do for you?"

"Malta," said the girl in her clipped, clear tone. "I need to go to Malta tomorrow. And sadly it's got to be as cheap as you can make it."

"Last minute flights tend not to be cheap," I said, though I didn't want to. I wanted to say she could have it for free. Or that I'd pay.

"I know, I know," she said apologetically, vaguely flustered, biting down on her plump lower lip. "God, I know. I'm sorry. I'm not usually this disorganised. It's..." She glanced at her watch. "Shit. I've got to be quick. What's the best price you've got?"

The girl's raw energy wafted over the desk as she leaned closer. My heart beat faster.

I scanned the booking system.

"When will you be returning?" I asked, squinting at the screen, almost unable to concentrate.

"I don't know exactly."

I told her she'd have to get a one-month return and I gave her the price.

She sighed, very sexily, and then looked pleadingly at me.

"It seems awfully expensive."

"Short-haul flights are. It's almost cheaper to fly to Asia. How about it?" I said. "Northern Thailand's nice this time of year. We could...I mean you could..."

She smiled.

"Thailand's tempting, but I need to go to Malta."

My heart rate notched up another few bpms. Did she mean us in Thailand? Oooh. I thought fast. I didn't want her to leave disappointed.

"I'll tell you what. If you've got time, I can phone the airline direct and see if they've had any last-minute cancellations. We might get you a cheaper deal that way."

She looked at her watch, mounted on a slender wrist, and bit her lower lip again.

"Yes, please," she said, getting her mobile out of her pocket. "I've got to make a call while you do that. I'll be back in a minute."

She got up off the seat and I watched her slender but shapely backside stride out onto the sun-drenched street.

I pretended to make a phone call. I could have called BA, but the system told me the cheapest seats on the flight were still available.

I held a seat on the flight and waited for her to return.

Kate threw a ball of paper at me. "Put your tongue back in your mouth."

"What?"

"You're all over her like a rash."

"I'm giving her my usual high level of customer service."

"Bollocks. Your normal service is one price – take it or leave it."

I frowned. Mock hurt. Daisy strode back in.

"Sorry about that," she said, looking more relaxed. "I've bought myself another fifteen minutes. Did you speak to the airline?"

I gave her the news.

She was happier but still not making a move to lean over the desk and kiss me hard on the mouth.

"I fly loads. All over the world. I promise I'll come back. I'll be a good customer. It's only this flight I need rock bottom. I don't normally. Normally I'm cool with any price."

I smiled knowingly and told her we could absorb the cost of the airport tax. "But that's as good as it gets."

"Good film," she said, with a smile. "Have you seen it?"

I nodded, blushed, and booked her ticket.

"Because you're flying tomorrow," I said, "you'll have to collect the ticket at Heathrow. I can't issue it here."

She looked concerned.

"It's no problem; we do it all the time. It's standard practice."

"If you're sure."

"Trust me."

She smiled wider, this time revealing her (usually private) lower teeth, along with the more casually exposed top set. This was progress.

"And that's it?"

"Apart from the money. Do you want to pay cash or card?"

She paid cash, flicking twenties off a roll of notes she produced from her back pocket.

"I hope you have a good holiday," I said.

"Actually it's work, but it should be fun." She glanced at her watch again. "Christ, I've got to go. Thanks so much for your help."

Getting up she noticed my stack of business cards.

"Oh, I'll take one of these," she said, picking one out with slender fingers. "Guy. That's you, right?"

"That's me."

"You've been brilliant. See you soon."

And with that she was gone. I watched her as she strode up the road into the cold, bright light. Then I looked at my screen. There was her name: 'DAISY WARNFORD'.

Whoa, I thought. What a beautiful name. Not the Warnford bit. The Daisy. I'd picked a Daisy. Ha! She was definitely the one.

Chapter Three

I barely watch TV. I know, I know. What am I thinking? It's the twenty-first century. There are a thousand channels. The TV guide is the size of the *Yellow Pages*. I could spend all day in front of it, but... TV? The fool's lantern. It's all repeats, isn't it? And even the stuff that isn't repeats are rip-offs of Seventies' shows. The only timc I switch on is for *The Simpsons* and sometimes *Top of the Pops*. And that's it. Oh, unless you count turning on the TV to watch a video, which I don't.

Kate and Debbie at work seem to have only one rule as regards television. When they're in, it's on. When they're out, it's not.

They watch every soap that's ever been aired. They also watch everything in-between, bar the news. Bar anything interesting.

This gives them a spectacular amount to natter about that doesn't involve me. I'm cool with this. But somehow they're not. They want my opinion on this, my view on that. They want me *involved*. Usually, I resist, claiming ignorance. But if anything happens at work, I'm stuck. I can't avoid it

So, Daisy. The new topic. Kate went on and on about her every day. It was clear she'd created her own soap opera. She watched them at home, so why not a *live* one at work? For Kate, it was perfect. For me, it was pure pressure.

It started from the moment Daisy left the shop.

"You terrible flirt!" she called from the opposite side of the office, our desks being in a U-shape with the customers surrounded in the middle, like penned-in sheep bleating for help.

I simply rolled my eyes. "Every time a good-looking girl comes in you say that."

"But you were at your best yet today. You were practically dribbling!"

"I was not."

"You were. Debbie? Wasn't he?"

"He was very attentive." She said this as if I wasn't there, and she sits next to me. Luckily, Carol, our boss, was out of the office at lunch and Ted was downstairs organising brochures or something. It didn't stop Kate telling him when he reappeared through the nylon curtain.

"Ted, you should have seen Guy. My God!"

I sat there and took it. Like Foreman vs Ali. The Rumble in the Jungle. There was no point denying it. Ted just smiled, said "So what?" and got on with some filing. I think he's still a virgin. He claims to have a girlfriend, but I've never met her. Nor has anyone else. He's very quiet, is Ted. If he were punctuation, he'd be parentheses, or a space. Something discreet.

Kate, on the other hand, is a double exclamation mark. When she started last year, she blew me away. I told Ben I'd met 'the one'. Natural blonde, aerobic-looking figure, usually clothed in tight-fitting, sweat-inducing garments. (My sweat, not hers.) Turned out she had a boyfriend. Shit.

When Carol got in it was the same. Kate carried on about me and Daisy. That girl has one hell of a big mouth on her.

"You wait until she comes back next month," she gasped at Carol. "You'll see I'm not lying. He was drooling at the mouth. Like a dog."

Carol laughed. "No harm in that, so long as it keeps the customer happy."

I flicked a 'V' sign at Kate. "I haven't seen you sell a bundle of flights today," I said. "Why don't you do some work, rather than spying on me?"

"And how much did you make on the flight you sold her?" she asked, eyebrows practically hitting her hairline.

"Not much."

"How much?"

"None of your business."

"I looked it up. You sold it to her for net; you didn't make a penny on it. And we can't deduct the tax."

Carol looked at me.

"I'm thinking of the future. She'll come back and then we'll make some money from her."

"Just so long as you do," Carol warned. "And I expect you to pay the tax."

"Of course," I said. "Chill out."

That night, back at the estate agent's worst nightmare, I cracked open a few cans of Stella and re-capped every part of my conversation with Daisy, trying to work out if she fancied me as much as I fancied her.

One or two things counted in my favour. She took my business card. She said my name with some shy emphasis. She said, "See you soon." My heart skipped every time I thought of that. "See you soon." It was the best 'see you soon' I'd ever received. I drank a few more cans of Stella thinking of the way she'd said it. Did she mean it, would we meet again, or was it just a phrase I'd distorted for my own benefit?

I gazed out of the window to ponder this crucial point. Below, in the night haze, I could see the guy next door preparing a fire. He really was a strange little fellow. And he looked just like a goblin, even Ben agreed. I drank and watched. He lit the fire and started prancing around it. I imagined Daisy and I dancing with him, and then (much better) without him, naked and free in a nicer, more private garden... with a swimming pool, gazebo, barbecue, cocktails... I receded from the window and into a complete reverie.

"Daisy," I said aloud. "You are definitely the one."

*****

I don't know what Daisy's month in Malta was like but my four weeks in Cirencester involved lost luggage, expired visas, missed (panic!) typhoid injections, double-booked hotels and delirious delays.

My job stuck to its well-worn routine, as did my body. The twin peaks of my existence were solid. Most people had a triumvirate of concerns – work, health, *love life*. Not me. I had no love life. It eluded me like a parking space eluded the white-knuckled London driver. It jinked past me like a frightened cat in a dark alley. It consistently sold me the dummy like George Best in his prime.

For the sake of symmetry, this was preferable. Two arms, two legs, two spots (one on my forehead, one on my arse)... two areas of anxiety. Two was enough, really. Two was...plenty.

So I had an okay month. Sold a load of flights, started sweating it in the gym with the other poor muscle-free souls (mostly so I could truthfully tell Daisy I went there) and got pissed every weekend. And most weekdays.

Ben came down at the start of spring. That's when I told him about Daisy.

I was desperate to see her again. But I also dreaded it.

As each day ended without her visiting, I felt sadness and relief. Sadness that she wasn't desperate to see me. Relief that I hadn't suffered the horror of trying to talk to her in front of my work colleagues.

But I missed her. And Kate didn't help. At least once a week she would say in a loud voice, so everyone could hear, "She hasn't come back then? The lovely Daisy. You must be losing your touch." Or, "You must be gutted, selling that flight at net and she still doesn't come back."

I ignored these jibes, busying myself with brochures or checking the special offers. Kate rarely let it go.

"No," I'd say. "Jesus, you're observant. I mean you should have been a spy or a detective, or something."

And she'd say, "Ooh. Tetchy," or, "I didn't realise you liked her that much," or, "You know if you're still thinking about her, she could be the one. She could be."

I'd nod distractedly and comfort myself with the thought that whereas I once fancied Kate, I could now see what a pain in the arse she was and actually pitied, rather than envied, her boyfriend.

Sometimes Kate would go too far and get the sharp tongue treatment from Carol. Then she would briefly shut up. Get her head down and look busy. She was scared of Carol, ever since the day she bawled her out for being rude to a customer.

Carol was good to work for but she wouldn't have anyone be rude to customers. To Carol the customer was 'King'. 'Top Dog'. 'It'. It was simple business practice. It didn't require a three-year BSc to work out.

But clearly this didn't work with Daisy. With Daisy, I couldn't have been more charming. And she hadn't come close to the Go Away again. She was the exception, as lecturers and teachers are liable to haughtily pronounce, that proves the rule.

"You've been away," I kept thinking, "now come back." I needed her. I needed to bask in the glow of her beauty once again. I craved her presence like a smoker craves cigarettes or a junkie craves junk. I wasn't getting it. And I was in withdrawal.

Between you and me, I'd adopted some very sad practices. So sad, I was scaring myself.

I was hanging out at places I thought she might show up. Pubs and coffee shops around town. DIY stores (you remember the paint on the jeans?) and (less likely) Natwest Bank. (I'd spotted a NatWest Visa in her wallet.) Not to mention the library, the gym, and all the usual places, like the park on a sunny day.

So in April and May I became a caffeine freak and an

alcoholic. I redecorated my flat three times, and opened two new savings accounts and a Current Plus Fast Track. Fast track to what, I didn't know.

I borrowed books from the library I never read. I paid to lift weights I couldn't lift. It was rarely sunny, and when the sky did brighten it was ice-cold and I got flu from being intangibly dressed in the park.

My life was in ruins. My obsession was killing me. And then she showed up. And it all got much, much worse.

Chapter Four

Spirits are not really my thing. I'm not talking about ghosts or apparitions. I'm talking about the hard stuff. Whisky, gin, vodka. I drink cans and cans of beer, bottles of wine. In the summer, Pimms and Martinis, champagne, but I try to stay off the liquor.

It's not that I don't like it. I'm a drinker. I like the strong stuff more than anything. That's why I don't touch it. Because if I do, it gets drunk by the half bottle.

In one of my kitchen cupboards I keep half-a-dozen bottles of red wine, at least twelve cans of Stella, two bottles of champagne (supermarket brand), and right at the back a bottle of vodka, a bottle of whisky and a bottle of ginger wine.

The stuff at the back is for emergencies.

Wednesday had been an appalling day. Yes, the customers of the Go Away were flying all round the globe, as they requested, but they all seemed to be heading for the wrong destinations. Carol was on her day off, Kate had PMT, and Debbie and Ted both seemed useless, or not interested.

At lunchtime, when I presumed nothing could get any worse, one of the low-cost airline's entire fleet decided to strike.

It was left to me to sort out the mess.

"Yes, Mrs Connor," I said to the old lady on the line, "I do appreciate you need to get to Dublin today; we are doing our

23

best to find you another airline. Can I put you on hold for a second?"

I jabbed at a button on the phone and slammed the receiver on the desk.

"Why can't she just swim there?" I wailed at no one in particular.

"I don't swim," came the crackling reply over the speaker phone. I'd hit 'hands free' instead of hold.

I couldn't apologise enough, but it didn't help. I was assured I would be reported to my superior in the morning.

At five o'clock, when it seemed the most likely outcome of the stress was to suffer a hernia, a regular and important client of mine rang to book a last-minute flight to New York. She had to leave the following morning. All of the flights and I mean all of the flights to New York were booked, except business class. She couldn't afford that. I kept trying, using the system to call the airlines. Eventually, just before six, I found a vacancy: flying from Stansted. I phoned to okay this with the client. It was not okay. It had to be Heathrow or Gatwick. It took me another half-hour to sort that out. And another hour to take care of all the other problems that had arisen, like the undead, during the day.

I got home at nine. The electricity was off.

"That's it," I muttered.

I fumbled my way to the kitchen and forced my hand to the back of the cupboard. It took me three attempts with the torch to get the right combination of bottles. When I found them, I ripped the tops off and threw them in the bin. Whisky and ginger wine.

I put my CD walkman on, lit a candle, slumped on the sofa and poured a drink.

"Cheers," I said, over the sound of hard rock crashing into my ears. "Goodbye day. Hello oblivion."

Much later, when I staggered up to piss in the sink, bladder on the brink of bursting its banks, I peered out of the kitchen window.

Below were the strawberry and mustard flames of a bonfire, and whirling round it a small, naked figure, softly playing a pipe.

The goblin, I thought, has had a bad day too.

*****

The next morning I woke half on, half off the sofa. My back a ricrac, or chicane. Bright sunshine slanted in through the half-closed shutters of the living room. My mouth felt as if some unknown tease had poured diesel into it and then filled it with charcoal. Looking at my watch, I saw it was nearly ten. This didn't bother me (I assumed it was Saturday), but as the chemistry in my brain remarried, I shot off the sofa like I'd been zapped by a cattle prod.

It wasn't Saturday; it was Thursday.

Ripping my shirt off, and hauling myself out of my trousers, I leapt into the shower. The electricity had been off all night. The water was stingingly cold. I expect they heard my screams in South Cerney.

I had no time to shave, organise my hair, or staunch the flow of effluvia from my pits. Ludicrously, on opening my wardrobe, I found no clean shirts. Not one. I had no choice but to re-use the one I'd slept in. My suit looked like a road accident.

"I am…" I said, as I downed a pint of water before heading for the door, "just… my own worst nightmare."

The timing of my arrival at work could not have been worse. If I'd arrived four hours late, it would have been better. As it was I arrived just as Carol said into her phone, "Yes, I do apologise. Again. And we will ensure this won't happen in the future… thanks. Yes, thank you for your call."

She put the phone down and looked at me the way a wife would look at her adulterous husband. With hatred, loathing, contempt.

"That was Mrs Connor," she said. "Mrs Connor who should be in Dublin at her friend's wedding, but is, in fact, in some second-rate hotel room in Stansted. I assume you have an explanation for this."

I bit my lip.

"For swearing at her over the phone... and for wandering in at ten-thirty looking like you've just been scraped off the pavement."

The office went dead silent. I've heard rowdier old peoples' homes on a Sunday afternoon after a heavy lunch.

I thought of saying, "Hey, but at least the sun's shining" with an Anne Robinson cheeky grin and wink, but fast realised this annoys anyone in their correct mind. Instead, I played it straight. I said, "My father phoned me at work late yesterday afternoon. My mother's taken a turn for the worse. He was stuck in London, so I went to see her. I ended up staying the night. That's why I'm late."

Kate coughed a muffled "bullshit" into her open palm. Carol fixed me with her most serious look.

"I understand your mother's ill," she said. "But... I think we need to have a little chat in the back office."

As boss and employee, Carol and I get along very well. She knows I work hard. She knows I do a good job, so she cuts me a bit of slack if I'm late or take a long lunch.

The one thing she won't stand for is lying.

In the back office, she said to me, hands on hips like a matron addressing one of her minions, "I'm going to give you one more chance to tell me why you were late and then I'm going to drop it. But I want the truth."

I took a deep breath and told her again. The same story. The same lie.

I didn't feel too bad. No one tells the truth now. Not with politicians lying every other word. Not in the 2000s: The Lying Odyssey.

You can't afford to tell the truth these days. If you did, you'd never get anywhere. You wouldn't get a job. You wouldn't get an overdraft, insurance, a loan for a car, sex... lying is a way of life.

She gave me a very hard look. It made beads of perspiration rise up on my forehead like tiny mushrooms in time-lapse photography.

She said, "I hope she gets better soon."

"Thanks. But I think getting better is out of the question. Staying about the same is the most we can hope for."

"Now about Mrs Connor."

I looked gauche. My breath became fricative. The lecture I got lasted fifteen minutes. The gist of it was: you're very good; you could go far; don't ruin it.

I nodded, agreed and looked chastened throughout. But I could barely hear what Carol was saying. The hum of my hangover was deafening in my ears.

"Now get out there, write a letter of apology and then get on with what you do best. Sell some flights."

I assured her I would and lurched back into the office, head down like a wounded bull, with no intention of doing anything but wallowing in self-pity for the rest of the day. And then dying.

As I began to feel the shakes coming on, the roaring DTs accompanied by head spin and dehydration, the door opened. Too-bright sunlight hit my desk and blinded me. Then she appeared, like an angel out of the transcendental haze... Daisy.

I plunged into a free-fall state of shock. I actually gripped the desk to steady myself.

She raised her eyebrows, easing herself gracefully into the seat opposite. My heart was lodged under my Adam's apple, attempting to climb into my mouth.

I croaked, "Hi," and then said hurriedly so I could get away and calm myself, "Would you like a cup of coffee? I'm having one."

"Oh," she said, surprised at the service (I think). "Thanks.

That would be... lovely."

I sprang off my chair and fled to the back office, flicking on the kettle and lighting a cigarette, all in one fluid movement.

I inhaled deeply, trying to calm myself. It didn't work. My heart hammered on as if I was about to give an unplanned half-hour speech to a packed concert hall the size of Wembley Stadium. On the perils of drink.

"Be cool," I whispered to myself, "be cool."

As I spaded the coffee into the cups, Kate idled in, fixing me with a hooded stare. Pure *femme fatale*.

"God, you've got it so bad," she said with near contempt. "It's embarrassing."

"I don't know what you're talking about."

"Look at your hands!" she said, as I splashed water over the Formica. "They're shaking like an old man's."

"That's because I'm hungover," I snapped, getting irritated. "I mean did you come in here for a reason? Or are you just intent on annoying the hell out of me?"

She put a hand on my shoulder and smiled.

"I'm only teasing," she said. "Actually I think it's quite sweet."

"Great," I said. "I'm so happy. Can you hold the door open for me? I need to get back out there without burning my hands."

Kate nodded and pulled the door open.

"Go get 'em," she said, rather too loudly, allowing the door to swing shut before I'd trickled through it, catching my elbow and nearly pirouetting me into the filing cabinet.

I tottered back to my desk, my nerves percussive in their throb and jangle.

"There you go," I said to Daisy's chest, not daring to look her in the eye, scared she'd see the desire there. "So how was your trip?"

I sat down and pushed my chair back so I could look at her; also far enough away so she wouldn't see the sweat or smell the whisky coming off me, like cartoon lines, above my aching

28

bonce. Then my chair got snarled in my computer cable and I nearly went over backwards, but luckily I only spilt half of my coffee. She laughed (with sympathy).

When she stopped, she said, "My time in Malta was very good, thank you."

"When did you get back?"

"Oh three, four weeks ago. Something like that."

I felt a twinge of... disappointment, jealousy, embarrassment? She'd been back all this time and hadn't come to see me?

"Anyway," she said, rubbing slender hands on clean, black combat trousers, which surely housed slender thighs, "I need you to book me another flight."

"That's what we're here for," I said, feeling used, taken advantage of. Like a hooker. "Where are we going to next?"

"Dublin. A holiday this time."

Cripes, I thought. Let's hope I don't do a Mrs Connor.

"Been before?"

"Never."

"You'll like it," I said, though I'd never been. "Beautiful city, lovely pubs, interesting museums."

"And the people?"

"Dublin's a city. With all that entails. You don't really get to meet that many people. You'd need to head out to the West Country for that."

"Oh," she said, looking disappointed.

"When would you like to go? The cheapest carrier is on strike at the moment. To be safe, I'd have to book you with BA. They won't be too much more expensive."

"That's fine." I noticed again the slight upturn of the nose. Very cute. "We'd like to go next week."

I busied myself with the booking system as I recovered from the shock of 'we'.

"Pick a day," I said, still looking at the screen. "They're all available."

It took some time for Daisy to decide when she wanted to fly out and when she wanted to return. I couldn't work out if she was trying to spend more time with me by dragging it out, or whether she was just naturally ditzy.

Once we'd agreed dates, I asked the dreaded question.

"Can you give me the name of the person you're travelling with?"

"Oh, yeah, that might help," she giggled. "The name's Oliver."

I choked on jealous bile.

"Claire Oliver."

Relief flooded my system. So much so I completely lost concentration and had to get her to repeat the name.

"You got it this time?"

I'd got it. "I had a bit of a heavy night last night. My head's pounding."

"Oh, where were you?" She sounded interested, like she had a busy social life. Wanted to know any good place to go.

I couldn't say at home getting pissed on my own, so I said, "I was at..." and then I felt Carol's eyes come up from her work and fix on me, so I stuttered, "I mean... sadly, I had to visit my mother who's not well. And I was up with her half the night."

"Oh dear." She looked genuinely concerned. "I hope it's nothing serious."

"Well, it's... under control. Most of the time."

The silence throbbed, like a submarine.

"Anyway. Do you want to come and collect your tickets, or shall I post them?"

"Ah." She thought about it. I considered either to be a good option. If she came in to collect them then I'd see her again. If she gave me her address, I'd know where she lived. I could find out what her local was and camp out there. *Live* there.

"I can probably come and get them, actually. When will they be ready?"

"Any time after two tomorrow."

"Okay, I might come in then. Or if not, Monday."

"Fine. Anything else I can do for you? Hotels, car hire?"

"No, we're staying with friends the first couple of days, then we're going to find B&Bs. Thanks anyway."

"No problem. How do you want to pay?"

She gave me a wad of cash. I felt like a thief taking her money. And then she was gone again.

"So the romance continues," said Kate, once the door had closed. "Is this going to be unrequited love?"

I raised an eyebrow.

"I mean if you don't ask her out, nothing's ever going to happen."

"You can't ask her out in here," said Carol. "It's unprofessional. You'll have to grab her off the street."

"I can't ask her out full stop. I can barely look her in the eye."

"Ah, how sweet," said Debbie.

"Chicken," said Kate.

Ted kept quiet. He was picking at a tuna sandwich.

"Besides, I haven't got time for a relationship," I said, heading for the loo. "I'm just too busy."

The office tittered at me.

I pissed in the bowl thinking that, with all the nerves and everything, I hadn't done too badly. At least I hadn't completely put her off.

Then I looked in the mirror. I had a bit of sleep in my right eye. It looked like a chunk of cheddar big enough to catch a large mouse, or even a rat. There was a whisky stain on my shirt, my hair was sticking up at the back like a greasy teepee and my teeth were as yellow as urine.

"You old charmer," I grimaced, and tried to sort myself out with loo roll and a nail brush.

It didn't work. I returned to work looking like Wurzel Gumage's half-brother. And not the better half.

Chapter Five

When I arrived home that evening, still feeling several fathoms below the sea level of 'good', there was a message on my answer phone. The red LED on the machine winked at me conspiratorially. I hit the play button.

"Guy," said the disembodied voice. "It's Mummy. Give me a call when you get in."

I'd planned to call my mother anyway. Whenever I use her as an excuse, I feel I have to. You see, she is ill. And not in a frivolous way. The doctors have never been quite sure what's wrong. It's serious, whatever it is. Sometimes she has to stay in bed for weeks. When I was at school, she often stayed in bed for months. She was worse then, but she's still not good now.

"Mother," I said, when I heard her pick up and give the last few digits of the number. "You called..."

"Oh, Guy, yes. How are you?"

"Hungover."

"Out last night?"

"Kind of." I didn't want to go into it. It would only upset her. "What did you want to speak to me about? I've been thinking about you. Are you okay, I mean, are you...?"

"I'm fine darling. We were wondering if you'd like to come to dinner?"

I asked when.

"We thought Friday, or Saturday, depending on what days you're working."

I suggested Friday.

"Lovely. I thought we'd do pheasant. It's been hanging around in the freezer since December."

I wasn't a great fan of pheasant, but anything was better than having to cook for myself. I succumbed.

"Daddy will be here," my mother said. "He's looking forward to seeing you."

I didn't reply.

"Are you okay?"

I said I was fine. I wasn't really. My mother sounded so weak it was upsetting.

"Are you okay?" I said back. "That's the important question. How are you?"

Now it was my mother's turn to fall silent. Eventually, she said, "We're looking forward to seeing you."

"Looking forward to seeing you too, Mum," I replied.

She said she had to go, I guess to lie down. I gave her my love and hung up.

The phone call over, I limped lazily to the kitchen, loosening the garrotte of my tie. I got a beer from the fridge, returned to the living room, and slumped, sloth-like, on the sofa.

What a life.

My mother was an angel and she'd been cursed with illness since I could remember. It wasn't fair. I deleted the answer machine message, breathed a heavy sigh, and lit a cigarette.

I surveyed my flat. Do you want to know what it looked like?

Well, it looked like this: nuclear fallout.

Every room was a terrorist's meeting area. The garden below, at the back, looked like a dugout.

Out front is Ash Road. It passes by this bombsite of a home, nonchalant, unmoved.

My bedroom is the only spiffy room in the house. Clearly the superior of the spare. The alloy, sneering down on the thin rubber band kept for emergency blow-outs.

No surprise in that. I live here. It has a double bed – antique, genuinely comfy and slept in by Charles II (my great uncle – deceased – was an antiques collector). On either side is an oak chest-of-drawers with clothes in, books on, and on rare occasions has had chicks across. The books consist of an atlas, travel guides, some P.G. Wodehouse, biographies of the Kennedys, and some classics I pretend to have read.

In the bottom drawer are some magazines I also pretend to have read but haven't: I've just looked at the pictures. *Club, Men Only, Fiesta*, that kind of thing. They're all quite old, if I'm honest. (Seventies-style women: nipples like fifty-pence pieces, a crop of hair between their legs three-times the density of Che Guevara's beard.)

I don't have the nerve for buying porn any more. It feels too dirty, too surreptitious, like fancying your mate's mum. If I were going to (and I might do yet, if my run of bad luck with the ladies continues), I'd have to motor off to Stroud or Swindon, or any of the anonymous places where buying porn is not only acceptable but actively encouraged.

But I didn't need porn right then. I needed Daisy.

I don't know what the hell she thinks she's up to. I can't for the life of me imagine what gives her the right. But she's constantly in my dreams.

I seem to get off to sleep okay. With the help of a few beers, I get off fine. It just doesn't last. At three or four I'm awake, my heart hammering, sweaty and agitated.

The dreams take various forms. Some are light, frothy, fairy tales. The sunlight, the fields of corn, the floppy straw hats, the playful conjoining of still-clothed body parts.

Others are altogether more gothic. The bulging-eyed boyfriend, or husband, or amorous gardener poised over our naked, post-coital figures, twelve-bore cocked.

Or, more agonising and abstract, a blitzkrieg of questions on subjects of general knowledge from her father, for which (puce-faced and sweating) I have no answer.

And finally, her three brothers who are all taller/more intelligent/better paid/more humorous than me, with cocks the size of egg plants.

Last night I woke at four-fifteen. The dream I'd been having was the classic 'humiliation dream'. Perfect courtship, perfectly witty repartee, seamless move to the bedroom, followed by expert and tantalising disrobing, and then... not a hard-on in sight.

Nightmare.

Has it ever happened to you? Not you lovely girls, obviously; you just have to make sure you've shaved your legs, which you will part deliciously slowly when the time is right. I mean happened to you. The guys.

Ben swears he rarely lacks a stiffy, even during the day, so he certainly doesn't have trouble at night. I used to bomb around with a near-permanent hard-on too, when I was younger. When I was a teenager.

Now I sometimes have trouble. I must stress the 'sometimes' here. I am far from impotent. Once or twice, however, late last year, early this, I, well... you know what I mean. Frantically slapping it against the thigh. Nipping off to the bathroom to get the circulation going. Really yanking it about. It doesn't work. When the flag doesn't fly, it doesn't fly. That's it. That was the dream I had. I hope it's not a prophecy. I hope I'm not Nostradamus. The mad loon.

But hang on, why am I panicking? I must be at least a decade away from getting her into bed. Maybe two.

Chapter Six

Before I headed for work that Friday morning, I gave my appearance a check routine worthy of the armed forces. After all, Daisy might drop in to collect her tickets. I had to prove to her that Thursday was an exception to my usual high standard of hygiene and appearance. I had some lost ground to make up.

To summarise:

I got up an hour earlier than normal, at seven.

I showered and washed my hair twice, then conditioned it. With a towel around my waist, I meticulously ironed my best shirt – a blue-and-white striped number with double cuffs. I then ironed my red tie, followed by my suit and hung them all on the bedroom door, all the time listening to the radio.

I then shaved with extreme care, only cutting myself three times. It didn't matter. There was plenty of time for the blood to dry and be covered by spot cream.

Next, I towel-dried my hair. It's short, my mane, and blonde. Pretty manageable. I applied gel and tousled it to look spiky-ish but kind of 'who gives a toss?'

Now in my boxer shorts, I posed in front of the full-length mirror in my bedroom. I have to say, I'm not in bad shape. The gym isn't a total waste of time. Small hummocks have appeared on my arms and there's a vague swell about the chest. I'm looking good, with chiselled, enviable features. It doesn't help, though, with the confidence. The confidence still scrapes along the sea-bed like those fish with no eyes that you see in nature programmes. The confidence is, for whatever reason, screwed.

I put on my trousers, shoes and socks. Or socks and shoes. You know what I mean. I had breakfast. One bowl of cornflakes, no sugar, and toast with runny honey. I then had a strong cup of coffee, followed by two cigarettes.

Many people in this enlightened age are trying to give up, or cut down. Not me. I smoke twenty to thirty a day and have done so for some years. No, I'm not cutting down. If anything I'm cutting up. I'd like to get through two packs a day, ideally, but at present I'm not quite managing it. I need more time. I need to stay up later.

At quarter-to-eight, I returned to the bathroom and covered my razor cuts with cream, doused myself with Polo aftershave and finished dressing. The shirt and tie combination looked fantastic. The jacket hung from my shoulders, as the saying goes, like a rapist hangs from the noose (perfectly). I wore my best gold cufflinks with the family crest: a serpent coiled around a wheatsheaf. It means 'beware in the midst of plenty'. I was ready, absolutely ready for the day. I sauntered to the office, feeling good.

I spent the next nine hours with my pulse at a steady 130 bpm. Everyone, including the quiet Ted, took the piss out of my overdressed appearance.

Kate, always ready with the sharpest comment, said, "She'll think she's wandered into Burtons, you dressed like that."

"I don't shop at the same stores as your boyfriend," I retorted. Then I smiled and told her (in a chummy way) to get stuffed.

Daisy didn't show up. I was going to have to tolerate office jibes again all Monday. I could barely wait.

*****

My parents live in Southrop, a twenty-minute rally around some rural roads and tracks from Cirencester that are alive with wandering rabbits. If I don't fluff one on the way down, I'll thump one on the return. I try to avoid it, but they feign right, dummy left, pirouette and spin. And there's me, hunched and tensed at the wheel, trying to second guess, mirroring their mortal dance, which always ends in the screeched caress of moulded plastic on electric fur: 'Bumper meets Thumper'. Another episode in a series of short films to be shown throughout my life.

It's one of those things. It's life. I don't like it, but I've grown accustomed. I don't wince on contact the way I used to. Instead I rationalise. Plenty more where he or she came from, though I do care for them all individually.

The family home is set in seven acres of rolling Gloucestershire countryside. It's sixteenth-century, Cotswold stone, highly expensive to heat, but impressive. It can make American tourists squeal from half-a-mile. It certainly gives them something to think about as they head up to Bourton-on-the-Water, Stow-on-the-Wold and Stratford-upon-Avon.

"Gee, Gaad," I've often heard them say. "D'ya think a Lord lives there, or, like something?"

Well, a Lord doesn't live there. My father, vaguely pompous though he can sometimes be, is a plain mister.

"Darling, you're earlier than I was expecting," my mother said, as I wandered in. She was sitting with her feet up on one of three sumptuous plum red sofas, which trapped a vast square, glass-topped coffee table. In front of her was a roaring open fire, spitting and crackling at the stone hearth. She was reading, or thumbing a book, which she put down.

I waded towards her over the thick Indian rugs. The curtains on all four windows were drawn.

"Hi," I said simply, bending to kiss her on both cheeks. "How're you doing?"

"Oh you know," she said briskly, with a thin smile, "good

and bad."

My mother was a very attractive woman in her youth, judging from grainy black-and-white photos. Now in her early sixties, she still had something (poise, dignity), but the dazzle of her looks had faded. On a good day, mind you, a room would swoon to her smile.

"Where's Daddy?"

"Fiddling with one of his cars in the garage."

"I didn't see the lights on," I said. "I'll go and say hello."

"And bring him in."

I left the room, exiting via the long, high hall and out through the heavy front door to avoid Dot and her verbal diarrhoea. My feet creaked on the wooden floor as I went. The door groaned as I pulled the bolts and dragged it open. Old houses, they're all very well. They have character and all that, but too much. Sometimes, far too much.

My father was indeed in the garage lying prone under an old Aston Martin. A DB6, I think, or 7. Old cars, like old people, aren't my thing.

I made him aware of my presence and waited. I looked around the garage. There was more space than there used to be. More space, less cars, I'm sure.

I lit a cigarette and paced around. The remaining cars were covered in dust sheets. The only one of any interest to me is the Ferrari Dino. My father has never let me drive it. And I'm sure he never will, though he keeps saying it's because of the insurance. It's not because of the insurance; it's because he knows I'll prang it.

"Let's have a drink," he said, once he'd struggled up off the floor. My father is an impressive man. Six-foot-three, broad and not fat, but he's getting on. Sixty-four next year. Not as agile as he was. Last year he got stuck under one of the cars and was stranded for three hours before mother came out to look for him. She nearly died laughing. She had to phone the next-door neighbour to come and drag him out. He doesn't like to be helped, though. I wouldn't dream of offering. It would insult him.

Back in the drawing room, my father poured two lake-sized gin and tonics. My mother had a more restrained bird-bath of burgundy. We all sat. My parents unified on one sofa, I had to go it alone on another.

It reminded me of the 'meetings' we had when my prep school report arrived.

My father always opened with something staunchly ambiguous like, "Let's hear your thoughts first, then we'll tell you what we think."

I'd read the individual white slips with shaking eleven-year-old hands. One for each subject. Some typed, some hand-written in near illegible script. Every holiday I wondered why they bothered giving me one for each class; they all said the same.

"Well," I would reply in a ringing falsetto. "It's not bad, is it? It's not bad."

My father would raise his eyebrows at me, "But?"

I'd glance down at the rugs.

"There's always room for improvement. No matter how good I am, there's room to improve."

"What is it they all say?"

I'd hesitate and say begrudgingly, "Could do better."

"Mmm. And how long have they been saying this?"

"Ever since I started."

"So... four years."

"Yes," I'd quaver. "But they're hardly likely to say, 'could do worse', are they?"

My father always ignored my retorts.

"The question is, when *are* you going to do better?"

"I can't do any better," I'd sulk. "I keep trying and I can't."

"Well, we think you can."

At this point I would bolt from the room, short trousers spin-nakered from air speed. Later, I'd be reassured it wasn't all bad but more would be expected next term. I always promised to deliver. And never did.

"So," said my father, in exactly the same tone he'd used for my school reports all those years ago, "how are things with you and the travel game? Progressing up the career ladder?"

There was a hint of sarcasm in his voice. It immediately put me on the defensive. He didn't think much of me working as a travel agent, though he tried to hide it.

"Well, I sell the most flights. I get the most commission. I'm taking over when the boss leaves. So yeah, things are great."

"And are you still enjoying it?" my mother piped up. "Because that's the most important thing."

I nodded, taking a large slug from my drink.

"Oh yeah. I mean some days are hell. Everything goes wrong, every single person you speak to complains and it all feels pretty thankless. But on the good days," I couldn't help thinking of Daisy here, "you get lovely people in who couldn't be nicer. And they even send you postcards saying what a great holiday they're having. That's what makes it fun."

"How lovely," my mother said, with a beam. "Let's eat."

Dinner with my family is usually conducted in the dining room (yes, shocking): starter, main course, pudding, plenty of wine, cheese, cigars and whisky. End result: drunk and bloated.

Tonight was an exception. We ate in the breakfast room off the kitchen, with the lights low. We only had two courses and some cheapish plonk.

"Cutting back are we?" I joked.

My father frowned.

"If the whole family was here, we'd be in the dining room," he said. "As it's just you, we're not."

"Have you seen Vanessa recently?" my mother cut in, softening the blow.

"Not for a while. I've spoken to her on the phone a few times."

"Did you think she sounded okay?"

"Why?"

"No particular reason," said my father. "Just wanted to check she was okay."

"Why?" I asked again.

"Your sister is obviously a very sensitive girl. We're concerned for her welfare."

"You're making her sound like an emotional wreck. She's fine."

"That's not true, Guy," said my mother. "Has she got a boyfriend?"

"Not as far as I know."

My father sighed.

"What's the problem with that?"

"We just think it would give her some security. She's such an attractive girl."

"She's very picky," I said. "When the right guy comes along, it'll be fine. Anyway, after her last experience, who can blame her?"

The table fell into a sympathetic silence, before my father said, "Have you got a girlfriend yet?"

"No," I replied, but couldn't help a smirk.

Mother picked up on it.

"But there's someone you like? Someone waiting in the wings?"

I smiled broadly though I don't know why.

"Kind of. But I haven't done anything about it."

"Why not?" she asked, as if it was the easiest thing in the world to ask a girl out.

"Because I'm scared she'll say no."

"Nonsense!" my father bellowed. "You've got a job. You're good-looking."

"Ask her out, darling," my mother agreed. "What's the worst that can happen? She can only say no."

I sat there feeling about thirteen. It was embarrassing, talking to my parents like this. I wouldn't dream of doing it sober.

"Will you?"

"I will," I said in a very small voice.

"You can bring her over for dinner any time. You know we're always delighted to meet your friends."

"I know." I needed to end this little pep talk. And quickly.

"I might go for a walk as it's a clear night," I said. "Get some air. Anyone want to come with me?"

Luckily no one did. I took my cigar and drink, and headed for the back door. Dot had already gone home, the washing up all done.

Outside I looked up at the stars, so very far away, and thought of Daisy.

"I wonder what you're up to?" I muttered, taking another drag on the cigar.

Chapter Seven

Time has many speeds, don't you find? Monday, Tuesday, Wednesday drag on for what seem like aeons. Thursday and Friday operate on a vari-speed rota: sometimes fast, sometimes slow. The weekend has only one pace: flat out from start to finish. Spend too long in the shower on Saturday morning and you can come out to find it's Sunday night. No matter how aware we are of this, no matter how much we check our watch to try to slow the weekend's inexorable pace, Monday morning arrives quicker than the first drop of rain at Wimbledon fortnight.

And so it was again. I got up late Saturday morning, had brunch with my parents, a couple in the local, and it was Monday. Don't ask me what happened to Sunday. I've got no idea. Sunday went over my head. Sunday took the bypass, or the ring road. I don't know where it went, but it missed me. Completely. I didn't even have a chance to dream of Daisy. I swear, I didn't.

Bang. Monday. Action. Roll cameras.

Monday morning was much the same as Friday. Yes, I did all that preparation again, but this time with my second-best shirt, the ivory white one.

It was Daisy day. My pulse sat at a steady 140 bpm. The sweat glands operated on red alert. Everyone in the office could

44

feel my tension. I sent it out to them, over the ether.

"If she doesn't show up today," Kate jeered, "you're going to blow a gasket."

"Had a good weekend, did we?" I said, ignoring her sharp tongue. "Get your boyfriend something nice from Top Man? Spent all your money in the parade in Swindon?"

I knew this would hurt and I meant it too. Kate is a couple of rungs lower on the social ladder than she'd like to be but she loves her designer labels.

"I actually went to Cheltenham and got myself a designer handbag," she said, nose in the air.

"Oh good. At least you were still 'shopping'. I wouldn't like to think you were slipping. Have you thought of addiction counselling? I bet your credit card's racked right up to the hilt. I bet Tara Palmer-Tomkinson worships you."

She scowled, but didn't answer. I'd hit a raw nerve. She probably was terrifyingly in debt.

I moved onto the reserved one, Ted. Had he had a pleasing weekend?

He nodded.

"Do anything exciting?"

"My girlfriend and I went to London to see friends."

Now this was a shock, I must say. I'd assumed Ted had never been to London.

"Where do they live? Somewhere south of the river? Deptford? Lewisham?"

"West Hampstead."

"Oooh. Very nice. Very yuppy." Was he lying? Had he too caught the twenty-first century bug? I didn't pursue the line of questioning. Either he had a life worth envying, or he was an Oscar-winning deceiver. Both were too much for me on a Monday morning, but both aroused my interest. Yes, there was definitely more to this boy. No doubt about it.

"Debbie?" I pointed at her, even though she only sits a yard-and-a-half to my right. I was enjoying this forced Monday morning camaraderie.

"I worked both days," she said.

"Sell much?"

"I did okay."

"Fantastic. Great. You'll appreciate it when your commission comes in at the end of the month."

She nodded eagerly. Like I'd just paid her an enormous compliment. So I thought I would, to see what would happen.

"Your hair looks terrific, by the way. What have you done? New conditioner? New henna rinse?"

She blushed deep crimson and touched her crispy, flyaway locks self-consciously.

"It's the same as always," she said coyly. "It must be the light."

"Quite possibly," I agreed, and turned to get on with my work (I never ask Carol what she's been up to at the weekend, out of respect since the divorce. Q – "Carol, what did you do at the weekend?" A – "I cried into my pillow non-stop/made a voodoo doll of my ex and stuck pins and nails into it." I don't need to hear this. Do you?)

Anyway, I turned to get on with sending out my tickets and to my shock found Daisy sitting in my client chair opposite. I didn't even hear her come in. (I'm beginning to think she floats, rather than walks.) My heart immediately leapt into my mouth but my earlier arrogance with the staff somehow carried me through.

"Ah," I said, with great bravado. "And what happened to you on Friday?"

"I got roped into helping a friend move house. It wasn't a problem, was it?"

I shook my head. She was looking gorgeous. Hair down today, long and thick. Eyes clear and sparkling. Mouth pouting, nose still pert. Chest very much in evidence under a tight t-shirt from which protruded thin and sculpted arms, lightly tanned.

"You'll be wanting your tickets, then?"

"Yes, please," she said, scratching her nose nervously.

I contemplated my desk. I'd had them out on Friday so I could confidently hand them over. And now... I couldn't find them.

"They're here somewhere," I said tightly.

She smiled. "I hope so."

I was under my desk now, looking in the drawers, on the shelves, beneath the waste bin. They weren't there.

"Sorry about this. I'll just check out the back."

I darted into the back office to compose myself... where were they? I checked the incoming mail drawer, in case I'd put them there. I checked the outgoing mail. No joy. I went back into the office.

"Has anyone seen two BA tickets for Dublin?" I asked, sounding quite composed, I thought. Voice only mildly vibrato.

"What names?" Kate asked.

I looked at Daisy. In the panic they'd left my head.

"Warnford and Oliver," she said.

Kate took her time leafing through her paperwork.

"Oh, here they are," she said finally. "You must have misfiled them, Guy." Then looking at Daisy, rolling her eyes, "He's always doing that. Hopeless at organisation. Charming, but completely scatter-brained."

She offered Daisy the tickets.

"Thanks," Daisy said, and turned to me. "Thanks a lot for your help, by the way."

"Yeah," I said, feeling red in the face and totally deflated. "Have a good holiday."

"I will." There was an awkward pause. "Well, I'd better be going."

"Okay," I said, forcing a relaxed smile, which actually looked like a grimace as if I'd been recently circumcised and got my cock stuck in my zip. I went to shake her hand. She looked surprised but took it. The feel of her skin was electric. We made fleeting eye contact.

"See you," she said, and turned and left.

My pulse was racing again now. I knew I hadn't made the best impression but there was something there. A glimmer of hope in her smile. A sexiness in her touch. My mother's words looped in my head. The worst she can say is no… the worst she can say is no.

I stared at my desk, trying to pluck up the courage to follow her. Then I saw the plastic wallet and luggage tags she should have had with her tickets. It was a lame excuse but enough. I picked them up and legged it for the door. I spotted her straight away, further up the street, sashaying away.

"Daisy," I called, feeling criminal using her name in the street. Though also feeling intimate doing it. "Daisy!" She didn't hear me until the third or fourth time, at which point I was practically on top of her. She looked shocked to see me. Or just plain shocked.

"What?" she asked.

"You forgot these," I said, holding out my meagre plastic offering. Daisy eyed them like the vicar viewing coppers in the collection tray. With confusion, disdain, then amusement.

She took them.

I stared at her. Then up and down the street. I felt so nervous I couldn't speak.

"Listen," I said. "Err…I hope you have a really good holiday and when you come back…"

I saw fear in her face.

"…when you get back, pop in and tell me how it was. Will you?"

She looked relieved. She smiled.

"Of course I will. You've been great. Thanks."

We stood looking at each other. I couldn't believe what a chicken I was. I couldn't believe I'd bottled it. "Will you?" I repeated, my heart trying to jump out of my mouth.

"Yes!" she laughed.

"I've got to get back to work," I said.

"Yes, you should."

"Have a nice time."

"I will."

"Bye."

"Bye."

She turned and walked up the street towards the church. I watched her go.

The rest of the day, I castigated myself for my cowardice. No, make that the rest of the week.

And then I really beat myself up the following week, when she didn't turn up.

Chapter Eight

Meanwhile, my chequer board of dreams continued unabated. I hopped from good dreams to bad, from dark to dazzling. I was up and down more often than the big dipper on a bank holiday weekend. I could find no equilibrium. I hunted for it, in videos, magazines, in my drinks cupboard, but I couldn't find it. I looked in shops, mail order catalogues, on the internet. No use. Nobody sold equilibrium. There was none for sale. Not even on the black market.

And all too quickly the weekend that I was off to Reading to visit my sister, Vanessa, wound round. I'd hoped I'd be able to brag about my new girlfriend by then, or at least my hot date, but no, my sexual future still looked as barren as the vast expanse of the Gobi Desert.

Of course Ben got in on the act, didn't he? He's been trying to get it on with Vanessa since he was a teenager. Every time I try and sneak off to see her, to have a quiet chat, to check she's okay, he's on the blower asking if he can come down to Cirencester. It's like he has a bug on my phone.

"You can't this weekend," I told him. "I'm busy."

"Doing what?"

"Not seeing you."

"So you're going to Reading?"

"No."

"Don't lie. You never go anywhere, ever. And if you do it's Reading, or, at a pinch, London. But if you were coming to London, you'd have called me. You're so pathetic. Just invite me."

"Do you want to come?" I said, bored. "You'll have to hang around all those dull little university freshers, with their lack of sense, money, intelligent conversation..."

"...their lack of knickers, sexual hang-ups, ability to say no? I'm there, Guy. I'm there."

"I'll bet you are," I replied. "But I'm not picking you up in some ludicrous round trip so we can have a drink in your local at the start and the end of the weekend. If you want to be surrounded by fresh, young talent all weekend, you can drive yourself."

"I was going to suggest it," he said. "I've just got my new car."

My heart went into free-fall.

"What is it?"

"Wait and see, my friend," he laughed. "But, I can tell you, it'll suck those little uni chicks off the street and stick them to the windscreen; it's that much of a fanny magnet."

"Congratulations. And you wonder why you never get anywhere with my sister."

"There's always time for that to change."

"I'll see you on Friday. You remember where my sister's house is?"

"Oh yeah."

"If you're late, we'll be in the pub."

I put the phone down and breathed deeply. I'd wanted to go to Reading, see my sister, have a pretty chilled time. Now it was going to be one long pissathon. With Ben, it was never anything different. What the hell, I thought. I might even get laid. Get this Daisy chick out of my head.

Friday I managed to get out of work at five, right on five. I ran the three-hundred yards home and, panting, washed my car. Yes, my sleeves rolled up, my suit trousers still on, I washed my car. I like cars; I just can't look after them. This one, I swear, hasn't been washed since the beginning of time.

It may be over ten years old, but it still goes well. (In fact, it goes like a cat that's been pipped in the arse with a .22 airgun.) However, it looks like shit. The back bumper's hanging off. There's a dink in the front offside panel where it looks like it's been kicked. (I don't know how it got there. I woke up one morning and there it was. Like a spot the day before a hot date, it came out of nowhere.) The black trim is now pale grey. There's some lime-green slime round the windows. Yes, it's not looking its best.

So I washed it. And once I'd finished washing it, I wished I hadn't. At least the country dirt hid its faults; now they were exposed like evidence against me. A diary of neglect. A CV of abuse. If there was an authority for the protection of cars, mine would have been taken into care long ago.

"Sorry," I said out loud, as I threw the final bucket of hot water over it. "Sorry for not looking after you better."

An old man passed. All walking stick and grim determination. He gave me a funny look. Or maybe he just looked funny.

"And sorry to you, too," I said. "I 'spect you haven't had a good hosing down in a while either."

His expression didn't change.

"It never gets any better does it? Stuff still falls to pieces. We can't argue with decay. Degradation. I mean... look at you."

I was talking to the back of his head now.

"You take care. You go easy. Lock your doors at night..."

He was around the corner. I stood still for several moments, then put the bucket down and went inside. What had brought on that little outburst I didn't know. I think it's the pressure. Of getting older. And love. Love isn't as easy to handle as one may think.

*****

Cirencester is a market town. Some maps and guide books claim it's part of the Cotswolds. Don't be fooled. It's not. It's too far South. The Cotswolds don't officially start until Stowe and The Slaughters; not that the bus loads of Japanese tourists who come down every day seem to care. The video cameras still come out, the Nikons keep snapping. They don't give a toss.

The town has a certain charm. It doesn't have any fast food restaurants, for example. It has a large church. You can park right in the market place, though you'd better feed the meter. The traffic warden here is dedicated. Not a single bust slips through his fingers.

In comparison, Reading is loaded with burgers and kebabs, areas of tarmac to ditch the motor to chat among its own kind, and more forgiving parking officers. Plus it's good to get away once in a while to check out the scenery in another part of England's rich and fertile land. I was looking forward to it, really.

Amazingly, Ben was at my sister's house when I arrived. He was sitting gazing lazily at the TV, idly smoking a fag.

"Thank God you're here," he said, when I strode in, having hugged my sister in the doorway. "I'm gasping for a beer. Did you bring any?"

I held up two four-packs of Stella.

"This do?"

"It's a start," he said. "Let's get mindless."

I snapped one off the plastic binding and threw it at him.

"Oh wait," he said. "Before we get noodled, come and see the beast."

I glanced at my sister. She was looking stunning. Dressed down in faded jeans and black polo neck jumper, no makeup, raven hair dead straight, she couldn't help it – she looked breathtaking. Even with the fey look of those prone to depression.

"I assume he's bored you with his 'beast' already?" I said.

"Actually, it's very smart."

53

"See?" said Ben. "See? You know how picky your sister is."

Vanessa's flatmate Eve wandered in from the kitchen. A girl of average height, average looks, but funny.

"It is," she agreed. "Trouble is, you expect something equally impressive to get out of it."

I laughed hard.

"You girls take some impressing," said Ben, shoving me towards the door.

"Here it is," he said, after we'd walked thirty yards up the road. It was a warmish June night and dusk was starting to fall, but we could see okay in the street lights.

I focused down.

"Nice," I said. I couldn't help it. I'd planned to be derisory and sarcastic, but I said, "Nice. Very nice... it's a TVR right?"

"Yup. It's a TVR Griffith. Racing green. Thirty-thousand on the clock, full service history."

"How does it go?" I asked. That's all I was really interested in.

"Get in," he said, blipping the alarm.

I got in.

"Full leather interior," he continued, "bucket seats, 250bhp, and nought to sixty in five seconds."

"You're kidding me."

He turned the ignition. The engine roared into life.

"I'm not," he replied. He pulled away, flooring it in first gear. The back-end wagtailed. The cars parked on the left side of the street seemed to cower, shouldering themselves a little closer to the curb. Ben slipped it into second. I think we were already nudging sixty. There was a T-junction ahead. Ben pipped the breaks and turned. The back slid some more.

"That'll do," I said, terrified we were going to have an accident.

But that wouldn't do. Ben took me for a twenty-minute tooth-grinder that took in a slice of the A329, a chunk of the M4 and a spaghetti of back roads. Almost all of it was on the wrong side of the road, and much of it bumper to bumper with some poor driver in front.

When we finally parked up outside Vanessa's house again I was catatonic with fear.

"See?" he said. "If this doesn't impress the girls, I don't know what will."

"Well, I'm no girl," I said, recovering mobility slowly, "but I reckon it'd be more likely to induce vomiting."

"Vanessa loved it."

"Yeah. Well. She can be weird. She even said you were quite funny once."

"Really?"

"A long time ago, obviously."

"I'm funnier now."

"You're fatter now. Not funnier."

"So you like the car?"

"If you can keep it on the road," I said, "I think it'll do just fine."

Returning inside we found the girls getting ready to go out. Clothes, hair, makeup, lots of noise coming from the bedrooms. For girls the preening is an important part of the pre-social night. For men, drinking does the trick. Enough until you think you look good. We find it's more fun than spending hours in front of the mirror. So Ben and I hogged the sofa, drinking beer with some trance compilation playing on the stereo.

"You know," he said. "It never ceases to amaze me. I mean, can you remember the kind of dump you lived in when you were at university?"

He had a cigarette in his hand, which he waved to encompass the area. Ben: definitely back on the baccy.

I nodded solemnly.

"And then you look around this place... times have changed."

I looked around. The sofa I was scooched down on was fabulously comfy and leather. It set the tone for the rest of the house.

Student houses – typically a minefield of stains, rotting food stuffs, pub-style carpets and nineteen-fifties free-standing cookers. Not this one.

No, this was the antithesis of student living. It was large, spacious, uncluttered. It was surfaced in pale carpets that had remained pale. The cream walls were not littered with posters or join-the-dot configurations of ancient bluetack. They were decorated with framed prints. The downstairs was open-plan. A nightmare to heat, but who worried about the expense? Certainly not my sister, or the unfailingly cash-rich Eve.

"How much does your dad fork out for this?" Ben asked.

"I have no idea. And I don't intend to ask. Vanessa is Daddy's little girl. He doesn't want her living in a shithole, and nor, quite frankly, do I."

"But what about the dive where you lived in Kent?"

"Doesn't matter. It had running water. Besides, I was drunk most of the time. I wouldn't have appreciated a smart place."

Ben nodded sagely.

"So long as you're not jealous."

"I'm not."

Vanessa came down the stairs.

"Come on guys," she said. "We're going to the pub."

At the pub we got very drunk. No surprise there. You drink, you get drunk. But I used to be able to drink *better*. When I was late-teens/early-twenties, boy, could I knock it back. Go all night with no blackouts, no memory loss, no out-of-control antics. These days I drink a four-pack and I'm halfway to being Keith 'Cheggars' Chegwin, or Ainsley Harriot.

I mean, I remember getting to the pub and shelling out for the first round. Egged on by Ben, we all had 'snakebites' for 'old time's sake'. I've never worked out what this means, but it always depresses me. I don't want 'old times'; I want new ones. Better ones. Being a student was fine, but it wasn't great. It wasn't worth revisiting. It's like school reunions. I could never see the point of them. Unless you've just had a nose job, or married a supermodel, what's the point? Isn't the future more important than the past?

I remember the second round, too, by which time the pub was heaving. Ben bought that one and I chatted up some friend of Vanessa's while trying not to spill my pint. She said she was studying the history of art – that's how they knew each other. She was short with a pixie-cut hairdo and a *Big Issue* sense of style. All was going well until she disappeared to the toilet and never came back to speak to me.

Anyway, I got talking to a willowy girl, about what I can't remember. I think it had something to do with beer prices. I wasn't really concentrating. I was still hoping for the pixie to return. I felt stung by her absence and couldn't help wondering what the guy she was probably talking to now had over me. But then I contented myself with the thought she'd had to go home for some kind of domestic emergency. That went some way to healing the bruised ego.

The pub was so busy by that point, a large crowd had spilled out into the beer garden, though the temperature was far from Mediterranean, and I couldn't see anyone I knew. Not Ben, not Vanessa, nor Eve or the four or five others I'd been introduced to. I spoke randomly to any group that would have me, and amused myself stealing unattended pints off the wooden tables when their owners weren't looking. Or sometimes when they were, causing some excitement.

After this interlude, events got distinctly fuzzy. You know the kind of thing: a snapshot here, a piece of slow-motion there. Laughter, music, another cab ride. Lights, more music (louder this time), an attempted snog, some falling over and then... complete clarity.

I was sitting on Vanessa's sofa with my shoes and socks off, smoking a joint, talking to a balloon-breasted girl about guest houses in Chaing Mai (another place I'd never been), thinking (with beer-induced bravado) that if I wanted to, I could bed this chick. Then it was like a record stopping, or the stylus suddenly jumping into the space between tracks, and all of a sudden everything went black...

Chapter Nine

Coming round with no idea of the five or six hours that preceded passing out is never a comfortable experience. The mind asks questions – come on you old devil, what did you do? But it gives no answers. You can approximate what you may have done, but it's never a patch on the truth. It's never halfway as outrageous as you actually were.

And so it was that I opened my eyes with pure dread the following morning, or afternoon, or whenever it was, and hastily drank a nearby can of lager. To steady my nerves, as it were.

Then I did what I always do in this situation. I hauled myself off the floor, cleaned my teeth in the kitchen sink, and went to see Vanessa.

Vanessa is great the morning after. She'll fill the gaps, supply the details, break the horror stories, all with amusement, good humour, and not a trace of blame.

"Don't worry," she'll say. "You were drunk! Everyone does silly things when they're drunk. No one cares."

When, of course, the five or six chicks you goosed, the other eight girls whose boobs you squeezed, and the three or four dozen whose bums you slapped with back-breaking force, do care. They care a lot. (Thank Christ the suing culture hasn't completely passed into this country yet. Every weekend would end up in a lawsuit or paternity case.)

So I dragged myself up the stairs, feeling actually pretty sprightly after my breakfast beer and even better with another can reassuringly clasped in my right hand. I flung the door of her bedroom open, simultaneously launching myself onto the bed.

When I landed, I heard not the dainty, uncomplaining cry of Vanessa, but a much deeper, terser, "Shit! You fuckwit, what the..."

And when I rolled over, I came face-to-face with Ben.

"Ben," I said. "What the...?"

And then I rolled the other way. Turned the other cheek, if you will, and found myself looking at a half-scared Vanessa.

All of my worries that I may have been out of order the previous night vanished.

"You are kidding me," I said to the ceiling, and then wasn't quite sure what else to say or do.

Neither was anyone else. We lay there like sardines, or soon to be extinct cod, not moving. Finally I said, "Who wants a beer?"

They both said: "I do" simultaneously and I got off the bed and hurried downstairs. My brain was in an utter spin.

I don't know what was said in my absence but, when I returned and handed out the drinks, Ben launched nervously into his speech. He said, "I don't want you to think this is a one-off, Guy. I mean, we didn't actually sleep together, anyway, but I mean, I wouldn't take advantage of Vanessa and well, it turns out we've felt pretty strongly about each other for ages and it's taken this long for anything to happen, so we hope, you know, I mean we're going to take things slowly, but it should, you know, we hope, work out, and we hope you're not mad, because I know what you've always said about Vanessa, that you'd kill any guy who broke her heart again, and that's not going to happen, I swear it won't, and..."

"Oh no," I said, sitting on the end of the bed, facing away from them.

Ben paused. "What?"

"So I'm going to have you as a brother-in-law, am I? What a nightmare!" But as I said it, I turned and smiled, and winked at Vanessa, who giggled.

"Are you surprised?" she said coyly.

"Surprised? I'm horrified. I mean, I thought you had some taste!"

"He's your best friend!"

"Yeah, so I know what he's like."

"I haven't been out with your sister before," said Ben. "This will be different."

"You're damn right it will," I said. "And if you do mess it up, don't think you're getting a second chance with any of my brothers."

Vanessa giggled some more. I have to say, I hadn't seen her as happy in years. There was a glow about her. A radiance. That it came courtesy of Ben was confusing, if not miraculous, but... you never can tell, can you?

"I will be best man, I presume?" I said.

Vanessa brought her knees up to her chin, making the duvet into a tent.

"Of course!"

"If you promise not to get drunk," said Ben. "You were in such a state last night. I'm amazed you didn't get slapped. Do you remember half the stuff you did in the club?"

"I don't remember being in a club," I replied.

"Ha! Then you don't remember getting your trousers off on the dance-floor? Waving them around your head, then wrapping them round that girl's neck?"

I looked blank.

"Vaguely," I lied. "Yeah, yeah."

"Then what about that girl you snogged who was with her boyfriend?"

"Err...the blonde?"

"Yeah."

I shrugged, not remembering. "There wasn't much to tell, was there? She was a lousy kisser."

Ben laughed hard and continued detailing my night's exploits for the next ten minutes.

"And then you this... after that, you that..." I'm surprised he had time to get Vanessa in the sack, all the surveillance he was doing.

"Anyway," said Ben, in his summing up, "at least you got some action, hey?"

Now this was news.

"Did I?"

"That chick with the boobs. She was all over you. Mind you, she had been on the vodka all night."

"When did this happen?"

"At the club. You brought her back here. Did you shag her?"

"Ben!" said Vanessa, shocked by his frank talk.

"I doubt it, don't you? The state we were both in."

"Anything's possible."

"Can you guys have this conversation later? I don't wish to know." Vanessa looked like she was about to be sick.

"Yeah, actually, neither do I," I agreed. "It's like we're talking about someone else here. I don't know any of this stuff. Let's move on."

"She's downstairs, Guy," Ben teased. "Do you want me to go get her?"

"No," I said, with some finality. "Do you want me to punch you for being in bed with my sister?"

He went quiet after that. I knew he was feeling guilty, and boy he should have been. The number of times I'd told him my sister was off limits. "Think of her as a priceless work-of-art," I'd said. "You can look, but you can't touch." And he'd gone right ahead and touched. Oh! Human frailty! Human wickedness!

*****

Several hours later, about 2pm. A pub in Sonning.

"Ben," I said, sipping my pint. (I was on my third, not counting the three cans of lager for breakfast.) Ben was drinking lager top as he was driving. A centimetre of lemonade in each pint and he thinks he can have five and still be under the limit. Such is an alcoholic's reasoning.

"Ben," I said, "I want you to promise me one thing."

He pulled his 'here we go' face but listened, if not intently.

"I want you to promise that you won't sleep with her."

A wasp circled my pint. We were sitting outside, at a table near the river. It was a perfect summer's day. A family of ducks swam past. Ben considered this. I considered the wasp.

He adjusted his sunglasses and said, "Can we hold hands?"

"Not now," I replied, "people are looking."

"Very funny."

I paused. I wasn't expressing myself at all well. "I mean don't bed her this weekend and then leave it at that."

Ben slowly rotated his pint on the table, leaving a damp circle in the wood. A circle. Like the universe. Never ending. Adventures begin and end, but the circle, it just keeps on going, like the wasp.

"Can you relax?" Ben said, after several revolutions. "Can you just chill out?"

"She hasn't had a whole stack of boyfriends," I pointed out. "She must really like you."

"She does. And I really like her. Can we just see how it goes? Give it some time?"

I breathed deeply. I knew I was acting weird, but I couldn't help it. Ben and I had always discussed our girlfriends, and not always in the most flattering terms. We wouldn't be able to do this with Vanessa. So much would have to change. All our relationships would change. I was scared. And there was something more important.

"Do you remember, about a year ago, Vanessa went and lived in Antigua for six months?"

Ben nodded. He was concentrating. He'd picked up my tone.

"Yeah," he said. "Didn't she have glandular fever, or something?"

"No," I said. "But what I'm going to tell you, is strictly between you and me, okay? Do not ever tell Vanessa I told you this."

Ben didn't say anything. He looked at me, halfway towards agape.

"She had a nervous breakdown," I said, moving in. "The guy she'd been going out with dumped her. You know – her first love. She hasn't been out with anyone since. She must really like you. Really trust you."

The wasp moved away from my pint and towards Ben's.

Ben looked pained. He said, "Of course you realise I will treat your sister as if she was my own mother."

Then he realised what he'd said. "I think that might be trying a little too hard," I replied. "But I appreciate the sentiment."

"What I mean is," said Ben, "forget about the other girls. This is different."

"I know it is," I said warningly. "And you'd better forget about them too."

The wasp hovered a little higher. I considered taking a swing at it. It was near Ben's face. It was a win-win situation. If I hit the wasp, we'd have no more annoying buzzing. If I missed, I'd hit the jackpot. I smiled. Ben caught me.

"Don't even think about it," he said, before slipping off into what Bertie Wooster always called a 'reverie'. I really think he was wrapped up in thoughts of Vanessa. Eventually I said, "That's all I had to say. Let's change the subject."

Of course Ben didn't change the subject. Not for ages. He wanted to know all the details, exactly what happened. I told him. I told him Vanessa became so depressed she was like a prisoner in her own mind. That finally got us onto something else. The train of conversation jumped the tracks. The wasp left us.

After a pause, Ben said, "Did you know Tiger was inside?"

I didn't. Tiger was a friend from school I hadn't seen for a while. A skinny, hippyish kid who liked travelling to unusual places. Not my thing, sadly, but I liked the guy.

"Where?" I said.

"HM Brixton."

"What for?"

"Repeated drink driving offences."

"Not cool," I said.

"Apparently he knocked down a kid on a zebra crossing."

"No way! They'll kill him in there. For them, that's almost as bad as rape."

"Yeah. Word is he's not too chuffed. I thought we might go and see him one weekend."

"Yeah, we should. I can't believe it. How's the kid?"

"Recovering in hospital. Multiple fractures, some internal damage. You know the kind of thing."

I didn't, actually, never having broken a bone in my body or worked at an Accident and Emergency Unit, but I could imagine. It didn't sound good.

"God. Yeah, we should go and see Tiger. Give me a call next week when I've got my diary handy. We'll organise something. Can we take him stuff?"

"Soap, cigarettes. Books, I think. Not much."

"How long's he in for?"

"Three months."

Ben turned another circle with his glass. Another damp ring appeared in the wood. Another endless line created in a second.

"That will feel like forever," I said, staring at it. "That will feel like forever."

Ben nodded and got up.

"Same again?" he asked.

"Sure." A duck's wings fluttered in the water, causing a disturbance. A butterfly left its branch. The world was changing. It was never going to be the same again. The wasp returned and this time I took a full force swing at it, missed and hit Ben in the kidneys, who responded by kicking me in the chest before running to the bar.

I rubbed my pectorals. The world would never be the same again. It won't from one second to the next. That's what's so great about it. And so terrifying.

Chapter Ten

Take the smallest object you can imagine. Go on. Imagine it. The tiniest little object and... it looks big, doesn't it? You've magnified it in your mind. It looks huge, because you've blown it out of proportion.

We all do this. Everyday.

Monday, Tuesday and Wednesday, Daisy did not come to the Go Away. She did not come. I did not see her. Her world did not pierce mine. We both existed, but it was as if we didn't. We didn't exist to each other.

Magicians often say there are two components to magic. The 'action' of the magic and the 'reaction' of the audience. Without the audience reaction, magic is nothing. Magic is 'so what, who cares?' Like the old 'if a tree falls down in a forest but no one's there to see it, does it actually make a noise?'

It's the same with most aspects of life. We live in a cycle of action and reaction. Even a simple conversation is based on it. Think about it. You can't escape it.

So what can we do if we can't escape the inevitable? We do this: we try to control our reaction to it.

This is what I attempted to do with Daisy. I tried to rationalise her absence, and accept it. But of course I couldn't. Love, when it strikes you, is too powerful a force to ignore.

I have to say, I was pleased she didn't show up on Monday. I mean that. I was pleased and relieved.

The weekend continued in the same lane it started: the fast one. By the end, I had lager and vodka flowing through my veins, not blood.

We went out again on Saturday night to another club. (Don't remember much. Just the usual slide-show and the obvious out-takes.) Then on Sunday I persevered with Pimms in Vanessa's garden until I passed out. When I woke up it was 2am and I was just about sober enough to drive. I arrived home at 3am, knack-ered, hungover, and with distant pangs of guilt. Oh, I didn't tell you, did I? I did bed the girl with the boobs: Friday and Saturday night.

On Saturday, she reminded me of Friday. "We'd better use a condom this time," she said, producing one. My stomach turned. I'd promised myself: no more 'bare-backing'. No more waiting for the phone call: "I should have mentioned that I have herpes. Sorry." Or (far worse), "You've given me herpes, you knob." I kept telling myself I was done with all of that. But clearly I never was. I must be addicted to paranoia.

So I got to bed at 4am, after three calming whiskies and half-an-hour scouring myself with a brillo pad. A question kept running a loop in my head, 'Did I give her my number? Did I give her my number? Did I give her my number?'

And: what did she actually look like, apart from the boobs?

The answer came loud and clear on the Tuesday night. A Tuesday night that followed a disappointingly Daisy-free day.

If I remember, I was watching *Dangerous Liaisons* on video. Slumped on the sofa laughing at John Malkovich's evil Valmont, Glen's controlling bitch, thinking these characters are so heart-less I can't care about them, but I'm loving it. And the phone rang.

"'Bonjorno'," I said into the receiver. With total irration-ality, I was hoping it was Daisy, having somehow tracked down my home number, desperately anxious to declare her undying love.

"Hello?" said an excitable voice.

"Hello," I replied, confused. Off-centred.

"It's 'Kathy'," the voice said, with a giggle. "Remember me?"

I didn't. And I said so. (I'd had several beers.)

"Duh," she said. "It's Katherine. We met last weekend. You were staying at your sister's."

My heart froze. I said jovially, "Well, I wasn't expecting to hear from you. How are you?"

The girl with the boobs had come back to haunt me.

Here we go, I thought. Who's given what to whom? The VD clinic looms...

"Fine," she said, much to my relief.

"Bonzai. Why are you calling?"

"Do I have to have a reason?"

"No," I lied.

"But I do," she teased, and then giggled.

"Go on." I went to the fridge as I said this to get another beer. Thank God I have a cordless phone.

"What are you doing this weekend?"

I wracked my brain for something. Nothing came.

"Possibly dinner with my parents."

"Cancel," she said. "I'm coming to Cirencester!"

"Great. Maybe we can have lunch," I hedged.

"Don't play hard to get. I'm coming to stay for the weekend. And that's it. Give me directions."

"Err..."

"Oh come on. We can cosy up in bed all weekend. It'll be fun, I promise."

I felt like saying, "Let's do this another time, shall we?" but instead I said, "I'll fax you a map tomorrow. Give me a number."

She gave me a number. I jotted it down.

"And Guy?" she said, before she hung up.
"Yeah?"
"Buy some condoms."

*****

I'm sure you've been boxed in too, at some time or other. You've snogged the odd boy you'd rather forget about, haven't you girls? This happens to you too, doesn't it? You can't always control life. We're all trying, but we're not succeeding. I'm not. You're not. We're all losing that battle. We are. There's no question.

Life is the transport and we're simply the passengers. I am a passenger. And I haven't even done my belt up. There are no airbags! (Well, there are now.) It's icy. The car's out of control! Help!

It's interesting to view my present situation dispassionately. I'm in the classic scenario – A wants B, B doesn't seem interested, C wants A, A doesn't seem interested. It's so common and screwed up – it's *normal*. The worst of all things to be.

I'd say ninety per cent of the population are with someone they don't really like, or at least like a lot less than they used to, while fantasising about someone else. Or fantasising about something else.

One thing's for sure. Friday will be a nightmare. Yes, she's coming on Friday and staying Saturday. I can't remember what she looks like. I have no idea what she's like to talk to. I tell you, unless she wears a tight t-shirt, I won't recognise her. I can only identify her by her chest.

*****

As I said, Daisy didn't show up on Monday, or Tuesday. Same deal Wednesday. And also on Thursday. Then came Friday. In my world, as in yours, Friday came.

By Friday, I'd got myself together somewhat. I hadn't drunk on Thursday or Wednesday. Sounds good, doesn't it? Well, not really. Not really, because I was saving my quota for the weekend. I reckoned I could get six beers down my neck before 'Kathy' even arrived in Cirencester. Well, before she darkened my doorstep. And I was going to need it.

Despite the impending doom, I spent the morning feeling ridiculously upbeat. Like I'd recently inherited a small fortune, booked a long and expensive holiday, or just the other night slept with a supermodel. Of course, I'd done none of the above. I was high on life, people. High on life's buzz. That rich octane juice we live on (but don't always appreciate) every day.

And, I have to admit, the three shots of tequila I'd necked before my first coffee of the day (a double espresso) had helped. It had helped considerably.

Even Kate noticed.

"You still pissed from last night?" she asked, mid-morning.

"I didn't drink last night, or the night before," I said. "I'm happy, that's all. In that childlike, innocent way we can all be if we let the world's troubles slide, like the tide, away from us."

She rolled her eyes.

"I guess you've got a date then?"

"I do. But not one I relish."

"Some boiler you met at your sister's?"

I gaped.

"When will you ever learn?"

"Well, I always think next week, but it never seems to happen. Perhaps the start of the twenty-second century? When they lift me out of cryogenics, a new, morally stable, but still breathtakingly good-looking, adult alpha male."

"Christ. I think he's gone mad."

Ted looked at me and smiled.

"What are you grinning at, Ted?"

He adjusted his glasses.

"That was funny," he said. "What you said was funny. And

it's made even more funny because it's possible. It might happen."

"Yeah," I said. I thought: like you getting laid. But actually this is a lie. I would have thought this several months ago, when I barely knew the guy, but now...? I retract all of that. Ted's quiet, yes. But he has a dry sense of humour. He's... sardonic. A good thing to be, I think, when you look like he does.

It was Carol's day off, that Friday. Thus unattended, I spent an hour making a paper clip chain, an hour sending e-mails, twenty minutes smoking in the street, and a half-hour unblocking the choked beige anus of the coffee machine.

I enjoyed my time on the street the most, watching the world do its thing. Jinking, jostling, fussing. I tell you, it might not be the hottest summer on record but it sure is sunny. Bright, clear sun all day. I like it. I'm not complaining. You girls have got your thrilling, skimpy tops on. Advertising your beauty in that carefree manner you have. Us boys are looking cool in shades. Life is good.

Oh, I also took a two-hour lunch. Had a couple of pints in The Crown. Wandered round. Bought some new shades. Sat in the park. Went home and watched a chunk of *Groundhog Day*. Yeah, all round it was a laid-back day. And guess who I saw on my way back to the office, still pleasantly amused by Bill Murray's chat-up lines? Mmm...the one and only. Chesney? Nah. Daisy Warnford.

I was strolling down my road, hands in pockets, new dark shades on, sleeves rolled up, tie pulled loose, when I saw her. She was on the opposite pavement. Hair up, also wearing shades. She looked like she'd been soaked in a bath of pheromones, as usual, and was walking fast, long legs striding out. I noticed she'd accessorised her outfit with silver bangles, plenty of silver rings and, Jesus Godzooks, some bloke.

I felt a rush of adrenalin, followed by a mild panic attack. I stopped and watched them, looking for signs of togetherness.

They weren't holding hands. He looked pretty tall and old. His hair was blonde, but greying. They were laughing, though. Like they got on well. My eyes followed them until they were around the corner onto Sheep Street and out of sight.

Cripes, I thought. I walked two steps further towards the office, then turned and ran down the street the way they were heading. At the junction with Sheep Street I spotted them. They were going into the Waitrose car park. I walked swiftly to see where they went, my heartbeat picking up and my interior monologue telling me what a freak I was, what a fool, but my curiosity egging me on.

I stopped at the roundabout at the car park entrance and made it look like I was attempting to cross the road. My eyes monitored their progress. If they went into Waitrose, I decided, I was going to leave them to it. No point showing my face there. I wouldn't know what to say. "Do you come here often?" And with a posh laugh, "Isn't it so much better than Tescos?" No, I didn't want to do that.

They crossed the car park, still not holding hands, or anything terrifying like that, and stopped at a black Range Rover. The guy (he definitely was pretty old, at least forty) opened the driver's side-door, while Daisy went around to the passenger side. When the central locking flicked open, she got in. There was a long pause while the old guy got his act together, got the windows down and his bum settled, and then they drove off. They came out of the exit right next to me, steering a good line through the mini-roundabout and then heading towards Tetbury. The Ranger Rover was a special edition, named after some semi-royal. Money, I thought. And they were gone.

As I trudged back to the office, I felt a wave of melancholy drift over me. I had glimpsed a little of Daisy's life and it wreaked of affluence. Oh, how I wished she'd got into a clapped out old banger, on her own. But a Range Rover? Tetbury, or perhaps worse, Bath? Ooh, this was money. This could be a problem. The one thing I could impress most girls with was my family's wealth.

If I couldn't do that, I was jumping without a parachute.

And who was the mystery man? For the first time, I seriously considered the possibility that she was married. This thought hit me hard. If she's married, I said to myself, that's it. You don't mess with another man's wife. You don't. You don't even think about another man's wife. Unless the door's shut and bolted. You certainly don't think about another man's wife in public. Never.

Chapter Eleven

"So, Katherine," I said.

"'Kathy'," she corrected, touching my thigh under the table.

We were in a pizza place called ...Face. I wouldn't come here if I had acne, but bar that, the name's kind of cool.

"'Kathy'," I mimicked her. "Are you ready to order?"

To be honest, she wasn't looking too bad. I mean, I'd had four cans of Stella and a large whisky before she arrived... but no, being fair, she looked okay. Hair pretty lustrous. Face cupid-like, open and giving. Boobs: eye-poppingly large, terribly frightening, but shapely. Personality: red-hot keen, thus somewhat off-putting (strange, but we all know it's true).

And in this restaurant, the lighting dim, the atmosphere conducive, she looked great. Of course, the convivial setting helped, the drink helped and my determination to make the best of an undesirable night also helped. It wasn't that 'Kathy' was a terrible date. I just wanted someone else, terribly badly.

I ordered another bottle of white, with the intention of having at least one more, along with beers in a pub after. Yes, I thought, I can get through this. I felt a twinge of satisfaction. There's no need to fear life. It can be so easy. If you let it.

'Kathy' ordered the double pepperoni, medium. I went for the seafood platter, medium, and we opted to share garlic bread, with much giggling.

"It won't matter if we both have it," she said.

I winked at her. I wish I hadn't. I did not want to sleep with her again. It felt like I was being unfaithful to Daisy. And I didn't want 'Kathy' to think I was leading her on. She didn't deserve it. No one deserves it.

"You know, if you rub it on your feet it comes out on your breath two minutes later?"

"Do you like rubbing feet?" she asked, slightly missing the point.

"No," I said. "I like having them massaged, though. You know, by a professional."

Her eyes lit up.

"I can do that," she said. "I did a course in massage last term."

I smiled weakly. It's amazing what you get to know about people if you're prepared to listen.

I poured us both (very) large glasses of wine. Everything around me was beginning to recede. Everything was a blur except 'Kathy', and she wasn't too clear.

"Cheers," I said. "Here's to a lovely weekend."

"Thanks for having me," she replied, with a charming smile. And for a moment, just a moment, I almost looked forward to bedding her.

But you just can't. Not when someone else is on your mind. Not when someone else has snatched your heart from your ribcage and wrestled it, whimpering, to the floor.

*****

"Do you like my body?" 'Kathy' asked, as I peeled off her knickers, having already freed her boobs.

It was okay, her body. I just didn't want it this close to me, or this naked. But my primitive drive seemed to be responding to her proximity. Whether I liked it or not, I was getting aroused.

"It's great," I said.

She laughed.

"I remember you saying you liked big girls. Not these anorexic types."

I smiled, grabbing one boob with both hands and lowering my mouth to its nipple. I didn't say anything. I couldn't. I had a pink teet in my mouth.

"Mmm," she moaned. "Let's go to bed."

She edged backwards and sat on the bed, pulling me on top of her.

"Aren't you going to get out of your clothes?" she asked.

I nodded weakly.

"Of course. I'm, I'm..."

And I thought, I'm awfully tired. Why am I allowing myself to do this? It's only going to cause more trouble. 'Kathy', for whatever reason, was just not for me.

I lay on the bed and she got on top of me, straddled me like I was a lilo. Me: the lilo. Her: the menacing cloud above, obscuring the sun. She leant down and kissed me, her tongue almost flicking my tonsils. I grabbed her boobs (they seemed to be getting bigger by the minute) and squeezed.

"Ow," she giggled. "Gently, please. They may be big, but they are sensitive."

I remained silent, moving my hands down over her back instead, moving on to her bum. There my hands came to rest, and I passed out. Or fell into a coma.

Who knows what despicable things she did to me while I was asleep? All I know is this: when I woke, I found her on top of me. Riding me like a bullock or a recently broken Mustang. Eyes closed, her breasts a blur of white jiggling flesh; I let her get on with it.

Cripes, I thought. I'm too nice to make her stop. I'm too damn nice to throw her off me. Or perhaps I was just too much made of man.

"Go for it girl," I slurred up at her, but she didn't hear me. She was far too wrapped up in the moment, perhaps hovering on the brink of orgasm. I watched her for a while until, hypnotised by the boobs, I fell into another trance and then a deep sleep. I didn't wake until lunchtime the next day. And then this little speech, delivered by 'Kathy', lying affectionately on top of me, the nipples of each breast gently tickling me under the armpits:

"I feel so close to you already, Guy. I know we've only known each other a short time, but I feel like we're incredibly close."

I kept my eyes closed and said nothing. Thankfully, the waft of garlic breath I was waiting for – as patiently as the 1.15 appointment in the dentist's annex, flicking through copies of *Punch* – never came.

She moved so her breasts were now lying either side of my throat. I have never felt more trapped.

She kissed me. A full and probing kiss on the mouth. Another tonsil tickler.

"Guy? Hello!" she tickled me round my hips, 'accidentally' palming my semi-hard-on. "Oh, I could make love to you all weekend."

"Mmm," I groaned, feigning sleep.

She wasn't having any of it. She took me in her hand. She rubbed me against her dampness and she shoved me inside her. I lay like a plank on the sweaty sheets.

"I love you, Guy," she said, as she ground her hot, sweaty hips against mine. "Does this feel good? Does it? Do you want it harder?"

I groaned again.

"Open your eyes."

"I can't."

"Why not?"

"Hangover," I said. "I need a beer before I open anything."

She laughed.

"That's what I love about you, Guy. You like to party. Hang on." She slipped off me, my knob thwacking against my abdomen like a wet cod. "I'll get us both one."

She did too. And I drank it without opening my eyes, while she skipped and jumped and slithered all over me until I felt I was going to suffocate.

I passed out again after. When I woke this time, it was four. I took eight cold and flu tablets. I was pleased to have slept most of the day away. Pretty soon it would be dark again and I'd find her more attractive. I could get drunk and we'd both be happy.

I'd like to say that through the rest of the weekend, I got to know 'Kathy' much better and started to fall in love with her. I'd like to say we walked arm in arm round the antique shops of Cirencester, pausing slightly too long in front of the dated bridal shop, squeezing each other's hands a little tighter in recognition of what was to come.

I'd like to say I found her better and better looking. That we shared the same sense of humour. That we clicked.

It would be a lie, though.

All I had in common with 'Kathy' on Saturday turned out to be a hangover. All I had in common with her on Sunday was a worse hangover.

I was relieved when she eventually left on Sunday night. There'd been hints of staying another night, the week, a month. I demurred. I was busy. I was grouchy after work. She'd have a boring time.

In the end, I had to hustle her out, saying I had to drop in on my parents, see if my mother was okay. She wanted to come with me. I told her I'd call.

At ten o'clock, she rang from Reading and spoke to my answer phone, "Guy, darling. Just phoning to say thanks for the best weekend ever! I'm on cloud nine. I've told everyone how great you are. All my friends want to meet you. How about next weekend? Hope your mother's okay. Speak to you soon. Love you. Bye."

I laughed without humour as I listened, and poured myself

Luke Bitmead

a half-bottle of whisky, no ginger wine.
    "Ah, love," I said, as I drank. "Thank God for love."

Chapter Twelve

Monday and there was a distinct air of tension coming over the airwaves. Its source: the desk opposite mine. Kate's desk.

Fiddle, fiddle, gasp. Shuffle, cough, sigh. Twiddle, sigh, twitch. Cough, sigh, scratch. And so it went on.

By ten, my hangover could take no more. I said, "Do you fancy having lunch today, Kate?"

She looked up, confused, distracted.

"What?"

"Lunch, today? Do you want it?"

"With you?"

This was all starting to sound too sexual.

"Yes. Let's have lunch," I said. "My treat."

"Oh," she said. Tempted, I think, to say no. "Err...okay."

We went at twelve-thirty. I took her to a little bistro. We ate in the garden at the back, out in the sun. Mine: Thai chicken curry. Hers: salmon fish cakes and salad. Plus: one carafe of house white.

"So what's up?" I said, after we'd ordered. (The waitress was so young and babyishly attractive, she almost made my voice warble.)

"Nothing," she said, lighting a cigarette.

"Just wearing scratchy knickers, then?"

"What?"

"All that fidgeting this morning."

"Nothing's the matter," she snapped.

"Something is the matter," I persevered. "Come on, you may as well tell me."

Kate put her head back and exhaled moodily. Then she sighed.

"If you must know," she said, fiddling with her cutlery, "Damon and I had a row at the weekend." She pulled on her cigarette again. "And he's moved out."

"Oh shit. How long have you guys been seeing each other?"

"Eighteen months. We've been living together over a year."

"So what happened?" I lit a cigarette and poured us both a large glass of wine, which had just arrived in a rush of hormonal nerves with the waitress.

"Well, we'd planned to go shopping on Saturday..."

"Mmm."

"But when we got up, Damon decided he was going round to Julian's to play *Tomb Raider*."

"Sensible guy," I said.

Kate scowled. Our food had arrived now and she was picking at it. Pick, pick, pick. Fiddle, shove, twiddle. I tucked into mine, throwing back more wine and ordering another bottle.

"And...?"

"So I went with Emma, a friend of mine."

"Buy anything nice?"

"Well, I got this sheer top from..."

I was already laughing.

"Okay, that's not the point, is it?"

"No."

"So when I got back, he was still out. I phoned Julian's and Damon answered, really drunk. I asked him when he was coming home and he said he wasn't."

"Oh."

"Then he said he'd had enough. He was going to move out.

He said he was too young for all this relationship bullshit."

"How old is he?"

"He's twenty."

"He's right, then."

Kate scowled again.

"It was probably just the booze talking," I said. "He'll get over it."

"That's what I thought." She took a sip of wine. I topped up her glass. "But he came round on Sunday and got most of his stuff."

"What did he say?"

"He was really apologetic. He said he was sorry if he'd hurt me, hoped we could still be friends, but not to call him for a while."

"Where's he staying?"

"He didn't say. But I guess Julian's, or his mum's."

"So what are you going to do?"

"Do you think I should call him?"

"No. Let him think things over. If he regrets his decision, he'll call you."

"But I want to speak to him so much."

I shrugged. "Don't. It'll push him further away." I had another glass of wine. It was sitting on my hangover pretty well.

"I don't want to be single," said Kate. "I hate going back to an empty house."

"It's not always the best, is it?"

"Do you get lonely?" she asked.

"Not on the whole, maybe sometimes."

"I hope he comes back."

"He will. Good-looking girl like you. He'd be a fool to leave you."

She smiled. She was very attractive. No doubt about it.

"Thanks, Guy," she said.

"No problem. More wine?"

Now I've only met Damon once. It was at a barbecue Kate threw last summer, in the back garden of their twee two-bedroom Lego house. He was the epitome of common good looks. The razor short hair. The gold hoop earring. The sulkily muscular body. The tight football shirt. The confidence that comes with knowing how cars work, and how to steal them.

I don't mind admitting, I was shocked. I thought Kate would have traded up to a financial analyst or trainee accountant. But instead she'd gone down to the working Chav. I thought it odd, at the time, but then I realised. Beneath all her sharp wit and cocksure turnout was a person bereft of confidence. And what confidence she possessed came to her from designer labels, an ability to eat virtually nothing, and an 'inferior' boyfriend. Now he'd rejected her, she'd be on very shaky ground. I made a mental note to keep a check on her.

"If you ever get down," I said, as we got up to leave, "you can always give me a call. I'm rarely out."

"Thanks, Guy," she said. Genuinely pleased, I think. "It's been good talking to you."

*****

"It's good to talk," Bob Hoskins said, in that dire ad campaign BT ran a few years back. But BT was right, of course. It is good to talk, but not generally on the phone. It's better to talk face-to-face. It's more human that way. It's more intimate. 'Intimate' is almost a dirty word these days. 'Intimate' is top-shelf stuff. Pretty soon, it might be banned.

I had a bit of luck that afternoon. The first bit of luck I've had in a while. Daisy came in. She sauntered in, in those black combats, and we shared an 'intimate' moment.

Her timing, for once, was impeccable. I was half-pissed from lunch and I was on good form. As she walked through the door, I delivered the punch line to a joke. The office roared with laughter. Even the cool, sardonic Ted.

The joke, for future reference, is:

What has two thumbs (you hold them up), speaks French, and likes oral sex?

The punch line, delivered with the thumbs arcing in to point at your chest is, "Moi!"

Fade laughter.

"Daisy, hi! Good to see you."

"You too," she said, laughing as well, even though she hadn't heard the joke. "You all seem very happy for a Monday."

"That's us," I said. "Happy in our work. Happy in our play. Happy nearly every day. Did you have a good time in Goblin...I mean Dublin?"

"Oh the best," her eyes sparkled. "The best. I've got some great photos. Do you want to see them?"

My phone rang. I answered it and put it on hold. It was an important customer.

"Oh," she said. "You're busy. Maybe another time."

"I'd say we could go for lunch," I said daringly, my heart suddenly starting to pump faster remembering I fancied the arse off this girl, "but I've been already."

"Oh, that's too bad."

"How about a quick drink tonight?" I asked, nearly passing out. I'm doing it, I thought. I'm actually asking her out. I stared at my desk.

"Ah, I can't tonight."

"Oh, don't worry," I said hastily.

"How about tomorrow?" She looked flushed now. Nervous.

"Tomorrow would be fine." I couldn't believe this was happening. It was like a dream.

"The Crown?" she suggested.

"Six o'clock?"

"Okay," she said. "I'll see you then."

She got up and bounced out of the office, very light on her toes.

My hands shook as I took the call. I didn't listen to a word the woman said. All I could hear was the samba of my heartbeat in my ears.

When I put the phone down, I caught Kate giving me a dirty look.

*****

Cirencester is a town of double-barrelled names, double-barrelled shotguns and, it would appear, blowouts.

I left work at five-fifteen on Tuesday, having spent ten minutes in the loo, getting my hair just right. My tie was pulled down casually, but not too much, my armpits freshly deodorised, my eyelashes wetted to make them look longer.

I was in The Crown minutes later, swilling a double vodka and tonic, followed by another, followed by a pint of Stella. Yes, I believe in Dutch courage. Double Dutch courage. Dutch courage with a dash.

I sat at a table near the door, a copy of *The Times* open but unread, the large ashtray rapidly filling.

Do you want to know how I felt at that moment? Do you?

I'll tell you how I felt. I felt like one of those electric fur rabbits on 'The Bunny Run', and my heart was going as fast.

First dates. Wow! They're tougher than interviews. They're harder on the heart than exams. They're tougher. Tougher than anything.

I sat, and smoked, and drank. I thought of amusing anecdotes, jokes, points of interest in the news. "Oh the price of petrol! The trouble in Palestine. I wonder what happened to Monica Lewinsky?" I sat, I smoked, I looked at my watch.

At eight, I faced the fact she wasn't going to show. I had two more pints to commiserate, bringing my total to six, then went home for a half-pint of whisky.

Before passing out, I went through every conceivable reason for her non-attendance at the pub. Forgot. Got held up. Had an emergency. Decided it wasn't a good idea. Had a car accident. Forgot. Didn't care. Got held up...

*****

I dragged myself into work on Wednesday as depressed and hungover as it's possible to be. At 10.15am Carol said, "There's a call for you on line three that I think you might be interested in taking."

I picked up the handset and croaked, "Hello, Go Away."

"Hi, Guy?"

My head throbbed. My heart back-flipped.

"Speaking," I said moodily, but my beat had already picked up. My heart had forgiven. It was besotted. Blinded by love.

"Hi, it's Daisy."

Like I didn't know. I tried to be cool.

"Oh right. Did you forget about our... did you forget we were going to have a drink last night?"

"No, I didn't forget. Something, err…it's terribly complicated, actually. Listen, I feel terrible about standing you up. Did you wait long?"

"Only till nine o'clock."

"Oh God! I'm so sorry. This is really not me. I'm not like this. Are you free Thursday?"

I paused.

"I think so."

"Brilliant. Shall we have dinner? My treat. To apologise. I can't have my travel agent hating me, can I?"

"No."

"Great. So, how about it? Thursday, I mean?"

"I'd love to," I said quietly.

She let out a short, relieved sigh.

"Harry's? About nine?"

"Perfect," I replied.

"That's great." She sounded rushed and breathless. "I've got to go. I'll see you there."

"I hope so," I said, and she was gone.

Chapter Thirteen

First dates (well, second time around in this case). You do every-thing you can to prepare for them but you're never ready. You can never be prepared. I mean, I thought I was prepared for mine. For Daisy at nine, but I wasn't.

It was last night, our second first date. And I tell you. I've got it so bad for this girl, it's killing me.

I've been bitten by the bug. I think its terminal. So now you're with me. I've filled you in. I've been open. I've given you the low down, warts and all. I've been pretty honest. I may have embellished the odd detail here and there, exaggerated the odd scene, but I won't from here on in. You'll get it just the way it happens. No more lies.

Last night, then. You remember it didn't start well? I told you about it before. I was on the floor covered in beer, the rugger lads laughing... well in these moments there are two possible outcomes. One: you both feel awkward. The evening dies. Rigor mortis. Two: you laugh. You make a connection. You become close.

Daisy and I didn't do one. We did two. She helped me off the floor, we sat down and she said, "Did you forget to take your medication?" in a perfect mock-stern way. We laughed. We laughed more than the rugger boys, who were, by now, chastened, mollified or shocked by Daisy's beauty, her aura. I don't remember them leaving. I don't remember hearing another word from them. I had tunnel vision. Tunnel concentration. There was nothing but Daisy.

God, this is hard to describe. Real infatuation, it's so powerful, isn't it? Like a madness. It's true. Right now, I'm mad. Koo koo. Bonkers. I can't think of anything but her. Right now, I should be in a straight jacket.

I suppose you want me to detail her appearance. It helps to have a picture, doesn't it? Well... when I saw her my heart actually stopped. It missed three or four beats. It quit. It was so shocked, it lost its rhythm. And when it returned, it had upped its tempo, as if trying to make up for the lost semi-quavers. It went from 0-140 in a tenth of a second. Like a DJ queuing up a dance track. No beat and then a very heavy beat. Yes, she looked gorgeous. Breathtaking. She looked like a fantasy.

And she hadn't even tried.

She was wearing a tight black polo neck, tight black linen trousers and black ankle boots with chunky heels. Her hair was tied back, as usual, but looked lustrous and shiny in the candlelight. Her long eyelashes were picked out with a hint of mascara, her lips were shiny with gloss (no colour), her complexion uncluttered by foundation or blusher, just healthy, scrubbed cheeks, a sprinkling of freckles across the bridge of her perky nose. The whites of her eyes were so white. Her teeth gleamed. Her jaw-line was straight and delicate.

Ah, it doesn't sound much, does it? But perfection needs no augmentation. It must not be tampered with. Perfection must be given a long rein, freedom to move.

My heartbeat picks up, even now, simply recalling it all.

"Bet you thought I wasn't going to show?" she said, in her clear, educated voice.

Show what? I felt like saying. But didn't.

She sounded confident, but I detected signs of nerves. The slightest tremble of the fingers, the light stroking of the nape of her neck. I was pleased. Me? I was so shook-up I could have played the maracas or the tambourine without moving.

"The thought had crossed my mind," I replied.

"Well, I'm here," she said mischievously. "And I'm up for some fun, aren't you? Do you like white wine? Let's get a bottle. They do a lovely Chardonnay here."

Before I could agree, or as I was agreeing, Daisy asked the waitress over with a confident, "Hi there!" aimed at the bar. The girl came over. The cuddly cute one. Daisy ordered. The waitress nodded. Daisy then added, "Can you make sure it's really cold?" The waitress said she would.

"Isn't the food great here?" Daisy said.

"Yeah, I like it. I used to come here with my parents years ago. I sometimes pop in for lunch."

Our wine arrived, giving us a moment of silence while we followed the uncorking and pouring process. I thought our first conversation was going well. Daisy seemed excited, eager to please. I was starting to relax.

"Cheers," she said, once the waitress had receded.

"What shall we drink to?" I asked, touching my glass on hers.

"To good fun. To doing what you want to do. To not being satisfied with the same old shit."

We chinked and drank.

"That's a great thing to drink to," I said.

She winked at me. "It's the only thing to drink to, don't you think?"

"Well, I usually drink to freedom," I answered, "but I think that's tied up with what you said."

"It sure is. To freedom!" She chinked my glass again. "And to the speedy release of those who, for whatever reason, in whatever way, do not, at present, have it."

"To the bored office worker..." I continued.

"To the downtrodden housewife."

"To the factory worker."

"To the closeted lesbian."

"To the political prisoners abroad."

"To us, prisoners of politicians."

"To tyranny!"

"To boredom!"

"To dissatisfaction!"

Daisy drank. "To getting another bottle," she said, draining her glass. Her eyes shone. "To getting to know you, too."

"We'll have another bottle," I immediately said to the waitress. And to Daisy, "Are you ready to order?"

She nodded and went right ahead. I liked the way she ran her finger down the menu as she did it and said, "Please may I have?" like she'd had an English teacher at her school who'd always corrected her from saying, "Can I have?" Answer: Yes, you can. But may you? (Yes, you can, baby. You can have it all. You 'may' have the lot. All of me.)

I can't remember what we ate. I was so high that we were connecting, that we appeared to have common ground, everything else faded into insignificance. I do remember her sticking a forkful of what she was having into my mouth, and it tasted exquisite, but I can't remember what it was. I can't. It didn't matter.

The end of the meal came all too soon. Before I knew it we were the only diners left. We'd drunk our two bottles of wine and Daisy was settling up. (I tried to pay, but she insisted and paid cash. Another roll of notes.)

"God, the evening has gone so fast," I said.

"It doesn't have to be over yet," Daisy replied. "The Great Escape is open till two. I know it's dreadful, but we can go and dance."

She said this with no fear that I'd say no.

"Let's," I agreed. "Don't you have to drive anywhere?"

She shook her head. "I took a taxi here. Do you?"

"I live on Ash Road."

Daisy shrugged. "That means nothing to me. I don't know street names."

"Where do you live?"

"Tetbury. I don't know the street names there either. I know the places I want to go. That's it. That's all I need."

Tetbury, I thought – I was right. I told her Ash Road was near where I work.

"Handy," Daisy laughed. "Come on, let's go. I'm desperate to dance."

If I remember nothing about the meal we ate at Harry's, do you expect me to remember anything about The Great Escape? Well actually, I do. Not the first hour, I admit, where I felt very drunk, but later on, after some dancing (don't worry, I didn't blow it here; I dance like a demon). I remember Daisy and I having a good chat at the bar, over bottles of Becks.

"So how come you get to go abroad so often?" I asked her, over the music. I was very close to her ear now, nearly nibbling her neat lobe.

"I have a company called Better Binge…"

The music was so loud, I thought I'd misheard. Oh no, I thought fleetingly. Better Minge? She's a travelling bikini waxer…

"We do catering for functions, fashion shoots, films, concerts, that type of thing."

"Oh," I said, relief flooding me. "How did you get into that?"

"I've cooked since I could reach the hob. I went to catering college in London. I worked at The Thames Garden Restaurant, The Boiler Rooms, The Liquid Lounge. I liked it, but I got bored of doing the same stuff every day. Now I get to create new menus wherever I go."

"That's fantastic," I said, feeling totally out-cooled. "I can cook a bit too…"

"And travel. Travelling is my favourite treat. If I could I would backpack for the rest of my life."

"Me too," I agreed, thinking I could actually conquer my fear of anything with this girl. "Perhaps we should."

"Maybe," she laughed. "Let's dance."

Feeling out-cooled: that's never one to relish. Man's role has always been to impress women, not have women impress them.

Not anymore.

This is the new world. Now we're trying to impress each other. I don't think there's room for it all, personally.

People in showbusiness say never marry someone else in showbusiness. It doesn't work. Two people can't share the limelight. Two people can't have it all.

It's true.

We can't have it all. We can't impress and hope to be impressed. It's one or the other.

Last night Daisy and I got to know each other. We told each other what we thought we wanted to hear. And the boundaries were set.

Daisy, from now on, would impress. And I would be impressed.

This girl was on top. I was flat on my back, holding her hips, letting her do it.

It's the way it was going to be.

At the end of the night, my hormone levels were so high that I looked like a glow-stick in a shirt. Daisy and I had danced, and were getting very close. I'd never been more desperate to sleep with a girl.

So when we popped out of the club onto the yellow light of the street and she stuck her hand straight in the air for a cab, I nearly fell to my knees and begged her not to go. It took all my self-control to remain standing.

"I'll give you a call," she said, as the cab pulled up.

In a trance, I opened the door for her.

"You look very drunk," she said, as she got in. "Will you be okay to get home?"

I nodded.

"Hey," she said, smiling up, the street-light showing the sheen on her skin.

"Yeah?" I replied, feeling sad, nearly angry; she was going.

"Come here."

I leant forward, my back stiff from all the dancing. My head throbbing. My ears full of sleigh bells.

"I've had a brilliant night," she cooed in my ear. And then she kissed me. A soft, tender kiss on either cheek, followed (magically!) by a light brush of her pillowy lips on mine.

I stared down at her.

"Me too," I said. And she was gone.

*****

On Saturday, the phone rang. It wasn't Daisy. It was 'Kathy'. 'Kathy' was not happy.

"Where are you?" she asked at midday, after I'd picked up the phone with shaking fingers and pneumatic heart, thinking it would be Daisy.

"I'm... at home," I said, thinking of the catch, and then remembering... she'd called earlier in the week and persuaded me to visit her in Reading at the weekend.

"Why?" she asked. Her voice was a mixture of hurt and annoyance. "You could have called."

I coughed loudly and started acting.

"Christ, what time is it?"

"Twelve."

"God. Really? I've had this flu thing coming on all week. I've been lying here practically delirious since eight last night."

"Oh, you poor thing! I thought you sounded funny."

I did sound funny. I was so hungover/newly drunk, I could hardly speak.

"Mmm...I think I'll have to stay here, sadly."

"Of course! Goodness. I can be there in an hour if I hurry."

"No, it's okay," I croaked.

"I insist," she said. "I've got every flu remedy known to man. With my care, you'll be fine by tomorrow. See you soon."

And with that she put the phone down.

My first thought was that I could go out. Leave a note saying my parents had picked me up and taken me home. It was tempting, but knowing 'Kathy', I guessed she'd track me down somehow.

"Bugger," I breathed, and got another can of beer from the fridge.

*****

Forty minutes later there was a knock at the door. Forty minutes! Christ, I thought, that's not possible. She must have flown.

"It's open!" I called. I was lying on the sofa, cradling 'medicinal' whisky, cocooned in a duvet with a box of tissues on the coffee table. I was drunk enough to feel nonchalant about her arrival. I was drunk enough to ignore her faults. I was as ready as I'd ever be.

"Hi, Guy," came a familiar voice. Familiar, but not the one I was expecting. I turned on the sofa, my mouth lolling open.

"Kate," I said. "This is a... surprise."

"You don't mind, do you?"

"What? God, no. I mean it's good to see you. Do you want a drink?"

She shook her head. "I'm driving. You've started early, haven't you?"

I put my glass of whisky back on the table as she came and sat next to me. She smelt of Calvin Klein's Escape. She looked like a model.

"There's a reason behind this," I said. "A very tenuous but, in my book, very good reason."

I told her the situation.

"But didn't you have a date with Daisy the other night?"

she asked.

I nodded.

"And how did it go?"

"Great," I said. "We got on well. We had a laugh."

"So why are you seeing this other girl?"

"Because she's very pushy," I replied. "And I'm weak. I barely even like the girl. What are you doing here, anyway?"

"I came here shopping."

"Find anything?"

"No."

"So you thought you'd pop in and see me?"

"Exactly."

"But the shopping's crap in Cirencester, you know that. Unless you want to buy a Barbour."

"Which I do not. I came here for a change."

"To forget about Damon?"

"Kind of."

"Any word from him?"

"No."

"Oh."

"Yeah, well. He's an arsehole, I've decided. Life goes on. I came over to see if you wanted to do anything tonight, really. I'm bored of staying in, and you're the only single person I know. But..."

A door opened in my mind. Light flooded the darkness.

"You know what?" I said with a guilty, red-eyed grin. "You could do me an enormous favour."

Kate smiled.

"Would it improve our chances of having some fun tonight?"

"Most definitely," I said. "You can act a bit, can't you?"

*****

When 'Kathy' arrived, Kate was under the duvet with me, her head resting on my chest. It worked perfectly. 'Kathy' didn't even bother to knock; she simply thundered up the stairs and barged in, laden with bags.

Kate and I didn't need to act surprised, we were.

"Who are you?" Kate asked, fixing 'Kathy' with a scowl.

I played my part. I sat looking embarrassed. It wasn't difficult. I was embarrassed.

'Kathy' put her bags down and without closing the door said, "'Kathy'."

"Do I know you?" Kate squinted.

"No."

"Have we met somewhere?"

"I don't think so."

'Kathy' was looking confused, bordering on agitated. She turned to me.

"Guy," she asked. "Is this a friend of yours?"

"I'm his girlfriend," Kate said. "Have been, God help me, for three years."

'Kathy' looked crestfallen.

"Oh," she said quietly.

I put my finger to my lips and rolled my eyes, cringing.

"I'm a friend of Guy's sister, Vanessa," she said, getting a grip of herself. "She wanted me to drop round some stuff for Guy's flu."

"Oh." Kate held out her hands. "Thanks."

'Kathy' offered up the remedies.

"Vanessa wishes you all the best," she said. "I guess I'll see you around." She gave me a look. A look that's at home in a Merchant Ivory film, but not in real life. It was a poignant, aggrieved look. I averted my gaze. I couldn't bear the heat of that expression.

"Thanks," I said. And then foolishly, "I'll call you."

"That would be nice," she said, and left. Her steps down the stairs were much quieter this time, more subdued.

"I see what you mean about her," Kate said. "She's no supermodel, is she?"

"But she is a friend of my sister's."

"So?"

"So, I feel bad about it," I said. "Let's go for a drink."

Chapter Fourteen

Game shows. There are many on TV these days, my friends tell me. They involve money, winning prizes, finding a partner, spying on people. I'm not a fan. I can do all of this in any pub. See it all for real, and get drunk.

I explained this to Kate. We were sitting at a quiet table at the back of The Crown, sharing a bottle of Chablis.

"I like them," she said simply.

Hm. She would. I let it go. I had more important things to discuss.

"I've been thinking about both our situations," I said. "I don't like 'Kathy' because I don't think I could live like her. Damon moved out of your house because he claims he can no longer live like you. Wouldn't life be easier if we all lived the same way – like we did at school?"

"Eh?"

"Life has too many options. And we all take different ones. That means, unless we're all very flexible and forgiving, we're unliveable with."

She inhaled and exhaled twice, her well-plucked brow furrowed.

"You know what I think?"

I didn't.

"I think you talk a load of shit half the time."

"You're probably right. Feel free to change the subject."

Kate did. She felt free to. She got talking about the new DKNY shop on Oxford Street. I nodded and shook my head at the right times, I think, and got more drunk. It seemed like the best thing to do. By the time we got back to my flat, Kate was drunk too, and the phone was ringing.

*****

"Hello," I said, "The Go Away Travel Centre." Thursday already. The weekend seems a long, long time ago. I've had an under siege day so far. I mean truly terrible. Constant shelling, screaming and shouting. "Hello," I said again.

"Who was that girl who answered your phone on Saturday night?" came a refined, but sexy voice. A voice I knew well, was getting to know better, and one that made my heart hammer.

"Daisy," I croaked, casting my mind back. "You phoned on Saturday?"

"Yes. At about ten-thirty. I was in town and wondered if you wanted to meet up."

"Oh, that would have been great." I could feel myself reddening.

"The girl said you didn't want to speak to me. Is she your girlfriend?"

"No!" I quickly responded. "I don't have one. God me? Girls? No, that was a friend of mine. The girl who sits opposite me here actually."

This attracted some attention from around the office, even Ted looked up. Luckily Kate was out the back, smoking. A cigarette. Not her personally.

"The blonde one?"

"Yes."

"She's very attractive." Daisy sounded a mixture of mocking and jealous.

"Mmm."

Shit. Why did I let Kate answer the phone? I thought it was 'Kathy' that's why. So did Kate.

"No, you can't speak to him," she had said. "He's asleep. Can I take a message? Okay then, bye."

"Do you want to have lunch tomorrow?" I asked. There'd been a long pause. There was an even longer one after the question.

"I can do Saturday."

I was working, but it didn't matter. I could take a long lunch.

"Fine," I said. "One o'clock okay?"

"Mmm...one's fine." It sounded like she was eating an apple.

"Great. Let's go to the pizza place on Castle Street."

"Where's that?"

I explained and hung up.

Carol looked at me as I put the phone down.

"I assume you won't be taking more than an hour in my absence?" she asked. It was her weekend off.

"Would I?"

"I haven't been too impressed with your level of commitment recently."

"I'm doing okay," I said. "Only Ted outsold me last week, and that was because his corporate client came in with a load of flights."

"I'm aware of that. It's your concentration I'm worried about. You seem on a different planet half the time. I think you and I should have a meeting tomorrow."

"Fine," I said.

Ted caught my eye and shrugged.

"I think he's doing great," he said to Carol. Carol ignored him.

"We can all do better. Some of us, much better."

Christ, I thought. She must have seen my school report.

*****

102

I phoned Ben when I got in that night.

"I hope you're treating my sister right."

"Mate," he replied. "Give me a break."

"Have you seen her recently?"

"At least three times a week since her party."

"Christ, you must be sleeping with her then." He laughed.

"So are you?"

"None of your business."

"Seriously, are you?"

"Like I said. It's none of your business."

"She's my sister!"

"Exactly. Ask her if you want to, but you'll get the same answer."

I phoned Vanessa.

"Guy!" she said. "As if I'm going to discuss that with you."

"You're my sister," I said.

"Exactly."

I put the phone down. I couldn't explain my extreme need to know if they were sleeping together, but I needed to know.

When I got back from the kitchen with a beer, the phone was ringing.

"Hi," I said.

"Guy." It was Vanessa again. "While we're on the subject of sleeping with people, what's going on with you and 'Kathy'?"

"Nothing," I replied.

"Did she come down to see you at the weekend?"

"Kind of. She turned up unannounced."

"But weren't you supposed to meet her here, in Reading?"

"Ish. She invited me over but I hadn't fully agreed to it."

"That's not her story."

"Two stories are never the same."

"And who was the girl you were with when she turned up?"

"That was Kate, a girl from work."

"And what's going on with her?"

"We work together?"

"Then why did she say she was your girlfriend?"

"She's weird?"

I didn't see why I had to explain everything when nothing was being explained to me. Answering questions with further questions seemed a good way out, if somewhat American.

"Hang on," said Vanessa. "Somebody here wants to talk to you."

There was the noise of the phone being passed over and some whispering.

"Hello." 'Kathy's' voice sounded nervous.

I nearly hung up, but knew my sister would kill me.

"Hi," I said. "Listen, I'm sorry about last weekend. I wasn't really ill, I was hungover. The girl wasn't my girlfriend, she was just a friend who popped over to see me."

"Then why did she say she was?"

"She's weird."

"So you don't have a girlfriend?"

"No."

"So you still want to see me?"

"Aah…well, I can't do anything this weekend I'm busy, but…"

"The weekend after. I'll come down and we can do whatever, maybe go to London. In fact, yes. We'll all go to London. With Vanessa and Ben. We can stay at his."

Oh cripes, I thought. But what I said was, "Okay, that sounds, yeah…nice. Umm…call me next week."

Vanessa came back on the line.

"That sounds like fun, doesn't it?"

"Are you deliberately trying to drop me in it?"

"Yeah, bring a sleeping bag. Sure, you can stay here on Sunday night, if you want."

"I'll take that as a yes."

"See you next Friday, then. Bye."

"Love you too," I said, and put the phone down.

I knew what my sister was doing. Clearly little 'Kathy' had said I'd slept with her. And my sister was punishing me for it. She didn't believe in casual sex. She believed in relationships. And that was what she was going to make damn sure 'Kathy' and I had. I loved my sister, but not unconditionally. She'd done this to me before and I'd let it go. This time it demanded revenge. With Ben as her boyfriend, I was sure I could think of something to upset her world. Something to show her who was boss.

Having wolfed down a pizza and several beers for supper, I felt as if I had several gas canisters exploding in my stomach. There was only one thing for it. Visit the Texaco garage and get some Rennies.

I fill up at this garage often and usually come out feeling like someone's pulled the plug on my life. It's a draining, if not totally depressing, experience.

The staff there are surly. Like bouncers. And there's this one guy... all-knowing glare, uninterested arrogance, full of scorn. He manages to make me feel like vermin whenever I go in there. I don't know what I've done but he despises me. Maybe it's the indigestion. Or life.

I mean. Indigestion. It's so common, isn't it? It honks of hurriedly eaten take-away, cheap fizzy beer, poor quality colon. It's all burps, farts, hiccups. It's just dead embarrassing.

So I went to the petrol station and hurried in. My heart sank. The young guy was on, listening to Radio One, arms crossed defensively. I skipped up the steps, grabbed the Rennies and popped back to the counter.

"How are you?" he said as I approached. Hey, this was new. I don't think I'd ever heard him speak before.

"Apart from the obvious, I'm fine."

He smiled. "What was it? A vindaloo?"

"No. Americana pizza."

"That's okay. You won't shit yourself later."

I laughed. Amazed by the boy's frankness. "Hope not."

"You know if you drank half-a-pint of milk before you eat, you'd probably be fine."

"I'll try it. Thanks."

"No problem." He gave me my change. "You take care."

"I will," I said. "I will."

People. You just can't fathom them, can you? For six months this guy looks like he wants to kill me, then he's as sweet as a cold beer after a hot year off the piss. And the nice guy next-door who walks his dog every night, and gives you a cheery wave each morning, kills his wife.

But that's life. Don't try and work it out. Just go with it. Be that Pooh stick on the river's current. And if you come out winning, great. And if you come out behind – who cares?

*****

I sometimes wish I were a DJ. Not one of those guys who dashes around eight clubs a night spinning stomach-churning hard house tunes with unpronounceable names and recording artists for thousands of pounds an hour.

I'd like to be a local radio DJ, or hospital radio DJ, or an in-store DJ. One of those bin-ear-phoned fat blokes with infinite patter and a total inability to get embarrassed. By anything.

Yes, I'd like to be like that. Not that I'd like to be on radio. I'd just like to have that personality. That indomitable spirit. That shameless *joie de vivre*. That unstoppable ability to be positive: "Yes, today listeners it's still raining, but not to worry: Woolies are doing half-price umbrellas, we've got all our usual comedy features, and we're still playing the best mix of music from the Fifties, Sixties and today. Next up... Doris Day..."

Yeah, he sounds like a prick. We know that. But he's happy. He's conditioned himself to be that way. He has fun.

I don't have fun. My main emotions are:

Panic. Paranoia. Shame.

I get through the day with:

Bluff. Lies. Fake bravado.

I can only relax when drunk.

I'm drunk now but I'm still not happy. And there is one person I blame for my lack of happiness. It's the tall guy I saw with Daisy. The one she went off with in the highly-polished Range Rover, revelling in his height and his blonde/grey hair. I've been doing a lot of thinking about him, and none of it is good. I'm going to have to ask Daisy about him. Soon.

*****

My meeting with Carol on Friday took place in the back office. Not in The Crown, or Harry's Hairy Hare, or the little coffee shop round the corner, or even Viners the cake place. It happened in the back office, with its smell of stale smoke, its carpet ornamented with out-of-date brochures, its walls tattooed with oily bluetack and browning parchment posters. I wasn't even offered a coffee. I knew it wasn't going to be good.

Carol cleared her throat and cast her eye over a sheet of A4 paper she had on a clipboard, kept close to her bosom. I knew what it was. It was a staff assessment sheet. Something she hadn't used on me in months.

"I like you, Guy," she began.

I nodded. She sighed.

"And I know you're doing okay, but... if you're going to take over from me in a couple of months, I need to see that you're responsible."

I nodded again.

"Do you know what this means?"

I did. It meant always using condoms, never drinking and driving, and getting your tax return in by the end of March. I said, "It's response and ability. My ability to respond...to customers' needs...err, quickly."

"Don't try to be funny. It means..." and here she did that

pointing with her thumb first patented by Bill Clinton and taken on by Tony Blair, "…it means arriving for work on time. Looking smart. Dealing with all enquiries politely and efficiently. Being able to help your colleagues with difficult flights."

"Knowing how to get Kate to shut up."

"Well that comes into it, yes," she smiled, the tension coming out of her. "You know what I'm talking about, Guy. I don't know what's going on with you at the moment, and I don't want to know the details of your private life, but when you come in looking like the groom after a stag party every morning, I do worry."

"I don't come in looking like that every morning."

"But not far off."

I shrugged.

"I promise to do better."

"I know you will, if that's what you want. But I'm not sure this is what you really want, is it? The job, I mean."

I shrugged again.

"Who knows what they really want? I like this job as much as I'd like any other."

"How do you know that?"

"I like other people to go travelling. I like to help people have a good time."

"And that's it?"

"What more is there?"

Carol tapped her pen against the clipboard and inhaled sharply.

"Hopefully, I'm going to find out in Cape Town," she said quietly.

"You do that," I replied. And our meeting was over.

Chapter Fifteen

I've barely travelled. Pick a place you've been to, or that a friend's been to, or a relative, and I can guarantee I won't have been there. I am not qualified to be a travel agent.

Trekking from Morocco to Ethiopia. Taking a four-wheel drive from Kenya to Sierra Leone. Hitching from Somalia to Saudi Arabia. Flying across Iran, Afghanistan, Pakistan, India, China, the entire Far East – I haven't done it.

Canada. San Francisco to New York. Mexico, El Salvador, Columbia, Brazil, Uruguay. Every northern European country there is. I haven't been there. I mean, I hate flying, and I got car-sick until I was twenty.

Christ, I haven't even been to Australia.

My favourite place? Spain. I'm not kidding. It's one of the three countries I've visited. The other two are Greece and Portugal.

Carol was right. I didn't want to be a travel agent. Seeing others set off for adventures round the globe made me insecure. It was like slow water torture. Like a tarantula, or a very hungry scorpion, crawling up my back. I could just about stand it but, sooner or later, something very bad was going to happen. I was going to get stung. And seize up. And die.

The truth was, I didn't have the balls to grab a rucksack and go. I needed my home, my creature comforts, my dull little life.

"Hello, Go Away," I said into my handset, the phone ringing for the first time in hours.

"Are you okay today?" Kate asked. I looked over to her desk.

"Why are you calling me on the phone?"

"For a laugh. You seem stressed out."

"I've got a lot on my mind."

"Like what?"

"Never you mind."

"If you need to cheer yourself up, try thinking about one of those amazing trips you went on. You know, Kenya, Thailand, Cambodia. That's what I do." She smirked at me.

"Yeah," I said, "got to go." A guy had come into the office and I wanted his commission. Like I could barely contain my excitement, anyway, casting my mind back to reading those guide books in my bedroom. It was better to get on with it. With the daily grind. With making money.

"Good afternoon to you," I said to the gentleman in my friendly travel agent tone, as I swung in my chair to face him. He looked down at me with kind eyes. He was tall, imposing.

"Hello," he said with a half smile, amusement twinkling in his eyes. "How are you?"

"Very well," I said. "I mean, it's summer, I have no broken bones, there's beer in the fridge..."

He smiled more broadly and then laughed.

"The beer in the fridge I like..."

"So what can I do for you?"

"Well as you say," he began, in a deep, educated, financially secure tone, "it's summer. Time for holidays."

"In which case, you've come to the right place. Holidays are what we do."

He had a light tan, like he'd recently returned from abroad. He had the look of someone who was on a permanent holiday. Not a hint of stress anywhere on his face.

"I'd like a couple of flights to Lisbon," he said, putting his elbow on the table and resting his chin in his hand.

"When for?" I liked this. Portugal was my speciality.

He told me.

"And how many of you will be travelling?"

"Just two," he said. "My girlfriend and I."

I kept my eyes fixed on the screen. This was not a guy, who looked to be in his forties, that I'd have reckoned on having a 'girlfriend'. A wife maybe, but not a girlfriend.

I continued eyeing the screen as I said (and I don't know how the hell I got away with it), "Wife getting on your nerves, is she?"

He laughed without malice.

"That would be telling," he said. "Who says I have a wife?"

"I was joking," I replied, suddenly feeling Carol staring at me in horror, feeling the heat.

"That's quite alright," he said, glancing at Carol and pointing at me. "I like this guy's style."

"There are flights available on the 16th. What time of day would you like to travel?"

"Oh, always after lunch, I think, don't you? You're relaxed, full, a little drunk."

"Definitely," I agreed. "Nothing worse than starting your trip with airline food."

"Quite."

"Two-thirty-five okay, from Heathrow?"

"Perfect."

"And flying back?"

"Around the 20th. Can't be any later. I've got an important deal going through."

"Cocaine?" I couldn't help myself!

"No. More's the pity. I've got this site I've been trying to buy for nearly a year and I think it's finally going to come off. A good rest before the big push, and there'll be no stopping me."

"Always helps," I said.

He wanted the flights.

"Okay," I typed the details in. "And your name is...?"

"Warnford," he said. "Mr Peter Warnford."

I looked up. My vision went like a film effect. The one where the character in the foreground stays in the same place but the background recedes rapidly, making you feel dizzy.

"Anything wrong?" he asked.

"No," I replied, blinking rapidly. "No. I thought a contact lens was coming loose, but I think it's okay." I touched my eye dramatically. "How do you spell that?"

He spelt it out as my head swam. Said he wanted the tickets posted.

He gave me an address in Tetbury, which made me quiver again, but I managed to disguise it. I felt like saying, "Do you drive a black Range Rover? Do you know Daisy? Are you related?" But I kept my mouth shut, and was serenely polite throughout the rest of our meeting. I even offered to book him accommodation. He didn't need it. He had his own villa. When he left, I bolted to the loo in the back office and locked myself in, furiously smoking and thinking, tapping my right foot.

*****

The little pizza place on Castle Street isn't called Antonioni's, or Bella Pizza, or Ristorante Italiano. It's called Packed With Pepperoni. Not much more original than the afore-mentioned, but ten out of ten, and a large candy floss for the small boy, for trying.

It's a casual joint. Battered pine tables, candles stuck in old bottles of Lambrusco, walls in need of a good painter and decorator (a grand, mate. That's as low as I can go for the whole job). It doesn't even have any cutlery. You have to eat the pizzas with your fingers.

"You been here before?" I asked Daisy. We were sitting at a table near a side window, drinking Peroni.

"I haven't," she said. This lunchtime her hair was in 'bunchies', cutely enough, which were complemented by a little pink t-shirt with a white rabbit motif on the front. I didn't see what she had on below the waist; I was nonchalantly smoking and staring at the ceiling when she arrived.

"Do you like it?"

"I love it. Is the food good?"

"If you like pizza, you should be okay."

She laughed. We ordered. I had the full spicy meat job. (Freshly slaughtered buffalo, giraffe neck, crocodile thighs, etc. You know, the usual.) Daisy had the mixed seafood. (Curiously: tuna, prawns, mussels, calamari. Wow! Exotic!)

I ordered two more Peronis. I had an hour for lunch. Well, forty-five minutes by this point, and I had to get drunk enough to ask Daisy the all-important question; the one which was squirming like an eel to come out of my mouth.

We ate and talked. The cheerful Italian waiters embarrassed both of us while creating the 'atmosphere'.

"Ah, the beautiful girl. She your girlfrien', ri? No? Wha' happen with you? Why no? You like de boys? No, I don think so with you. You like her right? Give it time, my friend, give it time!"

We laughed our way through it and ate our way through the pizzas. I had another beer. I swigged it back and said, "Hey, guess what?"

Daisy held up her hands questioningly.

"A guy called Peter Warnford came in the other day and booked a flight. Mad, hey? That's two Warnfords I've met this summer. You guys must be like comets. You wait a lifetime for one to fall to earth, then you get two at the same time."

"I think they only come in ones."

"Maybe you're right. Do you know him?" I said. "Is he related?"

"Oh," she said, examining her t-shirt now. The ears on the bunny seemed to droop as she pulled it. "Yes," she muttered in a small voice.

"What does 'yes' mean?"

She looked up at me with pleading, hurt eyes.

"Nothing," she said.

"He's related?"

"No. Not really."

"Come on, what does that mean?"

She took a deep breath, examined her fingers.

"Can we drop the subject?" she said at last.

"You're worrying me."

"Sorry."

I was getting a very bad feeling. Like an invisible force had attached a nylon line to the top of my stomach and was pulling it slowly down to my ankles.

"Is he your husband?" I said, looking at the top of her head.

She was shaking it from side to side now. Slowly, deliberately.

"Is he?" I repeated.

She looked up.

"It's more complicated than that." She looked at her watch, then at me. She looked very sad now, fragile, vulnerable. "I've got to go," she said, but she didn't move.

I sat there, numb.

"Will you call me?" I said, not wanting to push her any further.

She took my hand in hers and squeezed it.

"I have got some stuff I need to tell you," she said. "I just can't now."

"I understand," I nodded.

"I really like you," she said. "I like you so much."

"I really like you too," I replied. "I think about you all the time. Call me, when you want to talk."

"Thanks," she said, and got up to go. I watched her stride through the exit and onto the street. Soon she was out of view.

My heart dropped through my shoes, through the floorboards and into the basement, where it beat three or four times, then stopped dead.

"Shit," I said as I put my card on the saucer to pay the bill. "Shit."

Chapter Sixteen

Heart Break Hotel: Elvis at his sultry, drawling best. This is the song that played in my head for the next week. I must say, I found it very difficult to concentrate on anything much apart from being downcast. So much so, I almost thought of learning to play a musical instrument and forming an indie band. But I couldn't. I was too grief-stricken to do anything. Except drink and mooch.

I became one of those people you see in the twenty-four-hour Tescos, staring at the range of goods for what seems like forever, unable to make a decision.

I used to laugh at these people. Come on! I used to think. Choose! You're looking at the shelves like they're an 'A'-level, a degree course, a doctorate in microbiology... taught in Thai. Cripes! How difficult can it be?

But it was difficult. For my confused, depressed mind, it was hard. Choosing felt like learning a new language, or how to play bridge, or filling in a tax form. Simple tasks had become complex. I was living in the dead zone. All life was lifeless.

And, as is always the case, you get kicked while you're down. In the middle of the following week, my father called to say my mother had been taken to the John Radcliffe Hospital. Somehow, in her frail state, she'd caught pneumonia.

I went to see her on Wednesday. I have never seen her look

so pale and skinny. Her hand felt like a bird's claw in mine. Her face was pinched. Her voice got lost in the background noise. It was barely above a whisper.

Dad and I talked to the doctors. They said her condition was stable, that they were monitoring her closely.

"She's not a car!" I said tightly, drawing a scowl from my father. "She needs to be looked after. Not 'monitored'."

"We're doing all we can," I was told.

My father and I went into a huddle on our own.

"I'm worried," he said. "She looks very weak. Sometimes she gets confused and forgets what she's saying."

"So do I, Daddy," I said. "I shouldn't worry too much about that."

I stood by her bed and watched her sleeping, while my father went to find coffee and cake. As I stared down at the gentle undulation of her breathing beneath the sheet, I started to cry. Tears rolled down my cheeks and onto my shirt. I felt ashamed but I couldn't stop. By the time I'd pulled myself together, Vanessa and Ben were striding out of the whiteness towards me, their shoes clip-clipping on the bleach-smelling tiles.

"Hi guys," I said. It was strange seeing them together: *The couple*. They were holding hands. They looked like they were already married.

"Hi," they said in unison. I hugged Vanessa first and then Ben, slapping him on the back.

"You didn't have to come," I said.

"I wanted to," Ben replied.

"How is she?" Vanessa asked, eyes wide and wetter than normal, ready to cry, on full cry alert.

I told her what the doctors had said. She nodded.

"Do you think she's going to be alright?"

"Of course. You know Mum. She's a fighter."

Vanessa nodded some more, then put her head on Ben's chest. We all sat and took the coffee gratefully when my father arrived.

The edges of the afternoon blurred into a dreamlike state where time doesn't travel forwards or backwards, rather sideways. We all drifted into our own private comas, emerging only when it was time to go.

"You're still coming at the weekend?" Vanessa said, as we walked to the car park.

"If you insist."

"I do."

"It'll be fun," Ben chipped in. "Take your mind off all of this."

"I'll phone before I leave," I said, helping Vanessa into the passenger side of the TVR and closing the door before she could reply.

I waved them off. The noise of the engine almost burst my ear-drums as Ben accelerated away.

"Will you come for dinner some time?" my father asked, walking up behind me. "It gets awfully lonely in that big house. I'm afraid Dot's on holiday, so you'll have to make do with my cooking skills. Or lack of them."

"Okay," I said. "What are we having? Welsh rarebit?"

"Something like that." We were at my car now. "I'll see you at home then," he said, "when you come round." I watched him walk stiffly across the car park to the Aston. His shoulders were straight and forced back, but there was an undeniable vulnerability to them that I hadn't seen before. It made me sad. No one likes to see their parents going to pieces.

I got in the car and left. The traffic on the A40 was terrible. I overtook recklessly, horns blaring. I didn't care. Nothing else could go wrong. And if it did, so what?

*****

Daisy phoned me at work on Thursday. You know what she said? You'd think so, wouldn't you? Mmm...something like, "Come and meet me for a drink and I'll explain everything, Guy, sweetie."

But no. What she said was, "Guy, I hate to do this to you, but I need a flight, urgently. I thought I'd booked it ages ago, but I forgot."

"When for?" I couldn't keep a little bite out of my voice. I wasn't going to say, "Don't worry."

"The 16th."

"Where to?"

"New York. A promoter I know wants me to cook for this huge gig at Madison Square Gardens."

"What the crowd?"

"No, the bands."

"Shame," I said, "if it was the crowd you could get by with a couple of hundred thousand hot dogs."

Daisy laughed. I booked the flight.

"You can pick the tickets up at the airport, as usual," I said.

"Thanks, you're a darling. I swear to God, we'll talk when I get back. I really want to explain things to you."

"I want you to as well," I said. "I'll see you later."

I put the phone down. My heartbeat was up, as usual, but my spirits down. The highway of our romance was turning into a country lane. We were getting bogged down in some serious shit.

*****

My father didn't cook Welsh rarebit when I went around for dinner. He heated chicken Kiev in the oven, and served it with baked potato and broccoli. I was impressed. My father has never been much of a cook. He even managed a few peas.

An unexpected visitor was my brother Jack, who'd travelled down from London. He was looking disgustingly healthy and solvent. His hair shone, his eyes sparkled. He shook my hand like he intended to break it.

"Have you managed to even get on a plane yet, travel boy?"

he scoffed.

I nodded sagely.

"And of course, finding people to do other people's jobs is hard," I said. "You're like a middle-man, a 'go between'. Have you seen that film? You're Jenny Agutter."

My brother was still wearing an immaculate pin-stripe suit with a crisp white shirt. Not because he hadn't had time to change, but because he wanted to appear impressive, lord it over me. I stood there, with my t-shirt untucked and my combat trousers ruffled, and took it.

My father sat us down at the kitchen table.

"There's no point in eating in the dining room without your mother," he said quietly.

"How is she?" Jack asked, all deep concern.

"Haven't you even been to see her?" I asked.

"I've been busy."

"Yeah, like getting your hair cut and your suits dry-cleaned. Christ..."

We got through the meal, all of us, with some tension, but less as we drank more. In the drawing room, with whisky and cigars after the meal, the atmosphere was almost genial. Jack even suggested we get together in London sometime. I said I'd try and fit it in, not planning to.

Jack was taking the train back to London that night, so father gave him a lift to Charlbury station. It gave me some time alone. Some time I needed. I did what I always did with time at my parents' house. I went and sat out on the bench by the garage, drank my whisky, smoked my cigar and looked up at the stars.

I thought of happier days.

My father joined me when he got back. He'd driven his Aston to impress Jack. He took ages parking. Lining it up with tennis balls and floor guides, set squares and tramlines. I peered in as he killed the engine. I'm sure there was another car missing.

When he came out of the garage, I'd had time to get him a drink and another cigar. I'd had time to do an eight-hundred metre run, but there you go.

"He got away safely," he said, taking his drink with a nod of thanks.

"Big deal," I replied.

"We all know you two don't get on."

"Yeah, well. Are you surprised? He used to humiliate me at every opportunity. Every girlfriend I ever had he used to embarrass me in front of. Tell them I was a virgin or something. You know he used to get friends of his in London to phone me at work?"

My father nodded and drank. I don't think he was really listening.

"The first time they booked six business class tickets to New York, gave me all their details, special meal requests, asked loads of ludicrous questions: 'Are the cabin crew good-looking? What's the ratio of girls to faggots?' You know, on and on, and then the next day Jack phoned up and cancelled the lot. He thought it was hysterical."

My father seemed to have woken up. "That is quite amusing," he said.

"And what about getting one of the older guys at his office to phone up and say his brother had just died and he needed to get to the funeral in Sydney. And he didn't have much money. Could I do the ticket half-price? Blah, blah, then crying. Almost an hour on the phone before Jack cuts in laughing his head off."

My father was silent for a bit.

"Now that's a little shameful," he agreed.

"And they," I said, "are just two examples of a man's life spent dedicated to humiliating me."

"Hmm," my father noted.

There was a companionable silence. It went on for long enough for our thoughts to drift back to where they'd started.

I finished my drink. "Dad?" I said, feeling about five, "You don't think Mummy's going to die, do you?"

"No," he said, rubbing his thighs. "No, she won't. I really

don't think so."

I nodded and drank.

My father gave a long sigh, like a sea lion in mating season. Then he said, "I haven't felt like this since your Uncle Graham disappeared."

I kept quiet. This was not a usual topic of conversation. We never spoke about Graham. I'd never even met the guy. He'd had a nervous breakdown and disappeared shortly after my grandfather died. We didn't speak about Graham. It was like talking about sex in front of your grandmother. Not done. Never done.

"I still feel guilty about it," my father continued.

"It wasn't your fault."

My father sighed again.

"I can't understand why my father left all his money to me, and nothing to my brother. He must have done something awful."

"Perhaps one day you'll be able to ask him," I said.

"I doubt it. He's gone. Never coming back."

I shrugged.

"You never know," I said. And I certainly didn't.

*****

Families are like fake antiques. Families present a unified front to the world but, beneath the veneer, there's cracks and glue and dodgy bits of chipboard filler. My family is no exception.

The person who usually holds it all together is the mother: The Matriarch. Men in the family fight and brawl, make money and lose it, become alcoholics and sober up. The women ride it all out, all the while keeping it together.

I can't remember how many fights my mother refereed in her time, or how many more she will in the future. When we kids were younger there were regular fist-fights, chipped teeth, and possessions stolen, hidden or broken out of spite. My mother adjudicated all of the squabbles, as fairly as she knew how.

It was always Mum, not Dad, we went to for advice. Now we were older, and less scared, we could go to Dad too, for some things, but Mother was our first choice. My first choice. I had no idea what I'd do without her.

That night, though we're not religious, Dad and I dipped our heads and prayed. Under the stars, we prayed she'd be okay, that she'd be able to go on loving us for many more years, that we'd be able to love her back, the best way we could.

I'll never forget that night. It was the night my father and I showed our emotions to each other without fear or guilt. It was the night he admitted he missed his brother and couldn't handle the thought of my mother also disappearing. Fading. It was good honest, heartfelt stuff.

My mother would have been proud.

Chapter Seventeen

It was Saturday night. I was drunker than a poet who hasn't eaten in days and chased a bottle of Absinthe with Meths. Ben and I were shouting at each other in a random club over some whip-loud music.

"I... want... to... marry... your... sister!" he yelled.

"You're kidding me."

"I'm not."

I dragged him off to the side of the dance-floor to a table covered in drinks and full ashtrays.

"Why?" I said, holding his shoulder as I asked him.

"I love her."

"I know that," I said. "I'm not stupid, but why so soon?"

"She's incredible. We fit together like two bits of Scaletrix."

"Did they ever fit together?"

"You know what I mean!"

"Yeah," I nodded, "I suppose I do. When are you going to do it? I mean does she know about this?"

"Yeah, man. We've discussed it. Next summer. We want you to be best man."

"What do I know about being best man? Worst man, maybe, but best?"

"Nothing! But you'll learn. Will you?"

"If you write the speech."

"Nick off, you write your own speech. That's the only thing you have to do."

"And organise the stag do," I corrected.

"Yeah, I guess. Minimum of five strippers at mine, man."

"But no hookers," I said. "Not if you're marrying my sister."

"Yeah, fair enough. I can live with that."

"Let's go and find her," I said. "I want to know if this is true. If she's this mad."

We found Vanessa on the dance-floor with her housemate Eve and the ubiquitous 'Kathy'. (Yes, I did bed her on Friday. I know. I'm not proud. But I had to; I was so depressed about everything, I couldn't stop myself. She gave me a fantastic ear nibbling, too. An erotic pleasure I had hitherto not experienced.)

We fought our way through the sweating crowds just as a big dance hit came on. The crowd went mental. Or more mental. The pint I was carrying shot in the air like a flare. It orbited briefly, above the lighting rack, before re-entering the heavy dance-floor atmosphere on Vanessa's shoulder, spilling backwards onto some thick-set guy. He in turn blamed some scrawny kid next to him and gave him a going over. Poor kid was already holding a pint in either hand – clearly not guilty. Still, all credit to him, even after a good scuffle he still had over half-a-pint in each hand. That's students for you. They may be a lot of things but they've got their priorities right. They know what's important and they hang onto it.

"Vanessa!" I shouted, 'Kathy's' sweaty hands clasping at my face and her threatening lips trying to find mine. "Vanessa," I said, brushing 'Kathy' aside and getting close enough to my sister to shout the question. "Vanessa, are you marrying Ben?"

"Yes!" she squealed back. "What do you think? Are you happy?"

I didn't know what to think. I hadn't had time to think. So I said simply, "Yes, of course," and danced with her until 'Kathy' managed to grab me from behind and drag me off, her pudding bowl breasts squashed into my back.

The rest of the night was a blur. Little sticks in my mind other than 'Kathy' asking me if I'd ever thought about getting married. She did this once we'd piled into Vanessa's spare bedroom and were naked together.

"Only in the way I think of Snowdonia," I said.

"What do you mean?"

"With dread," I answered and passed out.

*****

I'm sorry to report that on Sunday morning, right off the bat, with teeth-loosening hangovers and biscuit-dry tongues, in the beautiful four walls of Vanessa and Eve's 'student' house, an argument erupted between my sister and I that I can only describe as *reality TV*, so regrettable was it.

Vanessa and I were going to see my mother, or so I thought. I was wrong. Yes, Vanessa and I were visiting, but so were Ben and 'Kathy'. Ben – no problem. He was my best friend. He was marrying my sister. He had every right. He had achieved the correct status.

'Kathy', on the other hand...'Kathy' was posing as my girlfriend all too frequently. And now she wanted to visit my mother? My poor, sick mother?

"Vanessa," I said, dragging her off to her bedroom. "This has gone far enough. I know you think I've treated 'Kathy' badly, but come on. I don't want her to meet our mother. She's not my girlfriend."

"Why are you still sleeping with her then?"

"Because..."

"She's coming with us. She'll be right there with us; and you will be nice. And do you know why?"

"Why?"

"Because it might teach you to be a human being, Guy. You're turning into a right... knob, do you know that?"

I stared at my sister, wide-eyed. She'd never talked to me like this before. I felt anger rising in my throat.

"Fine," I said. "So, yeah, fine! Now I should just do what everyone else wants, I suppose. Become a little robot that anyone can control."

"You've always done whatever you wanted," Vanessa said.

"That is not true!"

"It is! You were supposed to do geography at university, and you did sociology and anthropology. You got a job in the City, then decided you didn't like it. You didn't want to live in London anymore, so you moved to Cirencester. You've always done whatever you wanted!"

"Yeah, well. Things didn't work out... and why shouldn't I change my mind..."

"You've treated lots of girls like rubbish."

"Okay!" I said. "Drop it. And that's not true. For every girl who never got a call, there are plenty of girls I've had great relationships with."

"Hmm."

The tension eased a bit.

"We'll all go and see Mum," I said.

Vanessa paused and recomposed herself.

"Good," she said. "Give me a minute to get my bag."

*****

"What's wrong?" 'Kathy' asked in the car. We were halfway to Oxford. I hadn't said a word. I was sulking.

"Nothing."

"Oh come on!"

"Vanessa's getting on my nerves," I lied. What I meant to say was, "You're getting on my nerves," but I didn't have the stamina for it with my brain-bleedingly-bad hangover. And I knew she'd tell. "I mean, can you believe she's getting married? She's only a child."

"She's plenty old enough to get married. If you've met the

127

right person, why wait?"

"Common-sense," I said. "The divorce rate. The end of the honeymoon period. Actually bothering to get to know each other?"

'Kathy' fell silent.

"God," she said after a while, "you can be so negative."

I didn't reply. I kept my eye on the road. We came off the M4, then headed north on the A34. Ben had already powered on ahead, showing off in the TVR.

"Where have you been?" he asked as we pulled up the steep slope to the John Radcliffe Hospital.

"We stopped for lunch at Beedon Hill," I replied.

"Yeah, right. Come on, Vanessa's already gone inside. Enjoy the ride, 'Kathy'?"

"I think Vanessa got the better deal," she said.

Cheeky minx!

Mother was asleep when we arrived, or drugged up or something. She didn't say a word the whole time we were there. She'd been moved to a new room, which had a smarter bathroom and a bigger TV. She looked content.

I was relieved she was sleeping. It avoided embarrassment. It's bad enough introducing your girlfriend to a parent even when you like the girl and 'Kathy', I was fast realising, was not someone I liked. She was a person who was demanding things from me I wasn't prepared to give. Not good in anyone's book.

We sat around the bed, talking in hushed tones, hands wrapped protectively round polystyrene cups of bitter coffee. No one knew what to say. Vanessa looked worried. 'Kathy' kept putting her hand on my knee and giving me searching, sympathetic looks.

After an hour-and-a-half, after Vanessa and I had had a quick word with the nurse, we all headed into Oxford for an early supper. We were tired and hungover. The conversation wasn't scintillating. All I wanted to do was go home. I think

Vanessa sensed this.

"'Kathy'," she said, over coffee, "Why don't you come back to Reading with me and Ben in the TVR. Save Guy driving back."

'Kathy' turned to face me.

"If you don't want to drive back to Reading," she said. "I can come and stay at yours."

I choked.

"I think Guy's tired," Vanessa said. "You should come with us."

"Are you sure?" 'Kathy' asked.

"I think so."

"You'll have to sit on Vanessa's lap," said Ben. "It's only got two seats."

"That's fine," said Vanessa. "Let's pay the bill and go. I've got stuff I need to do before tomorrow."

On our way out of the restaurant I quietly thanked Vanessa.

"Don't thank me," she said, brushing it off. "It makes sense that's all." It did make sense, but she'd helped me out. She felt bad about what she'd said, even though she was dead right.

"I'll call you next week," 'Kathy' said to me, as she squeezed into the TVR, squashing my sister. "Give us a kiss." I kissed her reluctantly.

It felt so good to be free of 'Kathy', I actually whistled on the way back to Cirencester.

That night I dreamt I was the star in a porno film. 'Kathy' was in it. Daisy was in it. So was Kate. Thankfully, none of my family made an appearance. That would have been too Freudian. Very scary.

No. The film was quite pleasing. In it I had a go with all three girls and all of them were grateful, or acted like they were. They 'oo-ed' and 'aah-ed' in all the right places. I performed wonderfully. And I looked incredibly well-hung and handsome. Yes, it was all... pleasing.

The downside was this: once the director shouted "Cut!", they all dressed hurriedly and left the room without saying a word. I was left there, straddled on the bed, my enormous great schlong carelessly flung over one thigh like a plump bathrobe belt.

I felt embarrassed. All my bravado was gone.

On the drive home from the studio, I spotted them all having a drink in a terraced bar. They were laughing and joking, and me... I was left all alone.

So totally alone.

I hoped this wasn't a sign of things to come.

Chapter Eighteen

The following week brought more hangovers and a panic phone call from Peter Warnford. He remained calm throughout, though he "desperately" needed my help.

"I've phoned BA," he said. "They told me all of the flights are booked up."

"You were supposed to be flying back tomorrow, right?" I said, looking at the system.

"That's right. But I need to get back today. An urgent meeting has been called over this deal. Is there any way you can get me back?"

"I'll see what I can do." I took his number. I phoned BA direct. The system is often booked out when there are still seats available. I had a 'friend' at BA who might be able to help. I told her the situation.

"...and he only ever flies BA," I added.

"We've got a couple of business class seats available, that's it."

"Can you do it for a reduced price?"

"We shouldn't. Not if he's bringing his flight forward. We'd have to charge him."

"Can you put it up against all of the flights I sell for you guys?"

"Hang on." She put me on hold. Eventually she came back

on. "We can't make a habit of this, but we'll do it. This time."

"You're a genius. Give me the details."

I got straight back to Peter.

"I've managed to wangle it," I said. "Your flight leaves in three hours. You're in business class."

"Oh right," he sounded pleased. "That's about double the price, right?"

"I got them to give it to us for no extra charge."

"Brilliant. You're a miracle worker."

"On one condition. You always fly BA."

He laughed. "You know I always do."

I told him where to pick up his new ticket and let him go. He was supremely grateful. I enjoyed doing it. In spite of everything, I liked the guy.

*****

I'd spent the first half of the week praying Daisy would phone. This was irrational. She was in New York until today, busy working.

She phoned me about four o'clock from London, a few short hours after her plane touched down. I was delighted to hear from her so soon after her arrival, though it felt like she'd been gone a decade.

"Are you free tonight?" she asked.

Of course I was.

"You're very sweet."

"Do you want to go for dinner?"

"Actually," she said. "I'm shattered. Could I just come round to yours? I'll bring a couple of bottles of wine."

"I can get some Chinese take-away," I said.

"That sounds perfect."

I told her where I lived in relation to the Go Away. No use telling her the road name again.

"I wonder who that was," said Kate, after I'd hung up,

arching a well-plucked eyebrow.

"Don't piss on my bonfire, Kate. I'm happy. Last time I looked, being happy wasn't a crime."

"It should be for you," she said, with a narrowing of the eyes, and went back to her work.

"It's very sweet of you to have me round," said Daisy. "I mean, you barely know me."

"Are you a thief?" I said. "Are you casing the joint?"

She smiled. "There's not much to steal is there?"

We both laughed. There wasn't much to nick, no, but I'd spent the last hour making sure everything was clean.

"You seem sad," I said. "Or are you just tired?"

"Both."

I was opening the second bottle of Wolf Blass she'd brought. It was a tremendous white, kind of creamy. The Chinese take-away lay half-eaten on cold plates, the foil containers on the coffee table.

Daisy moved to the floor. She sat cross-legged, bare-foot, her hair tied back. She appeared to be looking for something in the bottom of her glass. I topped it up.

"Thanks," she murmured. We sat in silence. Some trance played quietly on the stereo. The lights were off apart from the lamp next to the TV. I lay back on the sofa, put a hand behind my head.

The atmosphere in the room tensed.

Daisy sipped her wine. Running a slender finger across her full lips, she said, "I am married."

I stared at the top of her head; her fingers moved like a millipede's feet on her glass. I said nothing. It wasn't an out-and-out shock but it depressed me. I felt like crying. These were not the three words I wanted to hear.

"I've been married for six years," she said quietly, sounding emotional, "...and I hate it."

I saw a glimmer of hope and lunged for it like the fat guy

grabbing the last cake at a tea party.

"So get out," I said. "If it doesn't make you happy, get out."

"I can't," she replied. She was crying now and not trying to hide it. "I can't. I can't. I have two lovely children and I love them more than anything. I can't destroy their home. I have a lovely home. I can't..." She put her glass on the coffee table and put her hands to her face. I leant forward and put an arm around her shoulders.

I didn't know what to say. I was devastated. Married *and* two kids? Talk about a fast mover. I hadn't even lived with anyone yet. I'd been pacing myself, waiting for the right girl. Waiting a little too long, as it turned out. My mouth, when I attempted to speak, wouldn't work. It was locked tight. So instead of saying something stupid, I simply got down on the floor, hugged her and cried right along with her.

It was Daisy who kissed me first. She put a hand behind my head and kissed me on the cheek, leaning in towards me. Then she kissed my ear, my neck and finally brought her mouth to mine.

After several minutes of exquisite togetherness, she broke off.

I looked at her lovely face, her doleful eyes.

"We shouldn't be doing this," she said.

"I know," I said. "I'm sorry. It's just... I like you so much." Understatement isn't usually my thing but this was probably the biggest understatement of my life. I didn't just like this girl, I prayed to her.

"I like you too," she agreed. "I'll tell you what..."

My heart stopped.

"If we sleep together tonight and promise never to do it again..."

My heart remained still.

"I think I could live with that," I lied, my instant hard-on snagging painfully in my jeans.

"I could too," she said. "No one would ever need to know.

Peter thinks I'm staying in London tonight."

I smiled; my heart gave a feeble beat. "You had this all planned out," I said.

She looked hurt, then a cheeky gleam came in to eyes.

"Well, maybe."

I got to my feet.

"Good," I winked. "Come on. My bedroom's through here."

To say Peter's a lucky man would be a second terrible understatement. To say I'd ever been to bed with a more fit, agile or eager woman in my life, would be an out-and-out lie.

Boobs! Bum! Toned, slender limbs, flat stomach! Oh, it was nearly too much. And we fitted together so well. Like Hornby or Lego Technic. Not that Scaletrix stuff.

The only downer, the only whisper of ill-wind over the bright, clear night was the agreement. The 'once-only promise'. It was like being given a Ferrari for your 18th birthday and told you could only take it around the block before it went into storage until you were thirty and responsible enough to drive it sensibly.

I put it to the back of my mind. We stroked, teased and caressed our way through the night. We whispered compliments to each other. You do, don't you? The difference here was: I meant them. And I wanted her to mean hers.

She said I was perfect. Sadly I'm not. You know, I've told you before. And there's other deficiencies I won't go into.

I said she was a goddess. She was a goddess and more. She was a perfect, tender, beautiful deity.

I made love to her. Well, I gave it my best shot. I wanted her to remember this night for the rest of her life. I wanted it to stick in her mind. Three crucial dates: birthday, Christmas and 22nd September.

"It makes me feel so good being with you, being around you," she said later, cuddling into my chest. I rested my hand on her head and smiled, her hips, stomach and breasts all in full contact with my body, closer than close.

"You do the same for me," I said. Soon after we were asleep. Safe in our secret. Untouched by the world.

But the cold morning light came all too soon, and with it the sharp chill of icy guilt. I was the first to wake and the first to feel it.

Lying reptile-still, with Daisy's head still on my chest, I wondered how she'd be when she woke. I strained my neck to look at the alarm clock I'd failed to set. It was eight o'three. I had to be at work at eight-thirty. If I was going to make that, I had to get up. Now.

I didn't move. I couldn't bring myself to shatter the glass bubble we'd cocooned ourselves in. I tucked my chin into my chest so I could admire Daisy's nose, her slender arm resting on me. I watched her for ten minutes before she stirred. She didn't surface gradually. One second she was asleep, the next completely awake.

"Morning," I said. She pulled her head off my chest and looked down at me. Her hair fell round her face, framing it. She said nothing for several seconds. Her large, almond eyes showed no emotion. I felt tense. I wanted her to say something.

"Did you sleep well?" I asked.

Still she kept quiet. She moved her left arm so her elbow was near my right ear, then her thigh slipped across my hips, and she was on top of me. Her breasts brushed my chest. Her face was very close to mine.

"Is it morning already?" she asked.

I nodded.

She shook her head, tucking her hair behind her right ear, revealing her delicate jaw.

"It's not," she said, brushing herself against me now, kissing my neck. "It's still last night."

Chapter Nineteen

"This is exactly what I'm talking about," Carol said to me, when I arrived at 10.15. She rose from her chair.

"And there are some opportunities you can't miss," I said. Nothing was going to get me down today. "I've spent the first half of this morning doing customer relations."

"Oh God," said Kate. "She didn't let you sleep with her, did she?"

"Shut up," I said, "and get on with your work."

"Back office," said Carol, pointing at me.

"Now listen," she said, when the door closed. "I gave you a friendly warning not so long ago..."

"I can explain."

"I don't want explanations..."

"You're looking very smart today," I said. She was. Charcoal-grey trouser suit. White shirt with flared lapels. Very Jackie Brown.

"I don't want compliments either."

"Sorry."

"What I want is someone I can leave in charge. Someone who, while I'm sunning myself on those gorgeous South African beaches, I know is not screwing everything up."

"I know," I said. "I apologise."

"It's too late for that. As of today, your position is open. The other candidate is Kate. The one who proves they're most competent will get the job."

"Shit," I said. "My dad will disown me if I don't get this."

"Exactly. So work hard. Starting today. That's all."

She left me in the back office, alone. I lit a cigarette and flicked the kettle on. This was bad news. This bit of bad news was very bad news. I may not have massive ambition to reach the pinnacle of personal travel agency, but I have pride. Damn it! I have pride.

As I was stirring my coffee, Kate came in.

"She told you then?" she said.

"Yes."

"I'm going to get it," she stated.

I must have looked shocked.

"Well, you're not more competent than me, are you? You're too busy chasing clients to concentrate on being any good."

"Who made the most commission last month?" I said.

"You did, but not by much. Anyway, you've been here two years. I've been here nine months."

"So?"

"So you get repeat clients after a year. By December, I'll be outselling you by miles."

"I doubt it. Not once I start trying."

"You seem to forget, Guy. I know one very crucial thing about you that could dash your career hopes onto the rocks."

"You wouldn't."

"I would, to get what I want, and let's face it, I don't have much at the moment. No boyfriend, no spare cash, no life. Yes, I'm prepared to mention your lack of *bona fide* travel experience. But I won't need to. I'm the girl for the job."

"No, I'm the girl for the job," I spat, lighting another cigarette off the last. "I mean..."

"No, you're just a girl. A very big girl."

"God, you irritate me sometimes, Kate."

"Do I? That's a shame, isn't it?" And with that, she walked back into the office.

"Fuck!" I said, very loudly.

Ted walked in.

"Problems?" he asked.

"Just one or two."

"Fancy a drink after work? We could talk it over."

Now this was a surprise. I shrugged. "Why not?" I said. "Why the hell not?"

I finished my cigarette and sipped my coffee. I went back to my desk and worked. Kate wasn't about to take my job. No way. There wasn't a jeroboam of ambition in my blood, but there was a good magnum of pride.

Just before closing, a familiar figure walked through the door, smartly dressed.

"Hello," I said, shocked to see her in the daylight. "What can I do for you?"

She smiled at me, her brown face now gashed with white.

"Hello," she said. "I wan fly back to Philippines." (This is how she said it.)

"For a holiday?" I said.

"No," she smiled. "I hab finished study here. I hab my exam in accounting. Now I can get big job in Manila. Take care my family."

So she wasn't a hooker. Just a keen amateur. Unless she pounded the bed with her fist late at night when studying.

"Where are you living now?" I asked. "You moved out, didn't you?"

"Yes, I stay with a friend now. Save money for flight."

"Very sensible," I agreed.

I gave her the best deal I could, only a few quid above net. I think it was guilt, guilt that I'd misjudged her.

"You have a good life," I said when she'd paid up.

"You too," she smiled.

*****

"Don't let her get to you," Ted said. We were sitting in The Crown, near the doors that lead to the beer garden. For the first time I noticed Ted's face. He wasn't exactly good-looking, but his features were… cool, I suppose… in an angular, sharp-edged way. From a distance I always thought he looked like a geek. Not so, friends, not so. I briefly considered verbalising this compliment, this upturn of his appearance in my estimation. Sensibly, however, it took me a nano-second to demur. Men do not talk about other men's physical features, not even when the comment is resoundingly positive. No, that department is still for the girls. A man does it, he's gay. A girl does it, she's jealous. Jealousy is okay, gayness is not (for a hetero).

"Does she get to you?" I asked. Now it hit me. Ted looked like the other terminator in T2, the one with the reforming metal body and determined expression. He cruised that fine line between enviable looks and, well… David Coulthard was another. Was he good-looking or did he look like a Thunderbird?

"All the time. That's why I keep my head down. I don't rate Debbie much either."

"Why not?"

"She hasn't got much of a life, don't you think? All she talks about is TV."

I nodded. And she should be talking about films. T2, for example.

"I used to be very friendly with Debbie," I said. "Right up until the night we got very drunk together and she admitted she'd always fancied me."

"Shit."

"Yeah. Then she snogged me. I can't remember exactly what I said to get her off. I tried to do it gently but, as I felt her arm snake round the back of my neck, I think I screamed, 'Get the fuck off me!'"

"Is that true?"

"Haven't you seen the way she looks at me?"

"I guess," Ted admitted. "That's really funny."

He sipped his beer.

"Talking of girls," I said, "what does your girlfriend do?"

"Oh right. She... well, she's got her own shop in the Regent Arcade in Cheltenham."

"Cool. What does she sell?"

"Clothes."

"Women's, I guess."

"And men's."

"Where does she get them from?"

"She imports from India and Thailand. She made contacts while she was out there."

"Where did you guys meet?"

"Phnom Penn."

I lit a cigarette. Shit. I didn't want to talk about travel.

"How often do you go to London?" I asked.

"Once a month."

"To see?"

"Friends from school mostly."

"Where did you go?"

"Cheltenham College."

"No way!" I said. "That's where I went."

Ted was as amazed as me. We bonded after that. We did the usual. Talked about various teachers, good places to smoke, how bad the dances were with the girls' schools. We drank some more beer and then he asked me about Daisy.

"Have you...?"

I smiled and raised my eyebrows Roger Moore-style.

"Man," he laughed. "You... I'm impressed."

"Mmm…guess what the bad news is?"

"What? She's got a boyfriend?"

"Much worse than that, my friend."

"Oh no!"

"Along with the added bonus of not one, but two bambinos."

"Ouch. You must be gutted."

"I'm livid."

We both laughed. I persuaded him to stay for more drinks.

We had three, four, five, six drinks. Followed by more drinks. I must say, I got to like him more and more.

He now comes with my firmest recommendation. Ted Thunderbirds T2 Coulthard. If he were a restaurant, he'd get three Michelin stars, a Trusthouse Forte shield and a glowing write-up in *The Times* colour supplement from AA Gill *and* Michael Winner. Yeah! He's that good. You should try him. I think even Gordon Ramsay would *fucking well* like him.

And yes, I did tell him he looked like the dude in the silly film, but I didn't say he was better-looking than I'd thought. I may have been drunk, but I wasn't ready to come bursting forth from the closet, hands full of pink pounds and Kylie CDs bulging in my pockets, or with a cod piece, or muscle vest. I was still enjoying girls breaking my heart too much to consider men. But after Daisy, I had to admit, that could all change. I knew the next few weeks would be hard. Perhaps considering a change in sexual orientation might help...

Chapter Twenty

Three days after she'd slept naked in my bed, Daisy phoned me at home. I don't know if I was expecting this or not. The morning after our adulterous night, we didn't talk much. We committed adultery twice more (though once you're an adulterer that's it, so numbers don't mean much, I guess), but we didn't have any discussion regarding 'the once-only promise'.

I hoped she'd call. I prayed she would, and I wanted her to, but it was always in doubt.

"Hi," I said, after she introduced herself. I was reclined on my sofa watching a video with the sound down while listening to an old trip hop album. A can of Stella was on the floor, in arm's reach. I sipped it. "How are you?"

Lame, I know, but I meant it. I was desperate to know how she was.

"Missing you," she said.

My heart, slow to react in my beer-sedated state, finally picked up the beat. 90, 110, 130.

"Where are you?" She can't be calling from home, I thought. Not with hubby there.

"I'm in my car," she said.

"Where are you going?"

"The official story is I'm going to see my friend Rachel. The one whose flat I helped paint. You remember?"

I did.

"But?"

"Can I come and see you. I really need to talk to someone."

"Of course. How long will you be?"

"Ten minutes."

"Right." That's fucking no time, I thought. I'm a mess. The flat looks like a squat. The bathroom... "I'll see you then," I said, thinking she's getting closer and closer as we speak.

"Guy," she said. "Thanks."

"No problem."

She hung up. I threw the phone down and dashed to the bathroom. One thing I can't understand: how do bathrooms get this dirty? Last time I cleaned it I remember thinking 'that'll stay spotless for weeks'. When I'd finished, the place shone. I didn't need a mirror. I could see my face in the tiles, the basin and the bath. And as for the mirror itself, it was like the portal that opens over a dead man's head for him to enter heaven. It was blindingly bright. So bright I had to shave with sunglasses on.

And now. Now the room looked like an operating theatre after a vasectomy. The floor tiles were dusted with pubes, as were the bath and loo. The place was carpeted. I wondered whether I had that many hairs to start with. Could I honestly afford to lose this many in a week? Do they make pubic wigs?

I wrenched the Hoover from the bedroom closet and set to work. Once around the bed. Once around the bathroom (towels in the laundry basket). Once around the kitchen surfaces, sucking up crusts and diced peppers and potato peelings. Once around the floor, sucking up more pubes. Once around the living room, sucking up beer cans, plates, rats, and discarded ties.

As I returned the Hoover to its home, the doorbell rang. The tacky buzz, like an elephant blue-bottle, filled my flat. Ooh, she won't be impressed with that lower-middle-class naffness, I thought. Even a Chav wouldn't rate that. I should have disconnected it and listened for the knock.

I ran down the stairs and pulled the front door open.

"Daisy. Come in." This was the last sentence I uttered for some hours. Beyond "yes", "mmm", "okay", and sometimes, "err, no", I had little opportunity to show off my competence at speaking, honed to quite an expert degree after many years of intense tutoring and practice. It didn't bother me much. Daisy interested me 100 per cent. And you can't say that about many people, especially not girls you don't know very well. Besides, it gave me a chance to drink beer without interruption.

"I'm so confused," she began and, by the time she'd finished her story, I believed her. She was confused, but she was charming with it. I mean, cripes, I was confused too. We're all confused, but listening to her I experienced a twinkle of clarity, a speck of light piercing the gloom. Yes, I realised something. This girl had pip-pipped onto my radar and I wasn't going to let her disappear. Whatever the situation.

"Peter has affairs," Daisy said. "He started about a year after we married and he hasn't stopped since. The first one was with a woman called Annabel Dixon. Annabel was my mother's name. She was killed in a car crash when I was thirteen."

"Oh Christ."

"Yes. That was number one. Now we're well into double figures. Just the ones I know about. By the end of our married life, I'm sure he's hoping to chalk up a full Test century."

"Not if you stump him out."

"God, I've thought about it enough times."

"Keeping children in a home filled with bitterness is not good for them. It's not good for anyone."

"I know," she said. "I watch *Oprah*."

"Sorry."

"No, I am."

"How do you... I mean what's your relationship like now?"

Daisy took a deep breath, bit her lip, then exhaled slowly.

"Can I have a cigarette?" she said, eyeing the packet on the coffee table.

"Be my guest." I took one out of the pack and lit it for her.

She had several drags, then said, "Hostile civility."

I digested this comment slowly. I liked it.

"Do you hate him?"

"I did. I don't think I do now. I accept him for what he is."

"An arsehole?"

She snorted.

"He can be good to me. He buys me lovely presents. He's great with the kids, when he's there. Very occasionally we'll laugh and, you know, he sleeps with other women." She laughed without humour. "God, I wish he wouldn't do that."

I sipped my beer.

"So what are your plans for the future?"

"I don't know. Every day I wonder what to do, and every day I put off making a decision. Divorce... it's such an ugly word, isn't it?"

"But you've thought about it?"

"Oh yeah. All the time."

Daisy looked at her watch, then at me.

"I should be going soon. Peter's expecting me back."

"You're welcome to stay, if you want."

"No, I've got to go. I need to see the children."

She put a hand on my thigh.

"I feel like I've used you. You're very good to listen to my problems. I'm sure you've got enough of your own."

"Not really," I said. "I like hearing about you. I just wish you weren't married, that's all."

She nodded sadly.

"I know."

She got up, running a hand over the top of my head.

"Can I kiss you?"

She slipped both hands behind my neck and reached up to put her lips on mine. We kissed. Her mouth felt so soft and warm. When we came up for air, she was blushing.

"You send tingles up and down my spine," she said.

"I won't tell you what you do to me. Will you call me?"

"Of course I will. I want to hear about *you* next time."

"Prepare to be bored."

"Well, fair's fair!"

"You're right. You bore me senseless."

"Hey!"

We were at the front door now. Daisy kissed me again on the lips and then either cheek, like you'd kiss a child. We said goodbye and she skipped off down the road. I watched her go. The silky hair, those firm limbs, that lovely married arse.

"Fuck," I said as I closed the door. "Fuckety fuckety fuckety fuck fuck."

I ascended the creaking stairs to the kitchen and stared meditatively out of the window at the sky. The blow-bubble clouds changed lane tentatively, the sun took its fleeting moments to smile, and the trees did their thing of sounding like presents being unwrapped.

And below... below, the goblin, or Ewok, or Gremlin, was planting flowers around the edge of our bombsite garden. He was clothed in a duffle coat and Wellingtons, a few inches of beige trouser filling the gap. It was the first time I'd felt able to talk to him, this weird human being.

I retraced my steps down the stairs and went around the back to the garden.

"Hello?" I said quietly.

The goblin, pawing at the earth, stood up. He was no more than five-foot-three, with stocky limbs, and facial hair more like a gnome. Greasy hair slicked back. His nose was like a fallen Victoria plum.

He looked at me.

"Nice job you're doing here."

He nodded, his expression blank.

"I live upstairs."

He nodded again.

"Are you a gardener?"

He shrugged.

"Do you want some help?"

He shook his head.

"Well, if you change your mind, just ask."

He nodded.

I went back upstairs and watched him for a while. He worked quickly and efficiently with rapid movements, more like a mouse than a man.

Eventually I became bored and had a beer. When I looked later he was still working, scurrying about like an extra from *Oliver Twist*.

*****

Later that night, with a whisky and a half-pack of Bensons, I tripped my way along the *Yellow Brick Road* of Daisy's life, trying to work out who I'd play in this remake. The Scarecrow, the Tin Man, the Lion? Or was I the road itself, the stepping stone, which would lead others to a new life?

This much was clear: Daisy was in a tangled situation and I was getting caught up in it. Trouble was, I didn't have the will to cut myself free.

My father never gave me much advice about girls. The one tip he did pass on was, "So long as they don't have a husband, or children, you can't go far wrong". This made me laugh so hard tears ran down my cheeks. "Father," I said, "don't worry. I'm not a complete moron." He eyed me sternly and replied, "Sometimes the obvious is worth stating."

He was right. The biggest traps are the easiest to walk into. I was already too close to Daisy. The blinking dot of her existence had already reached the cross-hairs of my radar. What it would do there, I didn't know. It might stay, or it might move away. Perhaps I should simply switch off the monitor. Pull the plug.

I smiled to myself and swigged my drink. There was no way that was going to happen. We like danger, don't we? We like risk. We like the 100-watt rush. I'd had a wander around the amusement park. I'd tried the ride. Now I wanted the season ticket. I smiled some more. Yeah. Give me the annual pass.

Chapter Twenty-one

"What the fuck is TOOP?" Ben asked.

"You've never had TOOP with a girl?"

"I don't know. I may have."

"You'd know if you had."

"It's not a variation on a sixty-nine, is it?"

I laughed.

Ben slurped his pint. We were in The Old Bell. Dark, grim, so full of smoke that I was beginning to suspect it was on fire.

"I do like our Sunday afternoon sessions. Just you and me. It gives us a chance to get it all out. Tell it like it is. You know, without worrying we're going to say the wrong thing."

"I'm easily offended these days," said Ben. "So watch your step."

"Fuck off!"

"What's TOOP?"

"The once-only promise. You probably had it with my sister and wangled it from there."

"Don't talk about Vanessa. Vanessa is off limits in these conversations, right? I'm not having her name mentioned in the same breath as some of your rank fantasies, okay?"

I nodded.

"So you've slept with this girl... what's her name again?"

"Daisy."

"Yeah, Daisy. You've banged Daisy once..."

"I'd prefer it if you said 'had sex'. This girl is not a 'bang'. She's way better than a 'bang'."

"Man! How can you say that? Better than a bang? A bang is everything. A bang is what we're all after."

I put my hands up. "I know what you're saying; I appreciate it, but in this instance, no. Daisy is not a..." And I suddenly couldn't bring myself to say it, that horrible, disrespectful word, applied to my angel.

"If that's the way you want it."

"It is."

"Okay."

"Okay."

We both drank. The drinking helps. We all drink these days. It helps with the self-delusion we must live under. If we admitted the truth to ourselves we'd never get out of bed. We'd all stay in with the curtains closed, having sobbing nervous breakdowns.

"Okay?"

"Okay."

"Yeah, so we, you know, had sex, err...a few weeks ago."

Ben was laughing.

"What's so funny?"

He carried on laughing.

"Ben?"

"Oh man," he said. "I thought you were going to say 'make love' for a minute there. That would have been too much."

"What?"

"You heard."

"I know. I just can't believe you said that. There is no way I would have said that."

"You do love her, though."

"I..."

"You do. Christ. You're in love with a married chick with two kids. God help you."

151

"At least there's no danger of getting married," I said, raising my eyebrows.

"I'm marrying Vanessa, your sister; it's different."

"We're not talking about her. And it's no different. You're getting married and, as such, you deserve to have the piss taken out of you."

Ben wasn't happy, but he dropped it. I dropped it, too. I mean, I didn't want him jilting my sister at the altar because of some marriage joke I'd made. I was just getting used to the idea. Besides his parents were divorced so he was being brave. He'd seen how wrong it could go.

"The point is: what would you do in my situation? Forget about what you're doing; put yourself in my place and tell me what you'd do."

"I'd shoot myself."

"Over a girl?"

"No! Over the job. The life. The lack of... fun."

"Yeah, okay, ha ha. Get serious."

"I am being serious."

I huffed. "Sometimes you bore the shit out of me."

"Okay." Ben lit a cigarette – one of mine. I wished he'd just quit or smoke. Not this in-between shit. He smoked it in silence for several seconds.

"Yes?"

"In this situation, you've got to put yourself in the worst-case scenario..."

"The WCS?"

He raised his eyebrows. "If you prefer. Put yourself in the WCS and ask yourself if you can handle it. So... what's the worst that can happen?"

"Daisy's husband catches me in bed with her. He kicks the shit out of me, I never see her again, and he makes her life miserable."

"Is this likely?"

"Well, he does know where I work."

"Did you tell Daisy about that?"

"No."

"Fair enough. So there's a link. It's possible you could get found out."

"Mmm."

"Have you ever had your nose broken?"

"Not as I remember."

"That's not saying much. You've got a memory like a drain."

"Yeah. But I haven't had my nose broken. Look." I turned sideways. "Straight as a runway."

"And about as interesting."

"This conversation is getting us nowhere."

"They never do."

"What I want to know is, is it worth the risk?"

"And only you can answer that question. It's the same as an antique mirror, a Renaissance painting, whatever. It's only worth what you're prepared to pay. Do you know what I mean?"

I did.

"Besides. If she meant what she said about TOOP, you're fucked anyway. And not by her."

"You're so wise," I said, with a shake of the head, "you're so wise."

*****

This is a sad fact. In your late-twenties you require more than you did as a teenager, or as a twenty-one-year-old. When it comes to women, where a 1.1 go-kart would once suffice, nothing less than a Jag will now do.

When you're twenty, all you're interested in is dimensions and numbers. How big the girl's tits are, and have you got a shot at giving her mate one as well. It's simple.

As we get older, a previously undiscovered female trait becomes relevant: personality. My God, these people actually have shit to say! So life becomes more complex. You want the perfect body, yes, but now it's got to have the perfect mind. Unless you're Peter Stringfellow, big tits are not going to get you through life's dark underbelly. There has to be something more...

But please! Don't make the mistake of marrying the rough old boiler you think is your best friend. Best friends are best friends. Not chosen for looks. Wives have to have it all. Nothing else will do.

Daisy was the first woman I'd met who had it all. Trouble was, Peter had clocked this before me.

To answer Ben's question: to me, Daisy was priceless.

*****

Ben and I both had the Monday off work, officially. He'd taken the day off, and it was in my schedule. Rising at midday, we took our hangovers out to the town. We took them to the CD Shack and my friend Steve.

Two elements elevate the CD Shack over any other music shop in town. One is Steve. The other is Steve giving me free CDs.

You'll find the CD Shack in the market place. It's part of a small chain of 'cooler than your average' record shops that operate in the South-West. It's also one of the few record shops which still sells records 'for DJs'. Decked out in grey and black, it can look intimidating to those under sixteen who are used to a more Day-Glo look. This is the idea. It keeps them out.

Steve was behind the counter when we arrived, his long blonde hair covering his face as he attempted to drop the stylus on a twelve-inch. A young guy wearing headphones and a serious expression drummed his fingers impatiently on the desk.

"There you go!" said Steve, straightening up. Steve's hands were never steady. He didn't drink much but he was a caffeine freak. Permanently wired. It gave him his manic energy. That and the cheap Speed.

154

"Hi Guy," he said, as he noticed me for the first time through his pebble glasses.

"You remember Ben?" I said.

"Yeah, right." He held out his hand and shook Ben's, his wiry arms poking out from beneath a black Beatles t-shirt.

"So what can I do for you guys? Looking to stock up your boy band collection?"

"That'd be great," I nodded, smiling.

"Then you can fuck off to HMV!" he said, pointing at me and laughing.

Ben and I laughed too. Steve was a funny guy. Could possibly have done stand-up. In small clubs.

"The charts don't get any better, do they?"

"That's because only ten-year-olds buy singles. If we did it like the Americans, on sales and air play, we might get some reasonable shit in the charts."

"Don't bank on it. My dad's got crap taste, too."

"Big fan of The Eagles, yeah?"

"Don't talk to me about it. We're hungover. We thought we'd come in, have a mooch around..."

"Bum some free CDs..." Steve laughed again.

"Something like that, yeah."

The young guy with the headphones said, "Excuse me, hi. I'll take it."

"If you can afford it," said Steve. "It's fifty quid."

"Fifty quid?" The kid was incredulous.

"It's rare White Label, my friend. Not even Pete Tong has got this yet."

"Really?"

"No, fuck off! It's number eighteen in the buzz chart. How do you think it got there if no one can buy it?"

The young guy looked embarrassed. Steve laughed his laugh. "I'm only kidding, man; don't look so serious. It's £4.99."

The boy handed over the cash.

Steve put the CD in a bag and gave him his change. "Come

back soon. Bring all your friends."

"Yeah right, you freak," the boy said under his breath and hurried out of the shop.

"No sense of humour these days, kids," said Steve. "No sense of fun."

"Teenage society is certainly getting sucked ever further up its own arse. I'm sure I wasn't that much of a prick when I was his age."

Steve shrugged and made coffee.

With steaming cups resting on the stainless steel counter, he played us some of his favourite records. Ben and I recognised none of the names but it was good music. Some trance stuff, some South American percussive sounds, some thumping reggae. Steve played it all with infectious enthusiasm.

"There was a chick who came in here a couple of days ago that I wouldn't have minded giving a good hosing down," he said. "Very posh. Skinny, lovely tits. Dark hair, tied back. I could have rammed it right into her."

Ben and I looked at each other.

"Sounds just like..."

"No, it doesn't," I said.

"I could have settled down with her." Steve looked momentarily wistful. "I'd quite like to, you know," he said. "Live quietly, make meals together, listen to music, have a fucking good shag every night."

"Wouldn't we all? Wouldn't we all?" I looked at Ben. I looked at Ben for longer than he found comfortable.

"What?"

"Nothing." But there was something. It had suddenly struck me.

We weren't boys anymore. We were men, making our way through life. We were men, but we didn't quite know how to be one. That saddened me too. Adulthood seemed to always be just around the corner. Physically it had arrived; time was already doing its worst to the skin, the hair and belly. But mentally?

Mentally we all seemed to be stuck at about sixteen-and-a-quarter. Or perhaps sixteen-and-two-thirds. I'm older than you! So nahnah, nahnah, nah!

Chapter Twenty-two

Perhaps that's unfair. Ben may have worked out how to be a man but I certainly hadn't. If crying remains unmanly, I was definitely still a boy.

It couldn't have come at a worse time. It was the end of the summer, the nights were getting colder and longer, Vanessa had phoned me a day or two earlier saying she and Ben had had a serious argument. 'Kathy' was still on my case, Daisy hadn't phoned, Kate was outstripping me at work, the front bumper had mysteriously disappeared off my old banger, my cock, in the winter cool, had shrunk to the size of a cashew... oh! It was all crap. Then my father phoned.

He sounded detached, alien. His voice was metallic, clipped. Almost brusque.

"Guy," he said. "I'm afraid I've got some bad news."

He didn't need to say another word. I knew what was coming next.

"No," I said, not wanting to hear it.

"I'm afraid..."

"No."

"Your mother..."

"No!"

"Your mother passed away this afternoon."

"What time?"

"About four."

"Four? Why the hell didn't you call me earlier? It's almost six, Dad."

"I didn't want to phone you at work." His voice was quiet, monotone.

"To hell with work. Screw work! You should have told me."

My father was patient with me during that call. It couldn't have been easy for him, but he kept his cool. Once I'd calmed down, I apologised.

"I understand," he said. "Do you want to come and see her?"

"Of course."

"I think I'd better come and get you."

"No, it's fine, I can drive."

"You're upset. I don't want you doing anything silly."

"Daddy, I'm fine. There's no point in you coming all the way from the hospital and driving all the way back; you'll be exhausted."

"Well if you promise to drive very carefully. And I mean very carefully."

"I will," I said. "I'll see you in three-quarters-of-an-hour."

"Please be careful."

I hung up.

I hadn't cried yet. I was angry more than anything, full of anger that this should happen and guilt that I hadn't seen my mother enough in her final days.

I grabbed my jacket off the sofa and put my mobile in it, in case anyone phoned. Father had spoken to all of our immediate family. Jack and Vanessa were on their way to the hospital. Toby was attempting to get a flight back from Sydney.

In a state, I got my car keys from the kitchen, ran out of the door, slipped and clattered down the stairs. I landed awkwardly, my right ankle snapping inwards under my weight. I screamed and got up. I fell straight back down again. I pulled up my trouser leg and looked at my ankle. It was the size of a grapefruit. I tried to put weight on it. I couldn't. I fell on the floor again.

I wailed and screamed "Buuugggger!" at the top of my voice, following it up with a string of further expletives, starting with alternating 'F's' and 'S's'. I was crying now, all of the built-up tension and grief spilling out of me.

Still sobbing, I managed to drag open the front door and get to the street. It was raining but I pulled myself along on my arse to the car. Somehow, I hauled myself up and into the driver's seat. I got comfortable and positioned my right leg on the accelerator.

With gritted teeth I turned the ignition. The car leapt forward, smashing into the vehicle in front. I took it out of gear and tried again. The car started and roared, the revs shooting up to 6,000. I tried to ease off the accelerator. I couldn't. My foot was stuck.

I yelled and screamed, and beat the steering wheel with my fists, but it was no use. There was no way I was driving anywhere. Humiliated, I called my father and told him what had happened. Then I phoned the ambulance. It got to me with impressive speed.

*****

At Cirencester Hospital they told me my ankle was broken. I wasn't going anywhere for twenty-four hours.

"My mother died this afternoon," I said. "I have to see her."

The doctor was sympathetic but maintained they couldn't put my leg in plaster until the swelling went down.

I cried some more.

The hours I spent in that hospital were the longest ever. I wanted to make sense of what had happened, but I couldn't. I stared up at the white ceiling in Ward C and wished I were dying.

If someone had offered me a bottle of sleeping pills that night I would have taken them. With hungry, starving gratitude. There was only one person who could see me through this grief, and she was gone.

Lying in the hospital I tried to picture my mother's face. I couldn't. With my eyes open, there was only whiteness. With them closed, a deathly black, solid and infinite. I tried to recall the good times. I couldn't. I tried to recall the bad times. They'd gone too. The blackboard of my mind had been wiped clean.

I clenched and unclenched my fists in frustration. I wanted to throw myself off the bed and beat my head against the perfect white floor. How strange I thought, that a place of such habitual distress and mourning, of such blackness, should be rendered in glowing white. Hardly practical with all the blood being thrown around.

I think I ended up shouting because the next thing I knew a nurse glided over with a fixed smile and a heavy sedative. The white world turned black. The next thing I knew, Vanessa was by my bed. Tears rolled down her cheeks.

"I don't know what to say," she muttered, bending forward and giving me a hug.

I didn't either. I thought I might have lost the ability to speak. I'd certainly lost the ability to reason. Why bother to reason in an unreasonable world?

I stared up at her. I stared up at my dear, beautiful, troubled sister. I watched the tears roll down her cheeks. There was nothing I could do to stop them. I raised my hand towards her then placed it back on the bed. There was no use in trying to give comfort. We were both beyond that.

"It'll be okay in time," she said. "It'll be okay in time."

And then she cried some more.

*****

I remember one morning, I must have been six or seven, I decided to take my mother breakfast in bed. She was ill and I thought she'd like it. I boiled some eggs (until they split). I burnt

161

some toast. I fixed some weak tea and filled a glass with apple juice.

I managed to climb the stairs with the whole lot on a tray, holding my breath as I went, taking one step at a time. When I reached the bedroom door, I took one hand off the tray. Slowly I turned the handle. My left hand wobbled. The breakfast graffitied the carpet.

My mother called to me.

"Guy? Are you okay?"

I didn't say a word for a minute, ashamed at what I'd done.

"Guy!" my mother repeated.

"Yes?" I said in a small voice.

"Can you open the door?"

I opened the door and shuffled in, my dressing gown trailing on the floor behind me. I ran to the bedside and buried my head in the duvet.

"I'm sorry. I'm sorry. I was only trying to help."

"What happened?"

"I made you breakfast..."

My beautiful mother took my head in her hands and looked me straight in the eye. Sun streamed in through the window. She looked like a vision. "You didn't have to do that," she said, tears welling up in her eyes. "Mummy's okay. She can get her own breakfast. Mummy's going to be fine."

"But you spend so long in bed."

"That's because I'm tired."

"You're not going to die, are you?"

"No," she smiled. "Not until you're a very old man."

"Good," I said, with childlike simplicity. "I love you Mummy."

"I love you too, Guy. Come on. Let's go and have breakfast together. Just you and me."

*****

It always seems to rain at funerals and my mother's was no exception. I suppose it's good in a way. You can cry without people noticing. I don't remember too much about the day. My Uncle Robert gave the tribute. It was the usual bollocks, full of superlatives and corny stories, just like the one I've told you. Even so, it was highly moving.

My brother Toby made it over from Australia. We all stood at the front of the church in a line. Me, Vanessa, Toby, Jack, Dad. All of us cried in the stiff English tradition: eyes gushing, mouths set. I think I did a pretty good job. I never once wiped my eyes (I couldn't without dropping my crutches). My shirt didn't thank me, though. By the end, it was soaked.

My mother was buried in Westleaf Church, near the river. It was what she wanted. Afterwards, we all went back to the house and made polite conversation with relatives we hardly ever saw and whose names we could barely remember. I got very drunk and cried some more. Nobody minded. I think out of all of us, I was the closest to Mum. I'd been with her the most through the ups and downs.

That night in bed, with a glass of whisky on the bedside table, I had a long conversation with her. It was a bit one-sided but I told her how much I loved her, that I knew she was in a good place, and that I was okay with her being there. I'm not religious, but I believe in a force for good. I knew she was somewhere good. It was a help.

*****

Christ, did it rain in October. The 'Man Upstairs' turned on the taps and let 'em run. I fantasised he was crying for my mother. Could have been he was trying to clear a blocked pipe. Fair enough but, for us down here on planet piss, it wasn't much fun. Especially on crutches.

Don't get me wrong, crutches are a great invention. Wheelchairs and zimmer frames ditto. They're here to help, to make life easier, to give the immobile mobility. Or a semblance of it.

Every day I woke to the same shushing of rain on my window, the arrhythmic maraca on the roof, the 'thwap thwap' of tyres aquaplaning through puddles that grew ever deeper. Leagues and fathoms deeper, until the roads receded into an eternal gloom.

And so did you, I guess, unless you were taking an autumnal break in St Lucia, or Puerto Rico, or Acapulco, as many do. (And thousands do. I should know. I'm in the business.)

But for those of us left in Blighty, too poor, too scared of flying, or simply too patriotic to leave, we soaked it up, a big national sponge, full of bulldog spirit. We bore the brunt of it. It gave us the right to moan. We whinged and moaned every second we were awake.

I did my bit. I cursed and swore, and shook my fists at the plumped duvet of cloud. I cried my way through the lakes and oases, the water jumps and inlets that lined the steeplechase to work. Many times I'd teeter and fall. Back on my feet, I'd find an epaulette of gloopy sweet wrappers and fag butts stuck to my shoulder. I nearly returned home to bed, but I didn't. I carried on, bolstered by the team spirit. "You alright mate?" or a "Here, let's give you a hand." It made all the difference.

If you guys could do it, I thought, so could I.

Getting to work was only half the battle, however. Actually achieving something while I was there was quite another. To be honest, friends, I was having a hard time just *living* – getting my lungs to go in and out and the old ticker to pump out the required bpm.

Chapter Twenty-three

"Guy, Kate," Carol said to us. "Can I see you both in the back office, please?"

It was almost November, it was pissing with rain still, the office had been dead all morning – thirteen mornings less than my mother, who'd been dead a fortnight.

Carol was flying to South Africa on the 10th December. It was time to find out who'd got the job.

Carol looked uncharacteristically nervous as we sat down.

"Well," she said, "as you know I'm heading to..."

I put my hand in the air. "Spare us the preamble. We know where you're going."

She cleared her throat and dipped her head.

"Well, we have to announce this now, so whoever it is has time to train directly with me."

"Makes sense."

"After careful consideration, I've decided, along with the other store managers in the South, that Kate will take charge for the first six months of my absence, followed by Guy in the second six months."

I clapped lazily. "How very diplomatic," I said. "How wonderfully... fair."

"Good. I'm glad you agree. Kate will train with me and then help you, Guy, before you take over."

"Can I leave early to celebrate? Can I go now?"

"You can go at four if you wish," Carol said.

I glanced at my watch. "It's only two."

"Then you've got to stay two more hours before you can go." She said this with the forced tolerance she'd adopted in the last month when speaking to me.

"Great," I said, lighting a cigarette. "How do you feel about it, sexy?"

"I'm very pleased," Kate said. "Aren't you?"

"I'm pleased as punch."

"Good," said Carol. "Kate? Could you give Guy and me a moment?"

"Oooh steady. People might start to talk. Tongues may wag."

Kate thanked Carol and left the room. Carol fixed me with a curious expression. She took a breath.

"You can consider yourself very lucky, Guy. But if you carry on the way you're going, your luck may just run out."

"What does that mean?"

"It means, and let me spell this out for you, if you come back off your lunch break this drunk one more time, I will fire you."

"What if *I come in*to work this drunk?"

"Don't push it, Guy. Don't push it."

I stared at the floor. I could feel my bravado cracking. I put my head in my hands and sobbed.

"What if," I said, "what if I said I couldn't cope anymore? What if I said I woke up every day wanting to go back to sleep? What if I said the one thing keeping me going was the drink? What if I said I couldn't get through the day sober? What would happen then?"

"Then we could try and find you some help," Carol said, her voice softening. "But you have to want to help yourself."

"Can you give me a week off? I need a week off."

Carol looked at me. "Are you sure that's wise?"

"I can go and stay with my dad for a week. He could use the company right now. We need to talk. I'd like to do that. Please.

I could really sort myself out."

Carol considered this. I don't think she believed me for a minute but she relented. "A week. That's all. And when you get back, I want to see your old sparky self. Not this... mess."

"It's been a difficult time, that's all."

I got up and left.

Oddbins in the market place had a fruity little Australian Chiraz going at ten quid for three bottles. I bought twenty quid's worth and headed home. I had every intention of getting sober but first I had to celebrate getting off work.

*****

Life's pendulum swings back and forth, back and forth. Things get worse, then they get better. They deteriorate, they improve. This is the way life is.

My pendulum seemed to have taken a very long and louche swing to bad, without bothering to return at any interval to good. My pendulum 'could do better'. What a joke.

My mother's death on 8th October at 4pm, followed by me breaking my ankle at 6pm, was only the start of the pendulum's swing into the doldrums. Around the 10th or 11th 'Kathy' insisted on staying with me for *four* days. She was so sympathetic that it made everything much worse. In the end I had to order her back to Reading.

A day later I got gastro enteritis and nearly broke my other ankle rushing to the loo every two minutes.

My stomach ached. My leg throbbed. It rained and rained. The roof of my apartment gave in, flooding the kitchen. Vanessa called to say perhaps she wasn't getting married. Then she called back saying she was. Father phoned up one night drunk and rambling on about how much he missed Mum. I was on the point of phoning him anyway, drunk, to say the same. We slurred at each other for half-an-hour before hanging up, feeling emptier than before. Life, as they say in America, sucked ass.

And now this. Passed over for promotion and only a week to get my head straight. I opened the first bottle of Chiraz. It slipped down well. I opened the second with more enthusiasm, something approaching gusto, and drank that. I eyed the third. What the hell, I thought. It could be the last drink I have in a while. May as well go out in style...

The next lunchtime I wasn't feeling too clever. I'd spent the whole night on the couch, incurring neck and lower back pain in the process. I was in my dressing gown. I was halfway through a second can of Stella and I had more stubble than an Italian gigolo, or the proprietor of the local kebab shop.

The phone rang. It was Daisy. Daisy, who'd inexplicably maintained an icy radio silence since forever. No doubt she'd only recently 'found' my number in a bottom drawer.

"Can I come over?" she said, before I'd even had a chance to say hello.

"How did you know I was here?"

"I phoned work."

"Wanted to book a flight, hey?" I said, with a cynical laugh.

"I wanted to see you. Can I come over?"

"Be my guest. You'll have to turn a blind eye to the mess, though; I can't be buggered to clean it up."

I finished my beer and got another one. Daisy turned up as I was a third of the way through it. I hobbled spastically downstairs and let her in. She took one look at me, one look at the beer, and said, "What on earth are you doing?"

"Partying. I'm so happy, I party all the time."

She followed me up the stairs. I lit a cigarette and slumped on the sofa. The coffee table was covered in beer cans. Daisy remained standing.

"What's happened, Guy?" she said in a low whisper. "What's happened to you?"

"Life," I said, with a music hall smile. "Life and all its wonders."

"Come on, be serious."

"Okay," I said. "A – My mother died. B – I broke my ankle trying to get to the hospital before they put her in a body bag. C – this great girl I met never called me. D – I'm about to lose my job. E – The roof fell in. F – I can't think straight anymore. G – Life seems to hold no joy. H – Hope is a word of the past. J – ..."

Daisy crossed her arms. "Enough," she said, using a mother's sensible tone. "Your leg will be fine when it's out of plaster. The girl you met has come to see you, and," she said, plucking the beer can from my grasp, "we can soon get your head into gear by stopping you drinking yourself into a coma."

I tried to grab it back but she was already in the kitchen pouring it down the sink.

"You've got a hell of a nerve," I said. "I haven't heard from you in weeks, months maybe, and you come round here telling me what I can or can't do."

"Do you want to be an alcoholic?" Daisy asked. She looked upset. "Do you?"

"I'm not."

"You are."

I disagreed again.

"Right, I'm going."

I caught her arm.

"No. I mean, no. Of course I don't."

"Because if you do," she said, "I can take you round to see my father right now, if you like. He'll be on gin and tonics by now. He'll have had his vodka and orange for breakfast." She looked at her watch. "In another couple of hours he'll be on the whisky. Do you want to go round and have a drink with him?"

I gazed at her. There were tears in her eyes.

"No," I said.

Daisy nodded and began to clear away the empty cans. "Believe me. You don't want to do this to yourself."

"I'm unhappy."

"We're all unhappy. That doesn't give you the right to give up."

"I don't have a life."

"Get in the bathroom. Have a shave, have a shower, get dressed, and you'll feel much better. I'm going to tidy up here and make coffee."

"You don't have to do that."

"I'm doing it. You don't have a choice."

"Where have you been for the last month?" I asked.

"I've had some problems of my own," she said. "Shower."

"I can't shower," I replied, pointing at my leg.

"Then wash! God, you can manage that, can't you?"

"I suppose," I said, and went to the bathroom like a good boy. I bet I was better behaved than what's his name... Marcus, her son.

I shaved, cutting myself with every other stroke of the razor. I washed, getting more water on the floor than on me. I dressed, in a pair of new jeans I was happy to slit up the side (you can't cut up the old comfy ones, can you?) and a baggy shirt. It was all a struggle, but Daisy was right. When I was finished, I did feel better, bar the Grand National-sized hangover – all those thundering hooves and falling jockeys.

"Look at you!" said Daisy, as I came out of the bedroom. "A real human being was there under all that filth." She was on the sofa, two mugs of coffee on the table with plate of toast; the place looking immaculate. She looked more beautiful than ever.

I sat down next to her.

"Eat. You probably haven't in ages."

"You want some?"

She shook her head.

I took the plate and leaned back. I didn't feel like eating at all but I knew I should. I forced it in and chewed thickly. Daisy drew her knees up to her chin, hugging her calves.

"I'm sorry to hear about your mother. Were you very close?"

"Yeah."

"Had she been ill for a long time?"

"Since I can remember."

"What was it?"

"Pneumonia in the end. Her immune system couldn't handle it. Before that the doctors were never too sure."

"How long ago did this happen?"

"8th October."

"I'm sorry."

"Me too." I took a slurp of coffee. It tasted good. "How did you know I had milk, no sugar?"

Daisy shrugged. "I didn't. It's the way I have it, that's all."

I smiled.

"So what's been happening in your little life?" I said, trying to sound upbeat. "Anything exciting? Must have been something pretty special to keep you away from me all this time."

Daisy looked deep into her mug. "No, nothing too special," she said. "That night we went to The Great Escape, a couple of people Peter does business with saw us. They mentioned it to him and..."

"And what?"

"And he thought the worst. He's very jealous. Like most men who sleep around, he's very insecure. I just look at another man and he's livid."

"But you told him I was just a friend?"

"No. I told him you were a nobody who was chatting me up; I'd never seen you before."

"Thanks."

"I told him I was there with a few girlfriends. My friends don't like him, so they'd all back me up if I needed it."

"But he still flipped?"

"Yes. We had a terrible argument and he made all sorts of threats about divorce and the children, that if I behaved like this he'd take them away..."

"How?"

"Call me an unfit mother. Out enjoying myself when I should be with them, you know, drunk. Which is a joke anyway because we have a full-time nanny so I can work. And that took some doing, I can tell you."

"I bet."

"Yeah. Anyway I had to lie low for a while."

"You could have called," I said.

She scratched her nose. "My little girl had chicken pox. And actually... I have a confession to make. I've been trying to forget about you."

"Oh great."

"Mmm...but I can't."

"Good."

"Well... more trouble than good."

"Trouble can be fun. Where's your husband now?"

"He's spending the week in London. He's always got staff problems. I think he's interviewing."

"While the cat's away?"

"Don't say it like that. It sounds like I'm using you."

"Aren't you?"

"Oh, come on. You're using me too. Married girls who are still 'fit' are a dream come true for guys your age. You don't have to worry about getting dragged up the aisle. There isn't even any commitment. I'd say you've got it pretty good."

"How about if I want commitment?"

"You're a boy."

"How old do you think I am?"

She smirked behind her coffee. "Younger than me."

"Guess."

"Twenty-three."

"Guess again."

"Twenty-four."

"I'm your age."

"God. You seem younger."

"That's just immaturity."

"When's your birthday?"

"18th May."

"No! Mine's 6th May."

"Taureans always get on well."

"But you're still a toyboy."

"Hardly."

"Yes, you are," she said, laughing and pointing, jabbing me in the ribs. "You're a toyboy."

I poked her back. "Don't call me that."

"Why you baby, feeling a little young?"

"Right, you old granny," I said, grabbing her and wrestling her coffee off her. "Let's see who's stronger. The young man or the old woman."

We tumbled onto the floor and writhed around until I whacked my bad ankle against the coffee table and we had to stop while I cried.

"Silly boy," she said.

"Silly, but not stupid."

"Oh, I'm sure you're not stupid. You'd better not be anyway. One of us has to be intelligent."

"I can earn the money," I said, "if you can cook the food."

"Talking of which, I'm going to make us some pasta. A little late lunch."

She skipped into the kitchen and fiddled about. Twenty minutes later, we ate.

The lunch was exquisite. It didn't taste anything like any of the ingredients I had in the cupboard. It had an angel's touch.

Later, after we'd washed and dried up like an old married couple, Daisy left.

"I have to pick up my kids from school," she said. "Can I come back later?"

"Are you staying the night?"

"That's an offer!" she replied, and rushed down the stairs. "Oh. I know how many beers there are in the fridge, so I'll know if you've drunk any."

"What if I go to the pub?"

"I have my spies!"

I closed the door and went to my bedroom. I took the duvet off the bed, shook it, covered it in aftershave, then straightened it. It always paid to be prepared.

I even put a low-watt bulb in the bedside lamp in case we wanted to do it with the light on.

Chapter Twenty-four

Supermarkets are increasingly a unisex world. Pre-1970, if you spotted a man in a supermarket he was either a thief, a marketing manager, or foreign.

These days a man can stroll the aisles with full confidence, in the knowledge there are others of his species in the building, openly doing what he's doing: shopping.

Yes. Shopping!

Shopping isn't a dirty word in the male vocab these days. It's possible for a man to mention that he 'went shopping' when at his place of work on a Monday morning without being overly ridiculed. It still doesn't rank alongside football and competitive drinking as acceptable, but it's getting there. Year by steady year.

The reason for this multi-genderism is simple. We're all single these days. If we didn't learn to shop, we'd die. The caveman, 'homo-simplex', or whatever he was, brought home the bacon. Granted he didn't pop to his local Asda and return home with a pre-skinned, pre-plucked, pre-gutted, pre-shrink wrapped stegosaurus. He had to go out and kill it. But he still got his own food. Somewhere between the dawn of civilisation and the late-Eighties, man lost the skill to bring food home. Now it had returned. The wheel had come full circle. The wheel, like a supermarket, is a complete mystery to homo-simplex.

The wheel and the supermarket, however, are not a mystery

to us, 'homo-millenniae'. We drive on four wheels. We shop in the supermarket. Very few of us get this confused. One or two attempt to shop in the 'Offie', or drive on three wheels, but these poor fools are the exception rather than the rule.

One other observation about supermarkets: they attract the obese. You don't see stupendously overweight people in restaurants. Why? They're embarrassed by their size and the portions are two small. You don't see them in gyms because they have a hobby already: eating.

Not even obese people are what they used to be. Obese people are a hell of a lot fatter these days. What was considered vastly fat in the 1940s, during rationing, is now described as 'a bit tubby'. Believe me, in ten more years we'll have those moving walkways in supermarkets like you get in airports, so the big-boned can get all their groceries without succumbing to heart attacks on the way round. Every major outlet will be required to have a doctor on call twenty-four hours a day, ready to jump in with electro-shock treatment and mouth-to-mouth. In another ten years, these walkways could be extended to the pavements *so we never have to walk a single step*. It'll be cheaper for the economy. Cheaper than paying for all the liposuction and new hearts on the NHS.

So: Daisy went to pick up her kids. I went to the supermarket with the obese and the other alcos (but not the agoraphobics – they stayed at home, eating and drinking).

The Tescos past the Heart Lane roundabout in Cirencester is vast but, by modern (American) standards, microscopic. By that I mean it only takes half-an-hour to walk round. In the days of hyper- and mega-markets, 'super' seems strangely quaint, like saying 'super' when you mean 'that's fine'.

I entered the 'super'market with the confidence of a man who knows his terrain. I knew where the items were that I required and I knew how to purchase them. Then I stopped. All I ever bought in Tescos was a trolley full of booze, a family pack of loo roll. And bread.

I had a minor panic attack before following a middle-aged woman the whole way round. Any item she put in her trolley, I put in mine. Anything she squeezed, I squeezed. She liked the specials, so did I. We did well between us. The only problem was that she was shopping for a family of six. I was shopping for one. And Daisy (a half).

We parted company at the booze section. I paced up and down the double aisle for ten or more minutes. Christ there was so much booze. Bottles and bottles of the stuff. Two for one! Reduced!

I have to tell you, though, you'll be proud. I was strong. I bought a case of Stella and that's it. Oh, and a litre of Stoli (two quid off!).

A hundred-and-fifteen pounds lighter in the wallet and with my shopping safely stowed in the boot, I kicked off home. An hour later I had all the gear stashed and was ready for Daisy. It was nearly six.

Six o'clock is the watershed, isn't it? For most of us, six is the time we can crack open a beer in the sure knowledge we're not alcoholics. We haven't had a drink all day. We might go on that night to drink several more beers, a bottle of wine, a few whiskies. Yeah, it's way over the recommended units, but what are units anyway? I mean, who wants to live by the book? If there are limits around, I want to exceed them wherever possible.

So it was six o'clock. I was waiting for Daisy. I didn't know when she was going to show. I went into the kitchen and got a beer, and drank it very slowly. Daisy arrived half-an-hour later.

"I hope that's your first of the day," she said. "I mean the first since I last saw you."

"It sure is."

She gave me a hard look. "Well, you look sober," she said, taking a bag full of groceries into the kitchen.

"How were the kids?"

"Your shelves have got a lot fuller. Been shopping?"

"Your perceptiveness is astounding."

She cuffed me over the head. "Thanks. And yes the kids are fine. How's the big kid?"

"Happy you're here."

"You should be," she raised her chin, looking down her nose at me. "I'm going to cook you an amazing supper. You're going to love me after this."

I felt like saying, "I love you already; I've loved you since forever," but I restrained. "It'll have to be good," I teased.

She smiled. "Trust is the key to any good relationship. Trust me."

Daisy and I talked for a while about her children. I got her to sit down with a glass of wine and tell me about them. To tell the truth, I wasn't that interested (who is in other people's kids?) but I liked to watch her talk. I liked the way her eyes lit up when she told me a funny thing they did. I liked the way she laughed and the way she let her mouth fall open and the sound that came flowing out of her like a pure, cool stream. It was uninhibited and very sexual.

"Come on," she said, around seven. "Come and help me cook."

"I'm good at cutting and boiling stuff."

"That's what I'm looking for."

In the kitchen, I leant up against the units and watched her prepare the food. We were having chicken wrapped in bacon and basil, a tray of baked vegetables, noodles and some special sauce I can't remember the name of.

Watching her cook was an arousing experience. The way her hands moved. The concentration on her face. Even the way she yanked the oven door open and threw the stuff in. Her cooking style reinforced my opinion of her. She was gentle, careful, a bit scatty, but also no-nonsense; tough underneath that delicate, lovely body.

All I did to contribute was: I cut some potatoes, mashed some

garlic, oh and sliced some courgette. I did it pretty well, though.
It looked good.

"Done in half-an-hour," Daisy said, closing the oven door.
"Does this oven have a timer?"

I set it for her.

"Now all I've got to do is make the sauce."

I got the wine from the fridge and handed it to her. "So
cooking is a real passion, hey?"

"It relaxes me. I go into another world when I do
this. Problems disappear. If you talk to me when I cook, I won't
really be listening."

"I'll shut up then."

"No, it's okay. On this scale I can listen and talk. At work, no.
Not possible."

Daisy lugged some wine into the sauce and tasted it, sticking
her finger in and sucking it.

"Good?"

"More pepper, I think. And a little more cream."

I passed it to her. "Why are you doing this?" I asked.

"What do you mean?" She wheeled around to look at me.

"I mean cooking for me. Looking after me. Being here."

"Mothering instinct," she said, going back to her sauce.
"Here. Try this."

I tasted the sauce off her warm finger. It was delicious.

"I like you," she said, stirring. "I like to cook for my friends.
Are we friends?"

I nodded, suddenly overcome by sadness. "Have you done
this before?"

"I cook for people all the time."

"You know what I mean."

She stopped stirring.

"Your husband's had affairs. Have you?"

She began stirring again, slowly. "No, I haven't."

"None?"

"No."

"Why not?"

"It's not my style."

"So why now? What's so special about me?"

"You tell me."

"There is nothing special about me."

"You're wrong. You're charming, good-looking, intelligent..."

"So are a thousand other guys around here."

"Well, I haven't met them. Or they haven't asked me out."

I finished my beer and poured myself a glass of wine.

"You're not getting jealous, are you?"

"Would you be jealous if I had a girlfriend?"

She paused. A flash of hurt dulled her eyes. "Have you?"

I shook my head. "There's this girl who likes me, but I don't like her."

"So you're a heartbreaker."

"Like you."

"I can't break hearts. I'm married."

I was standing very close to her now. Her eyes were vulnerable. She glanced down, then looked up. I slipped a hand around her waist and kissed her. She reached up on her bare toes and kissed me back, putting her arms around my neck. We kissed for several minutes, her breasts rubbing against my chest, her hips pressing in towards me. When we broke off, I said, "You could break hearts if you were a nun," and I meant it. I was chuffed I'd said it. I felt like a Fifties film star.

All through the meal I kept asking if she'd stay the night and I wasn't getting an answer. At nine-thirty I said, "I'm going to bed. You coming?"

She smiled up at me. I was sitting on the sofa. She was lying with her head in my lap. "Do you always go to bed before ten?"

"Whenever I can."

She laughed, knowing I was lying. "So do I."

"Are you going to join me, then?"

"Do you think I should?"

"What do you think?"

She gave me a quizzical look. "We said we'd do it once and that would be it."

"Rules are there to be broken."

"Some rules are there to be broken. Others never should be."

"Like?"

"Like you shouldn't open your Christmas presents on Christmas Eve."

"True."

"You shouldn't swear in front of your grandparents."

"True."

"You shouldn't wear the same underwear two days in a row."

"Err…"

"Oh no, you don't!"

"Oh yes I do."

"Eugh. That's horrible."

"No, it's not; it saves on washing. Which helps the environment by not wasting water and using too much soap powder."

She waved her hands in front of her face. "How long have you had your underwear on?"

"A week."

"Aaaah!"

"No. It was fresh on from this afternoon when I washed."

"So it's clean."

"Unless something terrible's happened that I don't know about."

"Good."

"Are you staying the night, then?"

"If you beg me to."

"I beg you to."

"Okay then. Lead the way!"

It's a girl thing, isn't it? Putting up resistance. If a girl asks a guy if he's staying the night, she'll get a straight yes or no. If a guy asks a girl, they do a ten-minute to two-hour charade. Ooh, naughty. I probably shouldn't. Maybe. Do you love me? And so it goes on. Girls think it's charming. It's not. If Daisy had played the girl any longer, I would have thrown her out. In my book, if you want to stay, great. If you don't, let me get some peace. Let me get the bottom drawer open. And let me get on with it.

But I was pleased Daisy stayed. As before, she was outstanding in bed. So good she could have turned professional. No. Scratch that. She was a keen and gifted amateur. National champion, Commonwealth record-holder, Olympic hopeful. But not a pro. You don't want to turn pro. Not in this game.

Ah, but every rose has its thorn. As we went at it, I began to wonder. About Peter. Here was beautiful, thoroughbred Daisy bouncing about on my hips, small perky boobs bucking above me, and I had her hubby on my mind.

If she's this good in bed, I thought, he must have taught her. He, Peter. They've done this all before. Everywhere.

I tried not to think about it. I tried to blank Peter from the equation.

It didn't work. He kept appearing, plum-faced and breathless, doing what I had not.

These were not good thoughts but soon there was another problem. I had a sore knob as we got down to it yet again and it felt like the plunger in a half-inch diameter syringe. I had to do something to stop this.

"Wait!" I said.

"What, is it hurting your leg?"

"No."

"What then?"

I felt embarrassed now. Coy. "I...err...I need to know something."

"Now?"

"Yes." This made her stop.

"What?"

"Do you still love him? I mean do you still sleep with him?"

"Peter?"

"Yes."

"Very occasionally."

"Is he good?"

"What does that mean?"

"Is he good in bed?"

"Oh good God, Guy!"

"Is he?"

"He's okay. Far as I can remember. Is that all?"

"Is he? Is he… you know… bigger than me?"

Daisy laughed. "I don't know! I never got the tape measure out."

"Does it feel any different with me?"

"Of course it feels different."

"Better?"

"Do you want a rating?" Daisy was laughing now, her shoulders shaking.

"No. I just want to know if it feels good."

"It feels great. Can we carry on now?"

You know when celebrities say stupid stuff? I mean, I heard some boy band half-wit talking last week on the radio about some 'song' he'd 'written' and he was saying how amazing it was that he'd written it because he just started playing chords, out of the blue, that he didn't even know.

Hmm…if you only know three chords, the chances of you playing chords you don't know are considerably higher than if a thousand monkeys typing for a thousand years finally came up with a Shakespeare play. Big deal. And I've never understood this because if a chimp did finally write *Hamlet*, what kind of achievement would this be? It would be repetition, or plagiarism, at best. Let the creature do its own stuff, I say, like snapping your aerial in the wildlife park, having one off the wrist in the trees and denting your roof with its little fists.

Celebrities say stupid stuff. But so do we mortals. I said something devoid of all intelligence to Daisy. When she said,

"Can we carry on now?" I said, "Yes." With a knob that looked like a turkey giblet, I said, "Yes." I tell you, I'll make a perfect celebrity one day. I am that stupid.

"Yes," I said.

"Good."

She started to grind into me again, lowering herself to kiss me. "You are so insecure, Guy, don't you think?"

"I don't know. Is that a good thing?" Tears were coming into my eyes. The pain was medieval.

"Provided it doesn't take you over, it can be sweet."

"I always thought of myself as happy-go-lucky."

"You're not that."

"What am I then?"

"You're very intense. Shy."

"And you? Aren't you insecure?" I was lacking security at this point. Security that my knob was going to remain attached to the rest of my body.

"Of course."

"Do you want me to tell you what you're like in bed?" It would take my mind off the agony, I thought.

"If you want. If it's good."

"Oh, it's good. I think you're fantastic. I think you're an angel. You're perfect."

"Thanks," she kissed me some more. "You make me very... horny."

I shuddered. She picked up the pace. I lay there gathering yards of duvet in my clenched fists, sweating out the pain. I think Daisy thought it was ecstasy. I let it go. I faked an orgasm and let it go. After she was asleep I crept to the bathroom and stuck it in some warm water. The burning sensation eased a little.

The first sight I saw in the morning was Daisy standing stark naked by the window, peering out at the world.

Christ, the curve of those high buttocks, the delicate straightness of the shoulders. I was mesmerised. She sensed me looking at her and turned. I expected her to leap for the cover of the duvet or drag a curtain across her nudity, but she didn't flinch; there wasn't a trace of embarrassment. Not even in the tiny, pale stretch marks. She was a woman. She'd had children. She was beautiful.

"Morning," she said, with a smile, turning to face me. The full glare of her naked body, so comfortably exposed, made me wince.

"I have to go home. The children need taking to school."

"Lucky them."

Daisy smiled and strode across the bedroom to where her clothes lay on the chair. I watched her dress. She was swift and efficient, the sexuality of the night gone completely – but the sensuousness still there.

She scraped her hair off her face, tying it back in one smooth action. She came and gave me a kiss.

"Do you want to have lunch?"

She narrowed her eyes. "Where?"

"Southrop," I said. "There's a great pub there."

She glanced coyly at the ceiling.

"Okay. What time?"

My heart skipped. I think I'm getting somewhere with this girl. Don't you?

Chapter Twenty-five

The Duck in Southrop is a mile from my parents' house. It's a true country pub, with a heavy beard of ivy masking its exterior walls, a cavernous but warm interior and even a skittle alley. It's the first pub I ever drank in and one of the first I ever got drunk in. Still, all these years later, it remains my favourite pub.

It's changed hands three times in the ten years I've been drinking there. Every new landlord has created his own style, his own controversy, his own problems with the locals. The atmosphere always settles. Change is not everyone's favourite tipple but the locals know how to drink through it. And you have to be able to drink through anything in this pub.

I liked The Duck. I only wished I lived closer. If I could swap The Duck for The Old Bell, I'd be a good ten per cent happier.

Daisy and I had lunch in the bar area, catching snippets of conversation from vegetable-gardening locals to route-planning Americans.

When we were done, I suggested we look in on my father.

Daisy gave me an alarmed look. "How are you going to introduce me? As the married woman you're having an affair with?"

"I thought we could say you were a friend and leave it at

that. My father never asks tricky questions, unless he's talking about cars. And he's always been a sucker for a pretty girl. You'd really cheer him up."

As I motored up the gravel drive to the house, I sensed Daisy's eyes widening.

"You live here?"

"Well, no. I used to. Now it's just my father. And the cook."

"Wow! You know I've only been to Southrop a couple of times and both times I looked at this house and thought how fabulous it was."

"Well, fabulous might be overdoing it. As far as I can tell, it's slowly falling down, but it is home."

The place had garnered exactly the reaction I'd hoped for. She was impressed. To impress Daisy was absolute heaven.

"Crikey. Will you show me around?"

"If you behave yourself."

"Daddy," I said, poking my nose round the door of his study. "Hi."

He was sitting behind his snooker table sized desk, elbows resting on it.

"Oh, hello," he said. "All my children are coming to see me. How wonderful."

I looked down at the sofa. There was Vanessa perched on the end looking, well, not her best.

"Hi," I said.

She nodded but didn't make eye contact.

"And who's this lovely creature?" my father asked, as Daisy followed me in.

"I'm Daisy," she replied, striding forward and shaking my father by the hand. "I'm a friend of Guy's."

"Well, he's kept you well hidden. Guy, you should have told me we were having guests; I would have set something up in the drawing room. Let's go through there now. It's awfully gloomy in here."

My father took Daisy by the arm and led her through. Vanessa and I followed behind. She raised her eyebrows at me.

"'Kathy' was wondering why you hadn't called," she whispered.

"I said a friend, didn't I?"

"Friends that good-looking don't stay 'friends' for long."

She looked depressed. I was immediately worried. I asked her what she was doing out in the country.

"Visiting Daddy."

"And?"

"I'll tell you later. What about you? Shouldn't you be at work?"

"I've got the week off for good behaviour."

My father busied himself at the drinks cabinet as we spread ourselves around the room. "I want you all to try this Uruguayan Cabernet," he said. "I think it's lovely and very reasonably priced. I was wondering if I should buy some more."

"Ask Daisy," I said. "She's the expert."

My father loved this.

"How wonderful," he said, handing her a glass, and they were off, chatting away like old friends.

"So what's up?" I asked Vanessa, beckoning for her to come and sit next to me.

"Everything."

"You'll have to be more specific."

"Okay," she sighed. "Eve and I had a row about Ben coming over so much."

"And does he?"

"Not really."

I paused.

"Okay."

She sighed again, more sonorously.

"My uni work is going crap."

"That's not a problem. Everyone's uni work goes crap."

"But it's still not good."

"True."

I paused again. She sighed again. This time more of a huff. There was a long wait.

"And I'm not sure if I'm ready to get married..."

Bingo, I thought. Finally. This is what she wanted to talk about.

"Sounds serious."

"Mmm."

"Want to talk about it?"

"I can't."

"Yes you can. Who else can you tell?"

"Okay, but you have to promise me with your life that you'll keep your mouth shut."

"I promise."

"Really?"

"Yeah. Tell me."

"But he's your best friend."

"And who's my best sister?"

Vanessa smiled weakly.

"Go on," I said. "You know you've got to tell me."

"Oh God," she whispered.

I waited. And waited. Then finally, after much prodding and cajoling, she said in the tiniest whisper, "It's the sex," breathing in as she uttered the words, rather than out.

"The sex?"

"Shhh. Yes."

"What about it?"

"It's not very good."

A smile was spreading across my face.

"Oh, I knew you'd be like this; I should never have told you."

"What?"

"I bet you love this."

"I don't. Why is it crap?"

"Oh, I don't know. It's okay, I suppose, a bit quick, but there's no feeling there. I love him, but I don't feel it when we're in bed."

This was Vanessa's usual level of intensity.

"Have you talked to him about it?"

"Mmm."

"What did he say?"

"He said it would get better."

"Well, he's right. It will."

"I know but... I've only slept with, you know, Charles before, but with him I really felt something..."

"Are you sure you're not expecting too much?"

"Could be."

"Are you having any other problems?"

"We argue sometimes. That's not a problem. I just don't think I'm ready for all this. I'm scared of getting hurt."

"Then call it off. Carry on seeing him, but cool it. Christ, you're still at university. You've got to relax. I'm surprised you got engaged in the first place."

"You know me. I need security. And I don't want to hurt him either. Hurting people is terrible."

"He'll get over it. He wants to be with you. That's the most important thing. You're not going to dump him, are you?"

"No. I've never dumped anyone."

"That's okay then. You know, under all that cockiness, he's a really insecure guy."

"I know that!"

"Do you want me to say anything?"

"You say absolutely nothing, understand? Nothing."

I nodded.

"Nothing," Vanessa repeated.

"You know, I remember when that pony you had died and you cried for weeks. You love too easily, Vanessa. And, when it's not perfect, you feel it too keenly. Give him a chance. Give yourself a chance."

"I will," she said in a small voice. "I will."

Daisy and I left late afternoon. She had to pick up her kids from school. On our way out of the drive, a green Audi appeared. The woman behind the wheel waved. I think she was some friend of the family's from way back. Not a bad-looking woman, for her age. I waved back, polite to a fault.

Daisy was very quiet on the way home. She must have overheard Vanessa banging on about keeping quiet. She said absolutely nothing.

"Can I see you later?" I asked, as we pulled up outside my house.

"I can't," she mumbled, and fled the car. "See you."

And do you know what? I think there was a tear in her eye.

*****

Pissing for blokes isn't as easy, or as fluid, as women think.

Urinals illustrate the point. They're curved at the sides. This is not to spare the urinating man's modesty (or shame, depending on size), because the person next to him can look down at his cock any time he likes.

No. The reason for the curved sides is 'splash'. Not *Splash,* the late-Eighties film starring the leggy Daryl Hannah as a mermaid and Tom Hanks as a walking hard-on, more what happens if you turn a tap full-on.

The penis is not always a reliable nozzle or dispensary. Where we hope for a single lucid jet, we are regularly tortured with an unwieldy twin spray, or fan-style sprinkler. There is no guarantee.

The curved sides of a urinal are therefore not only a clever, but a 100 per cent necessary, feature of the modern convenience. I can't ever imagine having to say, "I'm so sorry, I seem to have pissed all over your suit" to a perfect stranger. It's simply not done. It's not British.

But if pissing is a high tariff move, getting your knob back in your trousers is a quadruple back somersault with tuck and double twist.

Before you even begin, you have to perform the shake-off. Consider this: a cold day and an almost totally numb knob. You've let the urinal have it. And the wall, the person next to you, and the floor. Now you want to get yourself zipped-up as quickly as possible and fly off to the next thing, before the old fella turns blue.

Girls – to offer an example: you've all drained pasta in your time, I assume (provided you're not so totally emancipated that you force your grandfather to do the cooking). You tip the saucepan, holding the lid so it's open a fraction to let the water out, but not the pasta. You do this several times. When convinced it's dry, you serve. And...? There's always a load of water left in the bottom that splashes on the plates.

The shake-off on a cold day is like draining pasta. You think you're done, and you're not. Shake, zip-up and hello...? The dove grey of the pinstripe is now charcoal.

It takes aeons to dry a trouser leg with one of those stupid half-watt hand dryers. And you don't get any sympathy from the other punters, the proficient, the stylish, the expert pissers. No, they simply smile and say, "Do you mind if I cut in for a second? I've got an urgent meeting." Great. That's pissing. Definitely not a piece of piss.

In the home, there are no urinals. That's why, with a raging twin-jetter, I've just let rip all over my plastered leg, the wall, the left side of my trousers and the floor. Pissing is not easy when you're fully able-bodied. When you're on crutches, it's a lottery.

Daisy wasn't coming over. I'd been upset about this, but not now. I was pleased Daisy wasn't coming over, after all.

White Summer

I needed forty-eight hours to clear the piss off the ceiling, my chin and the lampshade.

Chapter Twenty-six

"It's terrible losing someone close to you," Debbie said, as she handed me a 'Welcome Home' card (with 'Home' crossed out and substituted with 'Back!') on my return to the office. "My boyfriend's brother drowned when he was only five."

"Oh Christ." I didn't know the lovely Debbie even had a boyfriend. Let alone one with a drowned brother.

"Mmm. It took him a while to get over it. You just have to accept that person has gone."

"I know. I'm getting there. Bit by bit."

"You'll be fine. It'll get easier."

"I know."

I did know. It's what I told myself every day. It will get easier. It was my mantra. It was the first thing I said in the morning and the last thing I said at night. Each day that passed – it will get easier.

It hadn't yet, of course. I reckoned I was looking at a five-year plan, maybe ten. All I could do in the interim was keep myself off the booze. (This was damn hard. I'd reduced myself from a swimming pool of alcohol a week to a birdbath but the urge was strong to plunge back in.) And to stay focused.

I needed something new – an attention grabber. And luckily for me, the perfect bait came along.

On my third day back at work, on a cold November morning,

a tall gentleman with greying blonde hair strode into the Go Away Travel Centre. He sat in the chair in front of my desk. My heartbeat hit 130 as I recognised him.

"Hi," he said. I'd never realised what a good-looking man he was. He was tanned, chiselled and lean.

"Lisbon," I said, feigning slow recall. "You booked your flight with me. Did you have a good time?"

"Marvellous. Marvellous."

"And your...?"

"Girlfriend?" he winked, sitting back in his chair. "She had a pretty good time."

"Good," I said, my heart settling. "So Mr Warnford..."

"Call me Peter."

"So Peter. Can I book you something else?"

"No," he said, fingering one of my business cards. "No... Guy?"

I nodded.

"No, Guy. I was wondering if you'd like to have lunch. Perhaps today or tomorrow. At your convenience. Preferably today, if you can manage it."

This threw me. This was outside my expectations. I took a deep breath.

"Don't look so scared," he said. "I'm not queer. There's something I'd like to discuss with you."

"What?"

"I'll tell you about it at lunch. When's it going to be? Today. At one?" His tone was friendly but firm.

"Today," I said.

"One o'clock then."

"Perfect."

"I'll come and get you."

"What was all that about?" Kate asked.

"Search me."

"Are you going to have lunch with him?"

"Why not?"

"He seems okay," said Debbie. "Not a psycho, or anything."

I looked at Ted.

"He seems cool. I'd go."

"I'm going," I agreed. "No two ways about it."

I couldn't concentrate for the rest of the morning. Every possible scenario of why Peter Warnford would want to speak to me went through my head.

"Hello again," he said, striding in through the door.

"Hi," I replied, grabbing for my crutches. "Sorry, you'll have to hang on a second."

"Done yourself some damage?"

"Broken ankle. Fell down some stairs."

"Drunk?"

"I wish. It would have hurt less."

"That's funny," he said. "Last time I was in, you said life was good. You had no broken bones."

"God, you're right. Must have tempted Fate."

He laughed. "Don't worry. My car's just outside. If you don't mind, I thought we could have lunch at my house. It's not far."

Panic rose in my throat. I could see the headline:

Travel Agent takes mystery trip. Fears escalated last night as Guy Chamberlain of Cirencester...

I took a breath. You're getting carried away, I thought. This doesn't happen. Not in Gloucestershire.

"This is my car," Peter said, putting on shades. It was a hefty, modified motor, with large bored-out alloy wheels. I followed him across the road and got in.

"I expect you want to know," he said, starting it up and pulling smoothly away, "what on earth's going on."

"Actually, I'm not particularly inquisitive. I see the sun come up in the morning. I see it go down at night. Why or how it does doesn't bother me. Stuff happens. That's all there is to it." This was a total lie but I wanted to appear off-hand.

Peter smiled. "That's what I like about you. That's what I

sensed about you when we first met."

I didn't comment.

"You know," he said. "I go up to London regularly on business, at least three times a week. I have a flat there, off Sloane Square. I like it, but I prefer the country."

"Me too."

"About a fortnight ago I had to spend a week up there. I was really ratty by the end of it. The cabs, the traffic, the smog..."

"I know. Criminal. You didn't run into the Queen or Prince Philip, I hope?"

"No, thank God," he laughed.

Peter drove carefully, hands correctly positioned on the wheel, and fast. We were halfway to Tetbury by the time I had my seatbelt on.

"Yes. I spent a week there. A wasted week in some ways, looking for people to work for me."

"Oh right," I said. "For your property company."

"Exactly. I went around all the agencies and came up with nothing. Well, almost nothing. There was a guy at DeLoitte..."

"Oh Christ, not Jack."

"He's your brother, right?"

"Sort of."

"Yes, he's cocky alright. Not cocky like you, but more obviously. Though he had his uses. He gave me your CV."

"Most of that's lies," I said. "Whoppers. And he had no right to give it to you. I'm not looking for a job."

Peter took this in his stride. "Wait and hear what I have to say before you make any decisions."

"I will. I don't want to talk myself out of a free lunch."

"There's no such thing as a free lunch," we said in unison.

The Warnford residence is a large Cotswold stone farmhouse, built in an L-shape, plenty of land, plenty of outbuildings. But I didn't like it. It felt cold.

"My wife's out for the afternoon, I think," Peter said, as we went in through the back door. It was shrouded in ivy. The sills were rotting and there was moss on the ground. "So, we shouldn't be disturbed."

"What does she do?" I asked. (Ha, ha.)

"Mostly, she pisses me off. But that's what wives do. You're not married, are you?"

"God no."

"Sensible man. Keep it that way for as long as you can. I married after I'd had some fun, which helped. But I'm still having fun, which doesn't. I do love her, though. I presume she still loves me, even if it isn't always obvious."

He took us through a hallway into a large kitchen.

"She said she'd leave something in the fridge for us."

I was relieved Daisy was out. I didn't think I could handle it with her there. I felt like a peeping Tom in her home, digging about for lunch.

"One good thing about Daisy, she knows how to cook."

"That can add ten per cent to a woman's value," I said, trying to sound laddish and off-hand.

"Ah. Here we go." Peter produced two foil-covered plates from the fridge. He put them on the kitchen table. "If you can undo those, I'll open the wine. Chablis, okay?"

"Fine," I said, unwrapping the plates. Daisy had done a cold seafood mix with salad, risotto and quiche. On one plate there was a note. It read, 'Peter, garlic bread in microwave, put on number three for two minutes.' Seeing it made me jealous. I put the bread in the microwave with numb hands.

"Right," Peter said, holding two glasses and a bottle, "follow me." I grabbed the plates and followed him into the orangery. It looked out over the garden and the fields beyond. It was raining but the effect was still dramatic. Large conifers and box-hedges dominated, interspersed by shaped flower-beds. The garden also had several levels of immaculate lawn.

I took the plates to the glass table and sat down. Peter put some jazz on, then joined me. He poured the wine.

"Cheers," he said. "I don't garden, by the way. I saw you looking. That's all Daisy's work. And the gardener."

"It's beautiful."

"Like my wife. If you do ever get married, make sure she's a looker. Come on. Eat up."

As we ate, Peter explained he'd been looking for someone like me for some time.

"And what am I?"

"You're a people person."

"I can't stand people."

"That's not the point. You look as if you care. That's all I need. I can't stand people either. People, ninety per cent of people, are a pain in the arse. You and I know that and we can handle it."

"I can't always handle it."

"That's okay. Losing your temper sometimes shows you're a man."

"Yeah, I suppose."

"The way you got me on that flight from Lisbon really impressed me. That's service. You kept cool. You got on with it. You used to work in the City, didn't you?"

"Yeah."

"Did you find it tough?"

"I liked it in some ways. But it didn't offer me enough freedom. I like to be more in charge of my own time."

"So what are you doing as a travel agent?"

"Biding my time."

"For what?"

"I wanted to travel."

"And now you've travelled?"

"Good question."

"You're treading water. Do you want to stop treading and start to swim?"

"Possibly. You're going to have to give me some details first. I only got my fifty-yard badge at school."

"That's what I'm going to do right now."

I took a slug of wine and topped up my glass. I filled Peter's too. As I brought it to my lips, I heard the back door slam shut.

"Jesus. She's as thin as a reed but she can't half slam that door. Darling!" Peter called, as we heard her clatter into the kitchen. "Come and meet my new friend."

My heartbeat hit 130. I slugged back my glass of wine in one and stared at my plate. As Peter said, "Ah! Here she is." I spun in my chair, got to my feet and shook her by the hand. I couldn't bring myself to look at her face.

"Hello," she said. "I'm Daisy." She didn't sound too shocked.

"Hi. Nice to meet you."

"Peter, aren't you going to introduce me?"

"Yes, darling. This is Guy. I'm hoping he's going to work for me in the near future."

Daisy and I sat down. My heart still kicked out a good beat. Not as jazzy as the music, but a good shuffle. I poured myself more wine and offered Daisy a glass. She refused.

"You'll have to be careful, Guy. He'll promise you the earth and then let you down."

"Don't believe her, Guy. It's not true. I'm a man of my word."

"This man of his word," said Daisy, pointing an elegant finger at him, "is the man who said we'd have a tennis court in the garden the first year we were married. Seven years ago. Do you see a tennis court, Guy?"

I looked up. Daisy was giving Peter a stern look. I kept quiet.

"Peter?"

"I don't play tennis."

"But I do. I mean did."

Daisy sounded much older with Peter. They were like the two adults and I was the little boy, caught in-between.

"Okay," Peter said, turning to me, a flare of anger in his eyes. "I told you she was a pain in the arse."

"I can be a lot bigger pain in the arse," Daisy warned. "Have you taken the stuff to the tip?"

"I don't think now's the time, darling."

"Last week was the time, Peter, when you said you'd do it. That old carpet is still piled high in the barn. When is it going to go?"

"When I get round to doing it."

"And I thought 'doing it' was your strong point," Daisy said with venom.

"Yes, but not here, anymore. We agreed that."

I tried to close my ears. This is not what I wanted to hear.

"Guy, do you want coffee?" Peter asked.

"If you're having one."

"Two coffees please, Daisy. I would do it, but I'm busy. Would you mind?"

"You're always busy," she said, getting up, and then to me, "Do you see what I have to put up with?"

The situation was all getting too surreal.

Peter sighed. "Gorgeous-looking girl. Trouble is she thinks it's her divine right to get whatever her heart desires."

"That's it. The better looking they are, the more they think they can take the piss."

Peter laughed. "You know, you're very astute. Very aware of how the world works."

"I read *Hello!*"

He burst out laughing. "I'll tell you what. Let's have a cigar. Do you smoke?"

He opened a box on the table. "They're not great, but they're not bad." I took one and lit it with my own lighter.

"Tastes fine to me."

"Not when you've had the best. Not when you've had the very best."

"But sometimes the best is not all it's cracked up to be."

"Jesus, you're right again. You're like a talking Japanese fortune cookie."

"What? Full of shit."

"No, that's me!"

We both laughed some more.

Daisy came in with the coffee and gave me a searching look. I took the coffee and thanked her, avoiding further eye contact. The best move was to get out of here.

"Peter," I said. "I've enjoyed chatting, but if we don't go soon, I'm going to get sacked."

"Does that bother you?"

"Yes."

"Good. That's the way it should be. Come on, I'll take you back right now." He took a quick slug of his coffee. "Bring your cigar; you can smoke it in the car."

I looked around to say goodbye to Daisy. She'd already gone.

"She'll be changing," said Peter. "She's painting the fencing this afternoon. She likes to get her hands dirty. She fixed the tractor last weekend. Remarkable woman."

"What have you got a tractor for?"

"Fun! What else?" He laughed. "Come on. Let's go."

Chapter Twenty-seven

"Guy? What the hell is going on?"

It was Daisy. She phoned the second I got back to work. I told her I had no idea.

"You must have some idea."

"He likes me. I did him a good turn and he wants to offer me a job."

"Don't take it."

"Well, I..."

"Don't take it. It'll ruin everything."

"Ruin what?"

"He'll find out about us, then we'll both be in big trouble."

"Hadn't we better meet and talk about this?"

"I'll try and come round some night this week."

"Okay. You're not angry, are you?"

"I don't know."

"This is not my fault."

"It takes two to cause a problem. Look, I'd better get off the phone. I'll see you later."

She hung up. I stared at my computer screen. On impulse I typed, 'OH FUCK' ten times.

It made me feel better. Kind of. And it doesn't take two to cause a problem; it takes three.

*****

Daisy came round on Thursday night. Peter was safely in London at his flat off Sloane Square.

We drank wine, sitting on the sofa. Coldplay were on the hi-fi.

"It flipped my stomach when I saw you having lunch with Peter in my house. I felt invaded."

"I felt like a snooper. It wasn't much fun for me."

"Why did you agree to it, then?"

"He's very persuasive, isn't he? Christ, I like the guy."

"Oh, that's just perfect. Why don't you have an affair with him too?"

I couldn't help laughing at this. Daisy couldn't either.

"Oh, it's too surreal. How does life get this strange?"

"Who knows?"

"Okay. You have to promise me one thing. Don't accept any more invitations to my house. I don't want to spend my life on tenterhooks wondering when you're going to show up."

I agreed.

"And don't take the job."

"Fine."

"You're so sweet."

I looked at my watch. I didn't know if Daisy was staying the night. "It's getting late..."

"Then let's go to bed. I'm bored of talking."

"Me too. After you."

Daisy skipped to the bedroom and had flung all her clothes out of the door by the time I'd limped in to join her. She'd passed a big test here, I can tell you. No teasing this time. Just straightforward. Exactly as it should be.

Later, wrapped only in the duvet, we huddled by my bedroom window and looked down. Below was the claret and old gold of the goblin's bonfire. The little man was cartwheeling around it.

"What is he doing there?" Daisy asked, in hushed tones.

"He's planting us a garden," I said. "A new symbol of hope."

*****

The plaster, like a stripper's stocking, came off painfully slowly. I went to Cirencester hospital and had it scissored by the staff nurse. My leg felt like an escaped convict. I felt like an escaped convict.

But the freedom was too much. As I rose for a celebratory jig, the old pin gave like a reed of straw and I tumbled, OAP-like, to the floor. The doctor said I should remain on crutches until the leg had strengthened. The muscles, he added, would have atrophied in the six weeks of incarceration. I looked at my leg. He was right. It was paler than my left (ergo, almost transparent) and about the size of a pipe cleaner.

There was a message waiting for me on the answer machine when I got home. It was from Ben. He wanted to know if I'd come up to London on Sunday. My leg wasn't the only thing to find its freedom that week: Tiger had been released from HM Brixton and was keen to start living.

I got to Clapham at eleven. The traffic around Earls Court wasn't locust-dense for a change so I arrived relatively calm, which is to say unrabid. I even enjoyed the jostling for position over Battersea Bridge.

Ben's flat is not far from Clapham Common. It's an old Victorian conversion. Once it was a four-bedroom house, now it's two flats. (The estate agent smiles broadly.) I think it's mortgaged, but he could be renting. Ben is cagey about his financial situation. Mostly, I think, to spare my blushes. He probably earns more in a month than I do in a year, or possibly a decade.

I parked outside and he buzzed me in. At his door, he gave me a forged resident's parking certificate.

"You should be okay with that," he said, handing me a can of Stella.

"So where is he?" I asked.

"He'll be here about one."

"On good form?"

"Sounded it on the phone. I haven't seen him."

Ben's enormous flat-screen TV was tuned in to MTV. I settled in front of it on one of his blue corduroy sofas. Ben took the chair in the same style.

"So," I said. "What happened to the kid he ran over?"

"Made a full recovery."

"Excellent."

"Yeah, he's still banned for a trillion years, but he doesn't care. I think he's sold his car."

When Tiger arrived, he looked different. He was still skinny with a shaven head and a neck augmented with beads, but he was different. A look in his eyes said he'd come too close for comfort. Any remaining innocence he may have had was now gone.

We hugged and headed out to the bars on Battersea Rise. It was a cold November day, but miraculously the rain had given way to bright sunshine.

"Lunch is on me," Ben declared when we arrived at Big Joe's Bar and Brasserie. "You can handle the drinks, Guy."

"Since when does lunch not include drinks?" I said. "The drinks bill will be ten times the cost of three steaks."

"Okay," Ben sighed. "I will pay two-thirds of the bill, you pay the rest, okay?"

"I've got some cash," said Tiger.

"From being done in the arse in prison?" said Ben. "Fuck off, you aren't paying for shit today."

We sat down at a table next to the French window, which ran the length of the restaurant and overlooked Battersea Rise. A fit, young waitress bobbed up to serve us.

"My friend has recently been released from Her Majesty's

Pleasure," I said, gesturing to Tiger. "So I think we should start with a pitcher of tequila sunrise. You know. The dawn of a new day."

Tiger nodded. We drank all afternoon. I think we had some food. Don't ask me what.

"To freedom!" we kept shouting at each other. "To freedom!" and we carried on shouting it throughout the whole day.

I don't remember leaving Big Joe's; I don't remember spilling two consecutive pints in the next pub; I don't remember the sun rising or setting; and the night club... well it looked tiny due to my tunnel vision.

The one thing I do recall is Tiger repeatedly grabbing my shoulder and shouting in my ear, "Freedom is the most important thing you can have my friend. Freedom! Nothing else matters."

I thought about this as I drove back to Cirencester at six o'clock on Monday morning. Freedom! You certainly don't feel it at the crack of dawn on a November morning, I can tell you.

When I arrived back at my flat, with just enough time to shower and change before work, I checked my answer machine. There was another liberty-destroying message on it from 'Kathy'. She sounded uncharacteristically nervous.

"Guy," she said, "I know you've had a lot on your mind recently. I forgive you for not phoning. Let's get together. I'll call you next week. There's something I need to tell you."

I immediately phoned Vanessa. I got her answer machine. I was tired.

"If you're encouraging 'Kathy' to keep calling me," I said, "don't. I'd really rather not see her again. And I don't see why I should have to. It's like forcing me to eat a raw egg. I don't want one. It won't be good for me. And everything will end up scrambled. Sorry about the pun. I'm too knackered to think straight."

I showered and went to work in something approaching a deep depression – five fathoms down. I had a terrible, temple-thumping hangover. I didn't want to be at work and Kate was appearing more efficient than ever, revelling in her imminent rise in the ranks.

Just before lunch, I accosted her in the back office.

"Hey," I said. "Your promotion wasn't helped on its way by telling Carol about my lack of travelling experience, was it?"

"Grow up. I wouldn't stoop to that. I hardly needed to either. You've been about as useful as a rump steak to a vegetarian in the last few months."

"It's not like I haven't had stuff to deal with."

"I know, Guy, but you can't wallow in self-pity forever. You've got to snap out of it."

"I have snapped out of it."

"Then what's the problem?"

"The job. It's getting on my nerves. I'm better than this."

"Then maybe you'd be 'better' somewhere else."

"Yeah. Maybe I would."

Kate pushed past me back into the office. I stayed for another cigarette.

Chapter Twenty-eight

On Wednesday night, I drove over to Southrop, to the little church by the river, to visit my mother's grave.

It had been almost two months since her death. Standing in front of the headstone I bowed my head. I stood there praying for a vision or a sign or something, but nothing came.

"I really wish you were here," I said. "I feel lost. I need some advice... I don't know who to ask."

I stared into the silent darkness for ten, fifteen minutes. "I hope you're okay. I'll see you later."

On the drive back, snapshots of my childhood played across my mind: first day at prep school, learning to ride a bike, first party, birthdays, holidays – my mother played a part in all of them. Her face was ever-present, smiling, encouraging, loving.

Those days were gone. That safety was gone forever. I now had to make my own decisions. Christ, how must Daisy have felt when her mother was taken from her at fourteen?

We're all children underneath, aren't we? Little people who haven't quite grown up. Little, scared people who still like to be hugged and comforted. We can't hang onto our parents forever. No. That's why we have to find a mate. In many ways, I thought I'd found mine. Trouble was, I didn't even have her phone number.

*****

The phone was ringing when I got back. I dived for it, thinking it was Daisy. It wasn't. It was the anti-Daisy. It was 'Kathy'.

"Hi," she said, all (forced) bubbly and bright. "How are you?"

"I just visited my mother's grave."

"Oh."

"Yeah. I'm tired, actually. You?"

"Oh, I'm fine. Did you get my message?"

"I did. Listen. I think you should know. I have a girlfriend already."

"Not Kate?"

"No, someone else."

"Who?"

"No one you know."

"Oh."

"Mmm...I'm sorry 'Kathy'. I don't think I can see you anymore."

"Oh."

"You'll be okay. You'll find someone else."

"Oh. I... I suppose. Listen, Guy." And then it all came tumbling out. "Would you mind helping me through an abortion? I'm pregnant with your child."

Ouch. I said nothing.

All I heard from the other end was a big wracking sob, which lasted for five, ten minutes. When she could speak again, she said, "I'm so sorry. I don't want to put you through this. I kept hoping I'd come on. But it hasn't happened. I did a test last week. The doctor confirmed it. I need you to help me with this."

"Okay," I said. "Keep calm. Take a breath. Have you been to the hospital to book this?"

"No." Her voice was very small.

"Shall I come up tomorrow and we can sort it out?"

"That would be good."

"Okay," I said. "I can get there about eleven."

We talked for another ten minutes before I managed to get away. "Bugger," I said, when I put the phone down. I went straight to the kitchen and got the vodka out. Daisy and I had been at it without protection too.

*****

Condoms! The great liberating invention (along with the pill) of the twentieth-century. No more need for the human race to be troubled by unwanted pregnancies outside of wedlock. No more need to fear the spread of syphilis and AIDS. No more need to practice *coitus interruptus*. Or the 'rhythm method'. Or abstinence. No, from here on, sex was nothing but fun, frolics and as many partners as you could squeeze into a half-hour lunch break.

But wait. One snag here. They're no good in a bedside drawer. You actually have to put one on. And once you've got it on, sex is about as fun as bedding a bin bag.

When it comes to condoms, I and the jonnies are rarely in the room at the same time. Let alone in the right spot. I mean, I try. I have what Jules Winfield described in *Pulp Fiction* as 'best intentions', but they never quite come off. Sorry, 'come off' was a bad phrase there…

In my defence, I would like to say that if a young lady leaves the front door open, she should check the back door's locked. Err…no. That's not the right analogy. Again. If a girl allows a man into her house, she should make sure it's properly insulated… no. Okay. If a girl wants to go for it 'bare back', she should be on the pill.

I want to think this to shift the blame but know it isn't fair or of any help now. I've done what I've done and I have to take my share of responsibility. Christ, I wished it were Daisy who was pregnant and not 'Kathy'.

I tore the lid off the vodka and poured myself a large glass mixed with cranberry juice. I'd been doing so well with my drinking too. I hadn't gone over my six can limit in days.

*****

Carol was unimpressed that I had to take the day off work.

"What is it this time?" she said, her voice pure primary school teacher.

"A girlfriend of mine is in trouble. I have to go and help her out."

"Not the one who comes in here?"

"No! A friend of my sister's."

"Can't your sister help out?"

"Not really. It's more personal than that."

Carol shook her head. "You really have to grow up, Guy."

"Give me the map, and I will gladly follow the route to maturity," I said with feeling.

She sighed heavily. The disappointed parent.

"You'll be in tomorrow?"

"Definitely."

She pointed at the door. "The sooner you get there, the better, I suppose."

"Thanks, Carol. I owe you one."

"You owe me more than one, my boy."

"Where's he off to?" I heard Kate ask, as I left.

"Never you mind, Kate. You get on..."

But she was out of earshot now, and I was heading home with a heavy heart. There aren't many times I can claim I'd rather be at work but this was one of them. I had no clue how I was going to handle this. No clue at all.

'Kathy's' house in Reading is a shithole. I thought my flat was bad. 'Kathy's' house... well, if I had to live there, I'd commit a spate of burglaries until I got caught – HM Brixton must be more cheerful. It's not surprising she's always dossing on Vanessa's floor. The vibe of the place dragged me further into the ever-deepening pool of depression that I was trying so hard to climb out of.

When I arrived, she was all bouncy. As if we were off to Alton Towers for the day. I thought, cut it out, this isn't a cocktail party. She soon settled down, however, after I suggested we go straight to the hospital to sort the mess out.

To be honest, I'd had enough of hospitals of late. The inside of another was the last thing I wanted to see. I waited outside while she saw the gynaecologist.

I didn't ask her what went on in that room. I didn't want to know. She told me anyway but I blocked my ears. The salient point was this: if she wanted an abortion, she could have one. I told her we should book it. We did. Then she burst into tears.

Oh no, I thought, as I hugged her, her big tears staining my shirt. This isn't doing either of us any good.

"Are you okay?" I said.

"I'll be alright – with your help."

I cringed. "Do you want to go for a drink?"

"Yes."

I drove to Sonning, hoping the picturesque surroundings would lift our spirits. They did, in a way, as a counterbalance.

"Has this ever happened to you before?" I asked. We were lunching in The Ram, near the river.

"No." She looked much happier now she was eating some food. I was happy for her. I couldn't imagine what she was going through. All I knew was we needed to end this situation and fast.

"It'll be okay," I said. I was having the grilled trout. It eyed me with suspicion.

"Thanks so much for coming."

"We both caused the problem. We can both fix it."

"Do you think there's a chance for us?"

Oh crikey. We didn't need to do this.

"I don't think so," I said. "You're a lovely girl. I'm just

crazily infatuated with someone else."

"Really?"

"Really."

"Why?"

"I just feel when there's a clear sky... I look up and I see it's not written in the stars. You and me. It's not up there."

I know this sounded terrible, but I couldn't put it any other way. 'Kathy' and I were not meant to be.

She took a consolingly large bite of garlic bread and stared at her lasagne. I sat back and lit a cigarette.

"I'm sorry," I said.

"You're not sorry. You do what you want. You hurt people and then you leave them."

"Have you been talking to Vanessa?"

"No!"

"Well, that's her favourite line at the moment. And it's not true. I have feelings. Lots of them. They're just for someone else."

The waiter came to our table, a tall, thin guy in his fifties. I guessed he was the landlord. "Can I get you something else?" he asked. "Pudding, coffee..."

"I'll have the sticky toffee pudding and a cappuccino," 'Kathy' replied.

I passed. I just wanted to get home.

The sticky toffee pudding arrived and I changed my mind about coffee, ordering a double espresso.

Driving back to her house, 'Kathy' said to me, "You can stay the night if you want. It's not as if I can get pregnant again."

After all that had happened, I couldn't believe it.

"I have work tomorrow," I said.

"Oh wow! Work. At the travel agent's. How important!"

I was stunned. 'Kathy', the closet bitch. "If you want to hitch from here to your house, you're going the right way about it," I said, not looking at her.

She retracted her statement. I dropped her off and left in

a hurry. Christ, I never wanted to see her again. And the abortion was in two weeks.

*****

When I got back to Cirencester, I went swimming. It wasn't part of my usual routine, I admit, but the doctor had said, you know, for the ankle. And besides, I hadn't got my heart rate up in a while, except through hormones or nerves. No. It was time to do some exercise.

There's a twelve-step recovery program, I believe, for people with addiction. Whether you're been on the booze, coke, smack, or weed-killer, there are twelve steps to get off it. One step to get on – 'yeah, I'll try it'. Twelve to get off. Presumably twelve ways to say, 'No thanks, I'll give it a miss.'

For the reformed swimmer, there's also a step-by-step guide back to the pool (from the brink).

Step one. Find trunks/bikini/swimsuit.

Now, if you haven't been swimming for some time (most people over the age of eight haven't been for a decade), this can be the most challenging phase of your program.

For me, it ended with a jaw-gratingly irritating and expensive trip to The Cirencester Surf Shop. Having scanned the bottom drawer, surveyed the laundry basket, spent a stomach-churning hour under the bed (with the dead spiders, the pubes, the discarded pornography), I admitted it to myself – perhaps I'd never even owned a pair.

Step one. Yes, I'd agree with the addicts. It's by far the toughest.

Step two. Find the pool.

Not too arduous this one. I mean, I can't actually miss it. The building that is. Inside, I had more trouble. I paid up (with a hammering heart), then passed an agreeable, if fruitless, half-hour attempting to locate the man-made deep. Me and the Swiss roll of my towel, stuffed with garish surf shorts, simulating confidence and sports centre savvy, and I suppose, failing.

A young girl in the sky blue uniform of sweat-top and logo-emblazoned tracksuit bottoms eventually guided me, like a pensioner being helped across the road, to the turnstile – the gateway to heavily-chlorinated rebirthing.

But before the swim comes the shaming of the changing room. There is nowhere to hide. Banks of lockers, with their hunger for fifty pences or tokens, glare down at you. 'Come on', they seem to say. 'Get your kit off. Let's see what you've got'. And of course the guy standing next to you is a ripped Van Damme or bulging Schwarzenegger with a baseball bat for a knob and tennis balls for testicles.

On the out-run, I was fortunate to find the changing area almost empty bar a frail old buffer intent on keeping himself to himself. I changed quickly, only briefly getting my left leg caught between the outer fabric and interior netting of my new costume.

I must say, standing in front of the mirror (placed just before the foot spa to remind you of how crap you look, to sap you of the last grain of self-confidence in your already low sugar bowl of body image), even I was awe-struck by the boldness, the out-and-out face-slapping cheek of my swimming shorts. God! The vulgarity of the yellow swirls, the orange overlay, the quite obvious toplessness of the mermaid across my crotch. I pinned the locker key over her left breast. There was nothing I could do about the right one.

A first date is like swimming. And therefore swimming is like a first date. You want to look your best. Act cool. And impress. With this in mind, I took a breath and ventured on.

And so to the pool and the large laminated poster. Another program. This one the eight step guide to correct pool policy.

'NO! Diving.

'NO! Bombing.

'NO! Heavy petting.'

And other restrictions. But, strangely, no sign which said,

'NO! drowning'.

I nearly turned on my heel and headed back. I mean, the only thing that wasn't banned was swimming. It was like walking into a bar and being confronted with a barman who told you:

"NO! joke telling.

"NO! gossiping.

"NO! darts.

"NO! pool."

The water looked like a gallon of toddler piss was added every half-hour to top-up the litres the OAPs swallowed every other length. It was as yellow as my trunks.

I hesitated at the steps. Did pool etiquette allow a slow descent into the water via the plastic rungs or were these strictly for exiting? I returned to the sign to check. It seemed this mode of entry was permissible, so I glided into the shallow end. And the water came up to just above my knees.

Wading out, it wasn't long until I grasped the metal tubing at the deep end. The water was up to my collarbone. I nearly wept with relief. Chances of drowning: slight.

Confidence high, I flung myself forward, kicking off from the wall, windmilling my arms in the style of the crawl. I must say, those around certainly took notice, mouths open with... admiration, disbelief, envy(?) at my proficiency.

However, I cut short the display halfway through length two. Yes, friends, my style may have been spectacular, but my stamina was not in the league of the plucky bus-pass holders. Yes. I'd have to work up to their level of fitness and/or grim determination. Right there, I resolved to return the following month, if I could find the time.

Back in the male changing area, I showered and dressed, only momentarily flustered by a pack of rippling rugger types (did I recognise some of them from that night in the pub?) tearing off their clothes with the kind of relaxed abandon I could only dream of.

I stuck near to the back wall and removed my swimming long

johns, towel clenched in my teeth to cover as much naked flesh as possible. It took me twelve seconds to transform myself from bather to street citizen, wring out my shorts, bundle them back into my towel and do my hair.

My final ordeal was supplied to me by a cocky nine-year-old who attempted to administer a 'rat's tail' on my bum before I left. When I admonished him, he told me (with unnecessary aggression, I thought) to "get stuffed".

The language was not as colourful as some under-tens come out with these days, but it certainly shocked me. Cripes, the modern planet was certainly populated with some arrogant little tykes. It wasn't like that in my day!

I left the centre with my confidence bruised, but intact. The moral victory was mine, though having forgotten to pack deodorant, my musky armpits nagged at my self-esteem.

Chapter Twenty-nine

My father phoned the following week and said something extremely bizarre. I don't know if he'd been drinking, or reading too much astronomy, or whether I still had water in my ears from the swim, but he certainly rocked me back on my heels.

"Daisy is the girl for you," he said. I hadn't even said, "Hello." These were his first words.

"Dad?"

"Guy. She's simply charming. Beautiful, intelligent, feisty. You'd be a fool not to marry her. She's the one for you, I guarantee it."

"Why...?"

"She reminds me very much of your mother in her younger days."

"But we're just friends."

"Nonsense. You don't have to feel ashamed. She's a lovely girl. My advice? Propose. Right away."

I couldn't help laughing. "Dad..."

"If you won't, I'll say something. She'll make a man of you, Guy. She'll keep you under control."

I was lost for words. My father? A matchmaker? With his reputation?

"What makes you say that?"

"A feeling. And no, I haven't gone mad. I'm quite with it. I have a very good feeling about this girl. She's streaks ahead of anything else you've brought home."

My father was right here. My previous girlfriends had been... varied, unsuitable, tragic mistakes.

After what seemed a lifetime of snogging, my first serious relationship happened at university. She was stunning: tall, blonde, the greatest body you're ever likely to see. You could scour every strip club and brothel in the universe, rent every porno ever made, flip through every dirty mag ever printed, and you'd never find perfection like hers. Ever. But she had one great failing for someone like me. She was exceptionally intelligent. Very few men can cope with that. For the not-so-secure man, intelligence in a girl can only do one thing. Make you feel shit.

Tabitha, or Tabby, was very good about her intelligence. She tried to hide it as best she could. When asked a general knowledge question, she would frown and feign thought, and eventually say, "I think it's Caracas, or isn't it Capulet?" or (gently), "No, I'm pretty sure it was Henry Moore, but I could be wrong," when clearly she knew all along. If ever there was a candidate for University Challenge, Tabby was it. I loved her. I loved her for two whole years, but when she corrected someone on who was the Prime Minister of Thailand at a dinner party, I could take it no more. I had to say goodbye.

My second major romance was with a film producer's daughter. Her name was Polly. Polly was also blonde, but thick and extrovert.

Thick and extrovert, I remember thinking at the time. This is much more me. This is a match made in my own vision of heaven. But it wasn't to be. Polly broke my heart. When I asked her why she didn't want to go out with me anymore, she said, "You can be a bit dull, Guy. Nice, but... dull."

This put me in a spin, I can tell you. Working in London, I went about rectifying my dullness. I drank more, I socialised more, I smarmed my way into as many double beds as I could, all in the pursuit of giving my life some 'back story'. Something to make the biographer sit up and take notice. It didn't work. I became a boring socialite, rather than a boring homebody.

A girl called Luna restored my confidence with women. I met Luna in Spain (yes, we're talking holiday romances here) but she was Portuguese, thereby combining two of my favourite countries in one (out of the three, if you remember). Note: we never had family holidays abroad: a) because of my mother's illness, b) too many of us, c) my father had an addiction to walking holidays in the British Isles – Brecon Beacons, Lake District, Loch Lomond, Ben Nevis... yawn.

Luna and I met at a nightclub. Not a good one. One of the tacky, easy to get into ones. Luna was five-foot-nothing, had dark curly hair and a twin sister. They were very attractive in their own small, identical way. Once I'd bagged Luna, my mind soon raced onto the possibility of getting her and her sister into bed. Ben backed me up on this as much as he could, trying to snog her, but it never got off the ground.

Nothing much happened between Luna and me during the last few days of our holiday. Lots of snogging and holding hands and that was it. The last night we went out drinking and exchanged addresses. I got back to London and after a week thought nothing more about her.

That was until she wrote me a very sweet letter, informing me of her imminent arrival in London.

'And I am thinking is it being possible to meet with you again, and perhaps staying in your home for a short time.
Please write me soon. Missing you, love Luna.'

I showed the letter to Ben (at the time we were sharing a flat with Tiger in Walthamstow).

He laughed. "Go for it. It's not like she's a dog. We saw her when we were sober. She was tasty. Sweet."

I wrote back several days later, giving her the thumbs up.

A week before her arrival, I began to get cold feet.

"She could end up being a real pain," I said to Ben. "Her English wasn't that good. If she stays long, we might not be able to get rid of her."

"If she outstays her welcome, I'll tell her to nick off. I don't think she will. Relax. And if all else fails, we'll get rotten all the time to compensate."

Tiger was looking forward to it more than me. "I think it's really cool," he said. "I know everyone talks about holiday romances and shit but look at it this way, we'll have a Portuguese student living here for a bit. That'll be good for her, and interesting for us, man. We'll all learn something."

"Sod learning," I said. "What about the sex?"

Tiger laughed. "Yeah, well, that too, man. That too."

I met Luna at Heathrow. She came in on the 16.35 flight from Lisbon. Ben came with me to lend conversational support. That was the idea, anyway. All he ended up doing was winding me up.

"I hope she hasn't put on loads of weight... what if she's had a radical hairstyle change and you don't fancy her anymore?"

When she came through arrivals with her trolley and her charming smile, my fears were allayed. I said to Ben, "Yeah, stick you." Luna looked every bit as beautiful as she had in Spain, if not more so. Her English had also improved, the result of much study: "I think if I coming to England, I must studying very much."

I was impressed. So was Ben.

That first night, we all went out for dinner. Me and Luna, Ben and his girlfriend (short-lived), and Tiger. We went to a Spanish restaurant, for familiarity. We chatted, we ate, we got drunk. Luna slept in my bed. We played tonsil tennis. I won. Three sets to love.

Her visit started well and so it continued. She got a job in a nearby bar. She enrolled in an English language course. She made some Portuguese and Spanish friends. She allowed me to part those short but slim and silky legs. We fell in love. I even thought about marrying the girl.

Then came the kicker. Having lived with me for nearly eight months, she was summoned home by her family. Apparently, it was high time she got on with life in her own country and stopped fooling around in London. There was no getting away from it. Luna had to fly home.

I was strong at the airport when I saw her off but driving home I cried. Luna wasn't hugely intelligent, she wasn't massively extrovert, but she was simply a lovely, sweet girl.

"I think we'd better take you out and get you mindless," said Ben, when I got back to the flat. We went out and got noodled. I ended up crying in some toilet somewhere.

A year later, bored of the constant pressure to sleep with every woman I met, I kicked the whole London thing into touch. I decided to head nearer home, for a quiet, settled life with a fine, broad-hipped country girl.

Or alternatively, a lithe, married stunner.

"What do you think?" my father said. I think he needed a wedding, or some big event in his life, to take his mind off the recent tragedy.

"It's not that simple, Dad. As I said, we're friends."

"Bring her round here again."

"No chance!"

"Go on. If you haven't got the balls to ask her, I will."

"You? Remarrying again so soon?"

"Oh behave."

"Do you think that'll impress her? You asking her for me?"

My father ruminated on this. "No, you're right. You must do it. But get on with it. She'll get snapped up, and you'll regret it."

I laughed a hollow laugh. So hollow it sounded like I was in a baked bean can.

"You could be right," I said.

*****

Every year people get off a plane and drop dead on the runway. A blood clot forms in the leg during the flight. When they get up to disembark, the blood clot is dislodged and moves to the heart. It's called deep vein thrombosis and it results in a heart attack.

'On behalf of the crew, may we officially welcome you to London. The temperature is 10 degrees. There is a light drizzle and cloud cover. Thank you once again for flying with us. Enjoy your stay and we look forward to seeing you next time you fly...'

And that's it. No rip-off cab ride to the West End. No shows in Leicester Square. No Angus Steak House dinner. Nothing. Not even a stroll along Heathrow's long and tattered carpets. The holiday of a lifetime is over. Twelve hours in a plane. Three meals, four gin and tonics, an individual bottle of some unpronounceable screw top wine, and.... nothing. One black bag, zipped-up, to be flown straight home. Thank you.

That's holidaying. That's life. That is economy class syndrome.

"So what do we say to a passenger who has questions about this?" I asked. We were all sitting in the back office. The Go Away remained closed.

"Refer them directly to their GP."

"That's it?"

"That's it." Carol folded her arms. "We're not in a position to offer medical advice."

"But we could put someone on a flight that could kill them," Kate cut in.

"In the same way a car dealer may sell a customer a car that may kill him, yes."

"That's not good," I said. "Are there any carriers that are most prone to this?"

"The one that carries most old people, I'd assume," said Ted. We all laughed.

"So we shouldn't book anyone over sixty?" asked Debbie.

"It's business as usual. I had to let you know in case of enquiries. That's all for this morning."

We all shuffled around and prepared to get on with the day.

"How's the love life?" I asked Kate, whom I'd been trying to humiliate publicly since her promotion above me. "Still single?"

"As you know, Guy," she said, through gritted teeth, "I'm concentrating on my career at the moment. Which is more than can be said for you."

"The nights must be awfully lonely."

"Like your days at your desk. Your commission is going down by the second."

"That's because I've got my mind on other things."

"Like that married girl?"

"How did you know she was married?"

"Something I heard."

"No, it's not that," I covered. Everyone had left the room now. We were on our own. "If you want to know, I've been head-hunted."

"What?"

"Yeah. Double the salary I get here."

"Doing what?"

"Lunch and dinner most of the time."

"No, come on. Tell me."

I told her.

"You jammy shit. Are you going to take it?"

"I don't have to decide until next year."

"What's to decide?"

"There are complications."

"Oh?"

"Yeah. That's all I'm saying. Life's ice hockey pitch is not without its ruts and divots."

"I know that."

"So... I'm pleased you got the promotion over me. You deserved it."

"I know I did. I reckon you'll be better off somewhere else. You're wasted here."

"Thanks." And so, with one careless comment, I'd half committed myself to leaving the Go Away. On impulse, I phoned Peter Warnford. Daisy was away in Scotland. She'd never know. I'm pleased I did. He invited me to dinner at his club.

"It'd be good for you to get acquainted with some of the other guys," he said. "Might just tip the scales in your favour."

It was Friday. I had the weekend off.

"I'll see you there," I replied.

Chapter Thirty

It was one of those dark oak walled men-only clubs that smells of cigars and Polo aftershave. Girls you're allowed, but only by invite (not very Y2K). They're allowed as add-ons, decorations, some fun later on, after the real business of getting pissed and talking bollocks has been dealt with. (This is not a tradition I subscribe to.)

I met Peter in one of the many bars. He thrust a whisky in my hand and introduced me to a group of seven or eight guys, ranging in age from mid-twenties to forties. I was hyped on adrenalin and dazzled them with witty repartee. Everyone laughed at my jokes. Everyone paid me attention. I felt like a celebrity, a rock star, or *Countdown* contestant. We had many whiskies in the bar followed by a rich and heavy meal. We drank crisp white wine and velvety red, along with viscous Port. We laughed. We bantered. We told jokes.

I remember Peter saying the company was doing so well my starting package would also include a company car, "something with a bit of poke, some ooomph." A twenty-five-year-old told me he drove a sports car. Admittedly, it was a few years old, but it was mint. Went like stink.

Afterwards, we played snooker and told more jokes. Everyone agreed I was the man for the job. What the job was, I still wasn't too sure. But I was the man for it. That's what counted.

I slept well that night. My head hit the pillows of the comfortable bed and donk! I was out. In the morning, Peter had already left for a meeting. There was a message for me at reception. It said,

'You impressed me again last night. I hope you're giving this serious thought. Have some breakfast on me. Talk to you soon. Peter.'

I phoned Ben from my room. "Fancy having lunch?"

He sounded groggy. His voice was thick with sleep. "Err…yeah, okay. Vanessa's here. We'll all go out, yeah?"

"Shall I come round to yours?"

"No, err…we'll come and meet you." He told me the name of a pub off King's Road.

"Cool." I put the phone down and dialled room service. "I'll have the full English," I said in response to the polite enquiry. "No, actually, I'll have the Champagne breakfast."

"Very good, sir. Anything else?"

"If you could bring me a pack of Bensons, I'd appreciate it."

I had a quick shower. The waiter arrived just as I slipped into my robe. I watched some CNN and lugged back the champagne. This is the life I thought. This, this is it.

*****

"So, I'm trying to decide if I'm going to take it or not," I said.

"You'd be a prick not to."

"Go for it," added Vanessa.

We were sitting in the narrow pub. The lights were low and I was already drunk.

I took a mouthful of patatas bravas. "I haven't told you who the guy is."

"Who is he?"

"Daisy's husband."

"TOOP?"

"Yup."

"That girl you brought round to Daddy's is married?"

"Yup."

"Guy!" Vanessa was appalled.

"It's not a happy marriage."

"Well, it wouldn't be with you in it, would it? Does he know about this? You're sleeping with her, right?"

"No, he doesn't, and yes I am, on a part-time basis."

"God! You're terrible."

Ben was laughing.

"This is not funny," Vanessa said. "My advice is drop her like a stone and take the job."

"She's already told me not to take it. If I do, she could blow the whistle."

Ben continued laughing. "And you say your life is boring."

I gave him the hand-job signal.

"I can't believe you, Guy," Vanessa continued.

"Shall we get another bottle of the house white?"

Ben called a waitress over and ordered.

"What should I do?"

"What's more important?" said Ben. "A job or a good lay?"

"A good lay," I said, trying to forget what Vanessa had told me about him.

"So stick with Daisy and forget the job. I'm nipping out to get some fags. Don't drink all the wine before I get back."

Ben lumbered away. Vanessa gave me one of her searching looks.

"I think you should take the job and forget Daisy. An affair is an affair. A job could really take you somewhere."

The wine arrived. I refilled our glasses.

"Talking of which," said Vanessa, "while Ben's not here, do you remember Caroline Saunders?"

I sent out the trawlers to the furthest reaches of my mind.

They came back with empty nets.

"No," I said.

"She used to come over a lot when we were little."

"Oh shit!" I had a flash of clarity. "She drives a green Audi these days? She popped in to see Dad the other day."

"Yes."

Vanesssa was sliding her fingers up and down the rim of her glass.

"Well. Jack tells me they've been having an affair on and off for years. Her husband died of cancer."

"No way!"

Vanessa bit her lip.

"No, it's true," she said. "Jack used to spot them walking in Hyde Park."

"God. Christ. How do you feel about this?"

"I was shocked, but... Mum always said she couldn't provide Dad with everything a partner needs. You know, because she was so ill all the time. I think she knew. I don't think it was a problem."

"How could it not have been a problem? She never mentioned any of this to me."

"Perhaps she didn't want to upset you."

"I'm not the one who gets upset. You are."

I couldn't believe this. This was more than a shock. This was like having a hundred cattle prods stuck up my arse.

"Have you talked to Dad about this?" I asked.

"No. I haven't felt the need."

"Well, I think I feel the need," I said. "I think I need some answers."

I took my phone out of my pocket. Vanessa grabbed my hand.

"Relax," she said. "Don't call Dad now. Don't just think of yourself, think of him. When you're sober."

"I need to go for a walk," I said, and got down from the table.

Outside, on the street, I bumped into Ben.

"Give me a cigarette." He could tell I was on edge. I lit it with shaking hands.

"Cripes," I said. "Life is... mental, isn't it?"

Ben agreed. He knew better than to cross me in this mood. He had a cigarette too and listened to me whinge. It was good to let it out. When we got back to the restaurant I was calmer, but very thirsty.

We stayed late into the afternoon, attempting to drain the restaurant's wine cellar.

Chapter Thirty-one

In films, people can make decisions on the spot. They can sit back in a big leather office chair, rub their chin for a second or two, then lean forward, hit the wood with their fist, and it's done. "Sell," they'll say. Or "buy". Stuff like that.

I'm not one of these people. I change my mind every two minutes.

On Sunday, safely back home, with a can of Stella in my hand, my bum on my trusty sofa, and *Mission Impossible 2* on the TV screen (the action washing over me), I made up my mind.

It's got to be the job. I got a pen and paper and wrote it down, 'GO FOR THE JOB'.

But what about Daisy? The girl who entered my thoughts every morning when I got up and every night when I went to bed. The girl who raised my heart rate just by *being*. The sexiest, most charming girl I'd ever met. And that arse!

I crossed out my first sentence. Below it I wrote, 'IF YOU DON'T HAVE LOVE, WHAT DO YOU HAVE?'

I had another can of lager.

Double the salary. That would mean a new flat, a house maybe. The company car. I could meet a sexy girl who wasn't married. In a Porsche I'd be sucking totty off the streets. Yeah, the job would open up a whole new world. I wrote on a new sheet,

'GO ON. BE MATERIALISTIC FOR A CHANGE. YOU'RE YOUNG. HAVE SOME FUN!!!'

I had a whisky.

'But I love her', I wrote underneath in a scrawl. I wonder if she'll ever give me her number?

Then, in a state of drunken confusion, I cried. Nothing dramatic or girly. Just a tear. Then I thought of my mother. Then my father. Then Caroline Saunders. That whole situation was so confusing. Should I call Dad? Should I leave it? I didn't know. So I bawled.

I had another whisky. Then I went to bed. Christ, you don't want to hit Monday without a good slice of sleep. It was already 1am. I'd been drunk all weekend. Time to stamp my time card and head home... time to sleep. Time to switch life off for a second and romp through the fantasy world of dreams – naked, unashamed, uninhibited. In dreams, like in fiction, anything can happen.

But there are rules. Always rules. I mean, I'm not going to suddenly find a terrorist bomb under my bed, am I? That's taking it too far. There are rules, and we have to stick to them, more or less. More or less.

With a little tweak here and there. With a little greyish (nothing a bit of Persil wouldn't sort out) lie.

*****

Daisy called me when she got back from Scotland. She came straight over. I was thrilled to see her but at the back of my mind was this job of Peter's. We needed to talk.

"Ahh...it seems like months since I last saw you," she said, as she threw herself into my arms and gave me a big kiss.

"It's been a week."

"I know... but..."

"I know how great I am. You don't need to tell me."

She slapped me playfully. "Now don't go getting cocky. Your most endearing trait is your modesty."

"I know."

She followed me up the stairs to my increasingly (I felt) inadequate flat. I needed more money to take care of Daisy. But getting more money could mean losing her.

"Tell me about Scotland," I said, having poured us both a glass of Chardonnay. "Did it go well?"

Daisy spent half-an-hour telling me it had gone very well. So well she had future jobs from three other clients.

"Wow," I said. "You must be thrilled; you'll need to take on more staff."

She shook her head. "What these people love about me is I always use local staff. I am Better Binge. I organise, I do the menus, I guide, and all the labour is local. So clients get me and they don't have to pay for ten caterers to fly out to wherever; it's just me. That's how I'm so successful."

"That's mad. Isn't it really stressful?"

"Not as bad as it used to be. I know people in the places I go to now, so I can look them up again. A phone call a fortnight before gets them in place and it all works like clockwork."

"You're amazing," I said, genuinely impressed.

"Not just a pretty face, you know."

"Or a fab bum."

She laughed. "So come on. Tell me what you've been up to. Anything exciting happen in my absence?"

"Not really," I said, having already decided to gloss over my dinner with Peter. "I've been thinking about you."

"Oh, yeah?"

"Mmm. I don't want to get too heavy but our situation is, um, tricky, isn't it?"

"Yes." She nodded energetically. "Yes, it is."

"It's made more complicated because I'm in love with you."

Daisy stared at the top of her wine glass.

"I'm in love with you and nothing can come of it."

She guided her finger round its rim. She took a sip and put it on the coffee table. Then she pulled her legs up to her chin.

"Do you really love me?"

"Is it surprising?" I said, leaning forward to light a cigarette. "Are you surprised?"

"No. It makes things more complicated, that's all."

"How?"

"I didn't expect you to fall in love with me." She examined her toes. "God. I didn't expect to fall in love with you."

Coldplay was on again in the background – lyrics about 'stopping'.

"You've had a lot to drink," she said, with tears in her eyes.

"I need it," I said. "I need you."

We ended up kissing after that and soon we were in bed, the sex better than ever. I just couldn't get enough of this girl. I may have been drunk, but I did love her. She made me tingle all the way to my toes. If that wasn't love, I didn't know what was.

It must have been 3am when I said, "I don't know how much longer I can work at the travel agent's. The customers are killing me."

"Not me, I hope."

"I've just been there too long."

"You're thinking about taking the job with Peter, aren't you?"

"No. A change would be good, that's all."

"You can admit it, Guy. I've been thinking about it, too." She sighed.

"Peter can be awful. One thing I do have to say for him, though, is he's always looked after his staff very well. He's very picky but, when he employs someone he likes, he's a good boss."

"He's offering me double what I make at the moment."

"That's good. Listen if you want to take the job, go for it. I was wrong before. I panicked. I was being selfish. I can't stop you from getting a better job. God, I don't want to. I want the best for you. Same as I want the best for my kids."

"What about us?"

"Well, that's what I thought about. If we're going to have a relationship, we can get through it."

"Do you think you'll ever leave Peter?"

"I can't see myself staying with him forever but at the same time I can't rush into a decision. That's why I want you to get on with your life. We'll have to be very careful, that's all. I bought two mobiles today. From now on, we can use those."

"Wow! You mean I can actually call you?"

"Yes!" Her eyes shone.

"If you call me and Peter's around, I'll pretend you're a business call. I'll say I'm too busy that week to do it and hang up."

"My God. Were you once a spy? You've thought of every-thing."

"I don't want us to get caught, that's all. I have children to think about, remember? I can't have them getting hurt in all of this."

"I totally agree."

Daisy slipped out of bed and nipped into the living room, coming back with an Ericsson still in its box.

I felt an enormous sense of well-being wash over me. It was official: we were dating.

Just for fun, I called her then and there.

"Next week I can't do," she said into her phone. "I'm too busy with other projects, sorry."

We both laughed. Like two kids who've just got CB radios.

Then we had sex. Like two adults who are very hot for each other.

Chapter Thirty-two

Two weeks before Christmas, and two days before Carol was due to fly to South Africa, we closed the office early and went for a few drinks, followed by dinner at a Chinese restaurant.

Before we ate, I presented Carol with a designer holdall that we'd all chipped in to buy. In response (and with moist eyes), she said, "I know we've had our ups and downs. It's not always easy when you have clients on the end of the line, expecting you to perform miracles, not to get a little ratty. As you know, I'm going to South Africa for an extended break after my divorce and I'll be back in a year. I hope all of you will be here when I get back and I'll look forward to hearing about how you've got on. I've really enjoyed working with you all. Thanks guys."

We all raised a glass and toasted her good health.

"I think I can say on behalf of everyone, you've been a really good boss and we'll miss you loads," said Kate.

"Go for it, girl," I called. She was being so licky.

The food was 'finger lickin' good' (can you get sued by KFC for using this expression now?), if a little expensive. Still, the owner's got kids to clothe, and most residents in Cirencester have got a bob or two, therefore they can be fleeced with a clearer conscience. Taking money from the rich so that some of it goes back to the poor.

"Think of us while you're sunning yourself on the beach," I

said. "Spare us a thought as we shiver our way through another piss-cold winter."

Carol laughed. "Yes. That's one aspect of Christmas I'm not going to miss. Goodbye de-icer, and thank God."

"Yeah, and hello sunburnt nose," said Ted, with his dry sense of humour.

A little (and not that attractive) waitress brought our main courses to the table. The food was the usual. Chinese restaurants: the menus are all remarkably similar. Still, the Chinese probably think the same about fish and chip shops.

So it was sizzling this, deep-fried that, crispy whatever wrapped in pancakes, all accompanied by rice with coloured bits.

"Jules and I are thinking of taking a break in South Africa next year," Debbie said, helping herself to more chilli prawns. She asked if they could visit.

"Of course. Just give me some warning. I'm going to rent my own place and I'll make sure I have at least two spare rooms."

"So what are you going to do while you're out there?"

"I fancy doing some teaching. I have a TEFL qualification from when I first went travelling as a student. I'd like to use that, if I can. I'd also like to go on safari, explore the East Coast, you know, do what we put other people on flights around the world to do."

"What," I said, "die of economy class syndrome?"

"Guy!"

"Just make sure you walk around on the flight, keep those legs moving. If you feel the slightest tingle of deep vein thrombosis, grab a parachute and jump."

"I'm going first-class. BA are upgrading me."

"And so they should. You'll be fine."

I ordered another bottle of wine.

"Keep drinking," I said. "It thins the blood. That'll increase your chance of survival."

"Guy," Debbie interrupted, "Let's change the subject."

"You change it," I said. "Let's hear about your boyfriend."

Yes, friends, I was drunk again.

After the meal, I insisted we all went to The Crown. Carol stayed for one drink and left, though I tried to bully her friend who'd arrived to pick her up to have a drink. She was a foxy forty-something. I think she was vaguely flattered by my attentions but wasn't having any of it.

Debbie went soon after, no doubt being escorted home by Jules. That left me, Ted and Kate. Ted was on good form. After a few bottles of wine, he really started to loosen up. Some people reckon the drunk man speaks the truth, like some guru. Because he's uninhibited, he can speak his mind.

This I find to be untrue. The drunk man talks bollocks. Fill a man's head full of foreign chemicals and you're not going to get the truth. You're going to get a lot of exaggerated stories, half-baked plans for the future, and more bravado than you can shake a stick at. That's all there is to it. Remember the early tests with acid trips and psychiatry? Open your mind... all of that stuff. It stopped pretty soon after it started, didn't it? Then they made trips illegal. Why? Too many people talking too much shit that sounded too much fun for it to be legal. Remember Ken Kesey? *One Flew Over the Cuckoo's Nest*? He was one of them, my friends. He was one.

"What can you see?"

"Ooooh...I can see... I can... I can see girls all around me. They're... bats. And one's hand is..."

"Okay, we're going to take you off this dose. Try you on heroin or something."

Remember the law is there to protect those in middle management with 2.4 children, a mortgage and a good life insurance policy. To anyone else, the law is often a pain in the bum. The law says: live your life without fun. Don't hurt anyone, unless you're told to by your government. And then die.

"If you want my opinion," Ted slurred at me, then pointed at Kate, who was chatting to a couple of rugger jocks, "that girl right there is hot for you."

"Kate?" I slurred back. "She hates me."

"That's not what she tells me."

"What's she said to you?"

"I shouldn't be telling you this."

"We're both drunk. We won't remember in the morning."

"Okay. But swear to God you won't tell her I told you."

"Yeah, yeah, yeah. Come on."

"She fancies the arse off you. That's what she said."

"When?"

"Ages ago. After you spent the weekend together."

"Why's she so nasty to me then?"

"You know girls."

"No, I don't."

Ted laughed. "So what do you think?"

"What do you mean?"

"Kate. As a girlfriend."

"All that shopping?"

"No kids."

"True."

"Great body."

"Yup."

"So…"

I slugged my beer. I looked over at Kate. She looked at me at the same time. She raised her eyebrows sexily. God bless alcohol, I thought. And the inhibitions it muffles.

"It's your round," I said to Ted. Sod it, I thought. Let's get rip-roaring drunk... and see what happens. Let's get leathered and go with the flow. Let's get mindless, flick the autopilot on and just see... I mean, you only live once, right? And Daisy is married…

*****

Kate, I have to say, does indeed have a fantastic body. In her clothes she looks like she's got real potential, but that's not always a true indicator of what lies beneath. Girls, as we know, are masters of disguise. Clothes, hair, makeup. It's all meticulously planned to cover the bad and accentuate the good. Kate dresses very well. She has style. Pure girl magazine style.

But to look stylish naked... that's one hell of an achievement. I don't think even Daisy looks stylish naked. She looks... naked. Pure, perfect, unhindered by faults, but not stylish.

Kate looks stylish dressed. She definitely looks stylish naked.

And I wasn't even supposed to see her! She was in my bedroom getting changed and I accidentally caught a peak.

"You go first," I said. "I need to tidy up in the kitchen." Kate went into my bedroom, leaving the door open. I slugged back a glass of water before returning to within a couple of feet of the bedroom door.

First she was there in trouser suit and jacket, circling like a dog looking for a spot to lie down. Then, settled, she was in trousers and blouse, swiftly followed by blouse and no trousers. My heartbeat picked up. I moved closer to the door. Those legs were very shapely. From blouse and pants, we went down to pants. Yikes! The flat stomach, the well-filled bra, the pleasing (but not ostentatious) flare of the hips. Next the bra came undone and she turned, rounding her shoulders, away from me, letting it slip to the floor. Gathering a t-shirt, she straightened and swam into it. I caught a brief glimpse of boob. It was a brief, but enticing show.

"You can come in now," she said, over her shoulder, as she slipped into my bed.

I walked on the spot for four steps to give the impression of approaching from a distance, then entered.

"Are you sure I wouldn't be better off in the spare bedroom?" she asked.

"Like I said, it's a dump. No sheets, no duvet. You'll be better off here."

"You don't snore, do you?"

"No."

"Talk in your sleep?"

"Only share prices and Shakespeare."

"Wandering hands?"

"Only over my own body."

Kate laughed. I hung up my trousers in the wardrobe (usually unthinkable – I did it to impress), then cleaned my teeth.

I climbed into bed.

"Aren't you going to turn off the light?" Kate asked. She looked very young, lying there. Very vulnerable.

"Oh," I said, getting back out. "I suppose I should."

With the light off the world seemed very dark. I got back into bed and settled down.

"It's cold, isn't it?" said Kate.

"It's December."

"It's cold even for December."

She shivered. I went for it.

"Come here," I said, putting my arm up. "I'll give you a hug."

There was a nervous pause before I felt her warm head press gently on my chest.

"God, you're like toast," she said.

"Or a freshly baked muffin."

Her hand snaked up to my shoulder and rested there.

I hoped she couldn't hear my heart. It was beating faster. Not 130, but triple figures.

"Guy?" she said.

"Yes."

"Are you still seeing that girl, Daisy?"

"I've seen her a few times."

"She's married, isn't she?"

"Mmm."

"I wonder what she's doing now?"

"I have no idea."

"Probably curled up in bed with her husband, nice and

warm, like us."

My drunk brain took this sentence and ran with it, as it was intended to. Like a wide receiver chasing that spiralling American football, it ran. What were *they* doing? Curled up together, yes. Or perhaps...

"Shall we snog?" said Kate. "Just for fun?" Her hand moved down my body. "We won't tell anyone at work. It can be our little secret."

Her face was now level with mine. "Shall we?" she breathed. "Do you want to? For a laugh."

Chapter Thirty-three

Something occurred to me the next morning at work and it was this: Kate was now my boss. It wasn't a good thought.

Her phone rang. She said, "Yes, hang on." A short pause. "Daisy is on line two for you, Guy." This sentence was delivered icily, as if she stored her voicebox in a chest freezer.

I picked up my phone and hit button two.

"Hi," Daisy said, chirpily. "Why's your mobile not on?"

"My head's barely on. How have you been?" I asked, trying to give Kate the impression I hadn't seen her in ages.

"Nothing's changed since I last saw you. I'm fine. Still got four limbs, all my own teeth. And hair."

"Good."

"Do you want to have lunch?"

I did. I just didn't want Kate to know.

"One o'clock okay?"

"Yeah."

"Okay, I'll pop over."

"No! Err, no, let's..."

"Why not?"

"I'm really busy today; I might get held up."

"Okay. How about The Crown, at the back. The food's okay there, isn't it?"

I agreed.

"I thought you hadn't seen her in ages," Kate said, the second I put the phone down.

"I haven't." I could feel Ted looking at me.

"Let's have lunch," she said. "I think I need to ask you a few questions."

"I can't."

Debbie was paying attention now.

"Why not?"

"I've got plans."

"You don't have any friends here. How can you have plans?"

"My dad's taking me out to lunch. He gets lonely since my mother died. We're having lunch, that's it."

Kate looked apologetic, then said, "Could I come?"

"Another time."

She looked sulky.

I got on with sending out my tickets and catching up on the news on the system; see if anyone else had died of economy class syndrome.

Economy class syndrome. Which is the most important word in the phrase? Yes, you've got it. It's 'economy'. It's not 'business' or 'executive' or 'club' or 'top' or 'first'. Passengers in these classes don't die. They're too rich to die. They're saved by money. Typical.

I know what you're thinking. You're thinking, 'Hang on! This guy's got some nerve. He's rich. His family's loaded! What does he have to worry about?'

Well, my family's not rich, and I'm skint. I'm skint. Me. That's the only person I've got to rely on. Me. Do I travel business class? No. I don't travel full stop. But if I did, I'd be going economy. You and I would be sitting next to each other, comparing veins in our legs. Not a good thought, is it? Twenty hours in a plane to arrive dead. Tut, tut. 'Disappointed' wouldn't really cover it.

I thought about this all morning, between calls, and into the afternoon. A bit too far into the afternoon. I first looked at my watch at five-past-one.

"Shit," I said, jumping up. Kate was up and by the door at the same time as me.

"What's wrong?" she said.

"I'm late."

"Daddy won't mind. Where are you meeting him?"

This was a tricky question. If I said The Crown, Kate might follow me in. If I said somewhere else, she might equally accompany me there and cause problems. I hedged it.

"The Crown," I said.

"Oh wow. I'm meeting a friend of mine there."

We went out of the door and walked briskly down the street. I began to sweat.

Kate was keeping pace with me pretty well, considering her short legs.

"Who's your friend?"

"Someone I went to school with."

"Name?"

"Linda."

"I haven't heard you talk about her before."

"I haven't seen her in ages."

"Well, perhaps you can introduce me once I've finished lunch with my dad."

"Sure."

We were now twenty yards from The Crown, waiting to cross the road at the traffic lights.

Panicking, I turned to Kate. "I'm not meeting my father," I said.

"I know."

"Are you meeting a friend?"

"No."

"What say I see you later then?"

"You're meeting her, aren't you?"

"Who?"

"For fucksake, Guy! Daisy."

"Yeah, okay. Is that a crime?"

"You said we were going to have lunch today."

"I didn't."

"You did."

"I didn't." My memory of the previous night was hazy but I was sure I never said that.

"Shit, you piss me off. You don't mean a word you say."

We were crossing the road now. I wanted to scream as I was so tense, hungover and frustrated.

"Let's have lunch tomorrow," I said, and lunged into the pub, hoping she wouldn't follow me.

I walked straight in past the bar to the tables at the back. Daisy was looking relaxed with a glass of white wine.

"Hi," I said, trying to look calm but not succeeding.

"What's wrong?" she asked.

I eyed the door. Thankfully it had not reopened. "Nothing. Hectic morning at work, that's all. Sorry I'm late."

I went to kiss her.

"Don't kiss me," she said. "Just in case."

It took me a moment to register. Did she have herpes, glandular fever, a mouth ulcer? I was concerned for her health. Oh no. The spies. Had to look innocent in public.

"Oh right. I might get myself a drink. Want anything?"

She pointed at her full glass. "I can only drink one at a time, Guy. Try to relax."

At the bar, I ordered a double Bloody Mary, which I drank standing there (to solder my broken nerves), and a pint, plus a Jameson's (drunk back in one again). The door from the street opened, putting my heart in my mouth, but a young couple came in, not a short blonde. "Relax," I said to myself. "Relax. Your worst nightmare is not going to happen."

I was right. My worst nightmare – Kate coming in and having a bitch fight with Daisy – didn't happen, but something pretty bad did. She came in with Debbie as we were starting our meal and they sat at the bar, both of them eyeing me horribly.

Daisy noticed them, too. "I see half your office comes in here for lunch."

"Popular pub, isn't it?"

"Do you want to ask them over?"

"Oh God, no. I work with them all day. We were all out last night."

"They keep looking over."

"They're nosy, that's all. They want to see who I'm with."

"Why, is there a big choice? A selection?"

I laughed. "As if. I have eyes only for you, Daisy."

"You'd better," she said, and it all sounded so surreal, what with her being married and everything. It sounded unreal, laughable, insane. But we played along. We enjoyed our meal, packaged and bound as it was in (white, let's be fair) lies.

When I got back to the office, Kate said, "You're late."

"Only five minutes."

"More like ten."

"You were late this morning."

"We came in together, remember? That makes you late twice in one day. I'm warning you now, Guy. If you're late at all next week, I'm reporting you to head office."

"What?"

"You heard."

"I thought we were friends."

"So I have to let you do what you want? Grow up, Guy. We're running a business here."

I was shocked. I felt meek. Did friendship count for nothing?

*****

Talk about friction. Christ. And I know what you're thinking. You're thinking we kissed. One thing led to another, my boxer shorts slipped down my legs, her knickers suddenly felt 'restrictive' and we...

Well, we didn't. I hate to disappoint you, but we didn't. We kissed gingerly once or twice, we hugged, but we kept our clothes on. We didn't do 'it'.

I pulled away. That's what pissed her off. When it came to the crunch, I couldn't do it. All I could think about was Daisy.

I know. I can feel the heat of a few accusing looks. I shouldn't have snogged her. But she practically begged me, and she is very attractive. I've led her on. And now she's mad. Oh dear. I think I'm in for a rough ride.

I try to be a better person but I just can't manage it. I try to reform, but I can't.

I've let everybody down.

*****

Tuesday 12th December, at the hospital.

"I can't go through with it," 'Kathy' said.

"What?" I was already uncool. We'd been waiting for aeons in a room full of other crying non-mothers to be. The hospital atmosphere, as usual, was whiter than white, practically Day-Glo.

'Kathy' got up and headed for the lift. I jumped up and grabbed her back.

"Hang on," I said. "Hang on. This is the only alternative. This is one unpleasant moment to save a thousand others."

"What do you mean?"

"You think having a baby is some kind of picnic? You don't think it's hard work, a twenty-four-hour commitment before you've even thought about doing anything else with your life? Shit, being a single mother is damn hard work."

"Would I be a single mother?"

"Yes. I'm afraid I'm not ready to play happy families."

She looked like she was going to cry, but she didn't. I helped her sit down with the lines of other young girls. Some of them looked about seven. And they were the old ones. They all looked equally pale. Thankfully, a nurse at reception said, "Miss

Katherine Burke", and it was time for 'Kathy' to go. She was led through to the operating theatre. She left with a scared look. I remained in my seat looking (at a guess) guilty, worried and relieved.

While I waited, I tried to think of something helpful to say when she reappeared but nothing came. I felt bad. Very bad. And I only hoped she wasn't going to come out with the 'I've killed someone' complex. If she did, I had a reasoned response prepared.

Think 'Kathy': the hundreds of lives that have suffocated in condoms, the thousands that have drowned down loos and shower plug holes, the populations soaked up in tissues, splashed around bedrooms. All those wasted lives, and you've only wasted one. We've only wasted one.

The world will not be a poorer place because of it.

All this sounded reasonable in my head but I knew it wouldn't have much effect if I needed to use it. Grief is something that can't be washed off. It must hang around for as long as it pleases.

I waited in a state of high tension.

As it turned out 'Kathy' came out of the theatre looking paler still, but relieved. She had the option of a bed for the night but she said she'd rather be taken home. The nurse looked at me suspiciously.

"You look after her," she said. "She's going to be pretty fragile for a few days."

"I know. Thank you."

I took 'Kathy' by the arm and led her at OAP-pace to the car park. I opened the passenger door for her to get in.

"How did it go?" I said, as we drove hurriedly past the anti-abortion, pro-life crackpots demonstrating at the exit.

'Kathy' burst into tears. My mobile rang. The one Daisy gave me. "I can't talk now," I said, and hung up. I nearly hit a pedestrian.

"It'll be okay. You'll get over it."

"Will you stay with me for a while?" she asked.

"I will, but I have to be back at work tomorrow."

'Kathy' cried harder and louder than I'd heard anyone cry before. I ended up staying three days. It wasn't much fun for either of us.

*****

Kate was no better.

"I've put you on an official warning," she said, when I finally returned to work.

"What? I phoned and explained the situation, didn't I?"

"Your social life is obviously more important to you than this job, Guy. One more cock-up and I'm going to recommend you be fired."

"What does 'one more cock-up' mean?"

"It means being late for work. It means taking unscheduled days off. It means being drunk at any time."

I took a long breath and rubbed my face. I was tempted to tell her to piss off and storm out there and then. I'd had enough of this friction. It wasn't like I didn't have another job to go to. But that didn't start until January and I couldn't afford to holiday until then. I'd have to stay. It could only get better, couldn't it?

And Daisy. Daisy had a bee in her bonnet about something too. She came round to mine on Saturday night and was extremely bolshy.

"What's wrong with you?" I said, when I couldn't stand her silent channel-hopping any longer.

"Nothing," she replied, predictably enough.

"Except for?"

"If you must know, I'm rather upset that almost every time I phone you, there's some other girl either answering or in the background."

"That's not true."

"Why don't you just admit you're screwing that common little tart you work with and let me get back to my miserable marriage."

Well this was a revelation, I can tell you. I hadn't seen Daisy lose her cool like this before. This was raw, untreated emotion veering into pure rage.

"Daisy."

"I'm sorry," she said, burying her face in her hands. "Oh, I'm sorry. I shouldn't have said that. I know I don't have any right. I'm just very jealous."

"That's okay," I said, temple thumping. "Look, I know things have seemed a bit suspicious lately. Before I met you I was seeing this girl and... there were a few problems we had to sort out. That's all done now. I never even liked her. It was one of those things."

"And Kate?"

"It turns out Kate is a bit of a fan of mine but nothing's happened. It's all okay. I'm not seeing anyone else. Honest."

"You're sure?"

"Positive." I was positive, too. I was in love with Daisy. If I wasn't, I'd have bedded Kate when I had the chance. No, I loved Daisy. And I loved her even more, now I saw how much she loved me. Our affair was clearly causing her some trauma, but she wanted to carry on with it. She was right to. I mean, we had something special going. It felt special. I wasn't about to screw that up.

"I'm hopelessly in love with you," she said, throwing her arms around me. "You do know that, don't you?"

"I do now."

"You do feel it, don't you?"

"I do."

"And you love me?"

"I love you. I really do. Massively."

She kissed me warmly on the lips. "It'll all work out, won't it?"

"Of course it will."

She smiled. A smile that was more sad than happy. "Let's just enjoy it, then."

I looked deep into her eyes trying to work out what she meant. She leant in and kissed me, softly, and then more urgently. As her tongue entered my mouth, I gave in. It didn't matter what she meant, because I would never understand it. And even if I did, by the time I'd worked it out, she'd probably have changed her mind. That was life. A permanent game of trying to comprehend where no one understands a word the other is saying.

Chapter Thirty-four

Christmas is not my favourite time of year. The shopping, the insane over-eating, the tragic office parties, the cards... the brain reels. And this Christmas, naturally, was to be the worst yet.

Mothers handle Christmas. They're the only ones with the strength. Only a human who can give birth can handle Christmas. For the rest of us it's just too messy.

My mother was in charge of the turkey upstairs this year, in the big open-plan kitchen in the sky. For the Chamberlains, this left Dot and my father. Now Dot has her own family and her own Christmas. This meant, beyond making us a pudding and leaving instructions on how to cook the bird, we were on our own.

My father phoned me ten days before Christmas Day in a mild panic. We'd spoken several times previously. I hadn't mentioned Caroline Saunders.

"Your mother would usually buy all the presents, do the decorations, the lot," he said. "I don't know where to begin."

"Which begs the question, Dad..."

"I was at work, paying for it all."

Or, I thought, you were...

"Can you help out?"

"What about Vanessa?"

"She's agreed to do most of the cooking. I need you to do

some shopping."

"Food or presents?"

"Both."

"Who for?"

He reeled off a list of relatives.

"Dad. You could have given me more notice. This is a month's worth of high-street hunting."

"Sorry, I've been trying not to think about it."

"What about Jack?"

"He's working right up until Christmas Eve."

"So? I'm working until the day before."

"He's under a lot of pressure."

"And I'm not?" This always got to me. Jack's job was always more important. Well, if it weren't for me and my job, Jack would never go abroad. He always booked with me, insisting on net prices for flights for him and his mates. I didn't appreciate his customer loyalty.

"You know what I mean. Can you do it?"

"Yes. Have you got any ideas what I should buy?"

He gave me a few lame thoughts and then hung up. I phoned Vanessa straight afterwards. She was bound to have some good ideas. She did. Not only ideas but where to get them and how much they cost.

"We have to make it a special Christmas this year," she said. "With Mum gone, it'll be tough, but she'd want us all to pitch in."

"I know. How many people are coming?"

"All of us, so that's five. Umm…Ben…"

"Christ."

"What?"

"I never thought I'd see the day he was staring me in the face on Christmas morning."

"Yeah, anyway. Ben, Uncle Robert and Auntie Sarah, their two, and Mum's sister, Angela."

"That it?"

"And Caroline."

"What?"

"Yes. She'd be spending Christmas alone otherwise. Dad needs support too, you know."

I sighed.

"And Toby's flying over from Sydney, obviously. Oh, he's bringing his girlfriend as well. Apparently she's lovely."

"I'll bet."

"Are you bringing anyone?"

"No."

"It's finally all over with 'Kathy'?"

"It never started with 'Kathy'."

"And Daisy..."

"Is married."

"Yup. Okay, so that's all of us then."

"When will you be home?"

"Couple of days. If you need any more help, give me a shout."

"I will."

"See ya then."

"Bye." I hung up. Two minutes later an awful thought struck me. What was I going to buy Daisy? It had to be either something incredibly expensive or incredibly meaningful. Shit. I got a can of lager from the fridge and thought about it.

*****

A couple of days later I phoned Ben.

"What have you got Vanessa for Christmas?" I asked.

"Why are you bothered?"

"I was wondering what I should get for Daisy."

"Oh. How about one of those self-help manuals on divorce?"

"Ha, ha."

"Or..."

"Sensible suggestions, Ben."

"Okay. How about... flowers?"

"Wow. That's inspired."

"It's romantic."

"What's she going to do with them? She's married. You can't hide a big bouquet of flowers with a lovey-dovey message on, can you?"

"Okay. Clothes."

"She's not very fashion conscious."

"Underwear?"

"Could be dodgy again."

"A short holiday?"

"That's a point."

"Yeah, you just find out when she's free and book something up. With your staff discount, it won't even cost that much."

"You know how I feel about flying, though."

"So get the shuttle to Paris, or Amsterdam, or Brussels. It'll be romantic. Girls love all that."

"You're a genius."

"I know."

"So what have you got Vanessa?"

"I'm going to book a holiday too. I've been meaning to call you all week. Got any good deals at the moment?"

"Call me when I'm at work," I said. "There's bound to be something."

I got off the phone to Ben feeling somewhat happier. Not only was a holiday a good gift, it had the added bonus of being a present to myself. Like buying your housemate a CD you like, or your parents a wok. Both times you benefit. Guaranteed good music, good food.

Daisy and I hadn't spent any real time together. A holiday would give us the chance to see how it would work if we spent more than one night and morning with each other, without either of us having to rush off. I wanted to see more of her. A holiday was the perfect way to do it.

While on a high, I plotted my Christmas shopping strategy. There were eight days until Jesus' birthday. I had twenty-four presents to buy. That meant three per day. Lunchtimes and early evenings. Or one splurge at the weekend. Or a kick-arse session on Christmas Eve.

On Tuesday, I bought two CDs, both for myself. On Wednesday, I bought a vase for my aunt. It got smashed in the pub. On Thursday, I did okay. I bought my father a humidor, Vanessa a little t-shirt, and my aunt another vase. I also booked a week-long break in Cameron House Hotel, Loch Lomond. I booked it for mid-January but I could change it easily enough if Daisy couldn't get away.

That night she came round and she was like a kid. More excited about Christmas than I'd ever been. And I used to get up at 3am to open my stocking, with its tangerine, its chocolate coins, its Hornby railway carriages, and the Scaletrix track that went together like ice cream and gravy (not well).

"I've got you a fantastic present," she told me.

"You shouldn't have."

"I wanted to."

"What is it?"

"That would be telling! Have you got me anything?"

"I might have."

"Oh! Isn't it so exciting?"

"Your kids probably look bored in comparison."

"Oh no, they love it. Having kids makes it much more exciting. You see their little faces when they open their presents. You can't buy that for anything."

"No, I'm sure."

"I'd like you to meet them, but they chatter too much. It could be risky."

"How is Peter, by the way?"

"He's spending loads of time in London. I hardly see him. Has he spoken to you?"

"No. Have you slept with him recently?"

"No! And don't ask me that."

"Why not?"

"Just don't. It makes me feel like a whore."

"Sorry."

She intertwined her fingers. "I'm going to have to leave him. You don't know how terrible it feels being there and not loving him."

"Don't do anything hasty," I said. But what I should have said was, "Do it. Do it now."

"It won't be for a while. God, I never thought my life would go like this."

"Nobody does. I never had plans for this either. It's weird with Christmas coming up. I'd like us to be together."

Daisy gave me a hug. "Me too. You know what, though? I can't see you again until after. There's going to be too many dinners and relatives and children to cope with."

"Can you wait that long for your present?"

Daisy laughed, then gave me a kiss.

"You're the only present I want."

"But I have to wait until after Christmas to get my present, do I?" I said, joking.

"I'm afraid so." She kissed me again. "But I can give you a little something now." She pulled me off the sofa and led me to the bedroom. "Would you like that?"

Well, I couldn't say no, could I? That would have been rude.

*****

Christmas Eve: fuck. I had twenty-odd presents to buy. Vanessa phoned me at ten, asking if I needed any help.

"I bet you haven't even started," she said.

"Actually, I've only got two to get," I replied, with hauteur. Pride, and all that.

"So you'll be over for lunch? Dad's got some lovely ham."

"No, I've got to pack."

She put Ben on the line. "How's it going?" he asked.

"About twenty to go... I need help."

He laughed.

"I'll come over now. I could do with getting out of the house. Vanessa's trying to get me to put decorations on the tree. Not really my thing."

"Who else is there?"

"Toby and Mel."

"His girlfriend?"

"Yeah."

"What's she like?"

"She looks like Kylie Minogue," he whispered, "but better. See you in twenty minutes."

Ben arrived in fifteen. I went down the stairs to meet him.

"What's the plan?" he said.

"The plan is you're my driver. And we've got to be quick."

"Where are we going?"

"Cheltenham. Cirencester is too rammed. I'll never get it done in time."

Ben drove to Cheltenham, as I knew he would, as if in a Grand Prix. There wasn't a single car on the road we didn't overtake, lights flashing, horns blaring, tyres struggling for grip. There wasn't a minute when we weren't on the cusp of a fatal accident. We got there in twenty minutes. It's a forty-minute drive. Heart rate: getting up to a disco 120 bpm.

The shopping was done with equal speed and teenage abandon. I would call out a name as we hurried through shop after shop while Ben would grab anything off the shelf, or clothes rail or display stand, that he thought would suffice, which, as it turned out, wasn't much.

Ben had a fail-safe rule for Christmas shopping. Get the men garden equipment, the women kitchen utensils. Failing that, books. Anything on gardens or cooking. And, if desperation kicked in, clothes. Something you could wear in the garden, or while baking. If all else failed, gift vouchers. From Habitat or Homebase. You had to hand it to him. At least he had a theme.

Cheltenham proved a duffer for his criteria so we headed, via the A419, to Swindon. An hour there and we were done.

"I'm not even sure Uncle Robert has much of a garden," I said, as we drove back at the same speed we'd driven out: warp plus one.

"Fuck him," Ben replied. "With all this kit, he can *grow* one."

Chapter Thirty-five

Christmas Day: a battery house of turkey, Irish fields of roast potatoes, a trough of stuffing, crackers, party hats and indigestion. (Where's the Rennies?)

Not forgetting family arguments. *'Yes another potato, a few more sprouts, ooh yes, and another fizzing family force ten, thanks, lovely.'*

And so it was with us.

I've said it before and I'll say it again, I'm not a big fan of my brothers, particularly Jack. Individually they're manageable. Together, they're unbearable.

Up until lunch, our Christmas had been a rip-roaring success. If it had been a musical it would have run in the West End for three years (with no lottery grants to keep it going). I was even getting on with Caroline, who I pretended was only a friend.

Christmas Eve was so genial, you'd have thought it was a set-up. Vanessa grilled trout that was so delicious it tasted like it had been prepared by the gods. Father opened endless bottles of plummy red wine. And the atmosphere felt as light as a soufflé, made in space.

It was textbook stuff. So flawless, I was expecting a photographer from *Hello!* magazine to come in at any moment and start snapping.

To give you an idea: the dining room was decked out in lush, freshly-cut holly and ivy. There were gold and red candles glowing on the oak table. Crackers crouched on side plates, ready to be pounced on. The silverware shone in immaculate perpendicularity to the place mats. The fire posed like a peacock's tail feathers rendered in the colours of a sunset, hissing and spitting like a red-faced cobra. It was as near perfect as a circle.

If I'd been the photographer, I'd have got Mel to pose next to the fire with a glass of champagne. She wore a black backless dress that made her seem like a perfectly airbrushed Minogue. She was a sweetheart, too. I had no idea how Toby had managed to pull her; he had less charm than a bare-knuckle fighter thirty seconds before he gets into the ring.

So: we ate well, we got happily drunk, and were looking forward to having our guests the next day. I missed Daisy, but that wasn't the point. We'd had an excellent family time. Considering all of the one-parent families on the dole getting through the whole season on half a chicken Kiev and a pot noodle, we had a *sinful* time.

Christmas morning, we were all in the kitchen around ten quaffing ice-cold Veuve Cliquot. Dot popped in to check we were managing and to receive her hamper. While she was with us, we got her to stuff the turkey and slice some vegetables. Have you any idea how long it takes to prepare enough brussel sprouts for twelve? God! Don't bother. Have peas instead. The frozen sort.

By the time Dot left, the hands on the kitchen clock were gunning towards twelve. Some of us had already showered and dressed, others needed to catch up. I was one of those lagging behind but I caught up fast. (Getting dressed, for me, is not an Olympic sport. I find it quite easy. Call it a natural talent.)

Shortly before twelve-thirty, I was outside in my suit, having a fag with Ben and Vanessa. (One of the other things I love about Vanessa is her low maintenance. She can get ready almost as fast as me, which means she's always in the thick of it, unlike some girls who only ever arrive at parties shortly before midnight, not because they're trying to be chic but because they simply can't get there any earlier.)

Unremarkably, it was a foggy morning. No bright sunshine and fresh snow, thus no reason to hang around outside.

"Shall we go to the drawing room and have a gin and tonic?" I suggested.

Ben and Vanessa were in agreement. Ben was as warm in his suit as I, but Vanessa was starting to shiver in her lilac satin dress. He gave her a hug, but she didn't seem happy. Sherlock Holmes style, I detected some tension.

"Come on," I said.

The rest of the troops had had the same idea and were already boozing it up.

"Ah, here come the young 'uns," said Jack, in his patronising way. "Are you being wine-waiter today, Guy?"

I'd been serving the wine since I was about five, so it was kind of a tradition. Jack loved to continue it, knowing it belittled me.

"I am. And if you want any, I should cut the sarcasm."

"Ooh. The travel agent speaks."

"Yes, he does."

The scrunched crisp packet sound of tyres on gravel turned our attention to the large windows. It was my father's brother.

"Toby, would you go and let him in?"

Toby put his drink down and headed outside. I could see him open the doors of the Range Rover and make some comment, making the passengers laugh. Then they all came tumbling out, like toys from a box, clutching bags full of presents.

"Who are they?" said Ben, pointing at the kids.

"John and Lizzie. They're pretty cool. I think they're both still at university. Dad's brother's much younger than he is."

Ten or so minutes later, Angela arrived. She seemed emotional at the anti-presence of my mother right from the start. Pale, drawn, looking like she hadn't been eating properly. At the funeral, she'd cried throughout. It didn't look like she'd stopped crying much since.

We all had a drink and then sat down to eat.

Family gatherings always start off stilted and then, the more everyone drinks, the more clearly the arguments appear on the horizon, like the four horsemen riding in to do their worst.

The argument I fell into with Jack had Peter Warnford at its vortex. He'd been onto my brother in the last couple of days before Christmas, asking him to chivvy me up. Get me to accept his job offer.

As soon as Jack mentioned it, I said, "I'm thinking about it," and that was it. I didn't want to talk about it over lunch. It was then he turned to my father and said, in an exasperated tone, "Can you believe Guy, Dad? He's been offered a job working for this property tycoon. He's going to get double his current salary, a company car, and he still hasn't accepted the offer!"

The table went quiet.

"I'm still thinking about it," I said. "There's no harm in that."

"That's your trouble," Jack said. "All you do is bloody think. You never get on and do anything. That's why you're such a bloody embarrassment to the family."

Well, this was *harsh*.

"I didn't realise I was," I replied stoically.

"Oh come on. You're still driving round in the car Dad gave you on your eighteenth. Your salary is a pittance. You live in a tiny flat in a crappy street. You need to get a grip. Do something with your life."

"Thanks for the vote of confidence."

"Jack's right," said Toby, wading in. "You've got so much potential and you're just not using it. You're a bright lad. Do you think Mum would want you to pass up an opportunity like this?"

"You keep her out of it," I said. "Mum was the one person in this family who took me for who I am as a person, rather than for how much I earned."

"Yeah, but who are you as a person?"

"Someone who isn't going to prostitute himself for the sake of a few thousand quid a year."

"Very noble."

"Mmm…very bohemian."

"Well, this guy Peter Warnford saw something in me," I said. "Otherwise he wouldn't have offered me the job."

"God knows what he saw."

"He saw a guy who got him on a flight no one else would have been able to. A guy who helped him out without getting in a state," my voice was getting louder, "someone who did a good job."

"So why don't you accept his offer?"

"Because in case you hadn't noticed, Jack, the offer's been going up and up. Every time we have a meeting, he offers me something more."

"He isn't going to offer you any more now. He told me so."

"It doesn't matter. I've already decided to take the job. I decided I was going to take it last week. I've been planning to phone him after Christmas. So you'll owe me one. The commission you'll get on that won't be bad, will it?"

"It won't make a huge difference to my salary – maybe buy me a new suit."

"Well, if you don't want it, I'm sure we could bypass you altogether."

"Yeah, just try it, you little worm."

"I could take you on," I said, standing up and lunging across the table, grabbing his tie and yanking him forward.

"Get the hell off me!" he yelled.

My father had had enough of this. Everyone was watching, slack-jawed.

"My God," he said standing up. "Is this any way to behave? Both of you come with me to the kitchen."

We felt like five-year-olds as we followed him out of the dining room. After he'd finished his lecture, I think we felt about three. We'd behaved appallingly and he told us so.

"This is hardly the way to respect the memory of your mother, is it?" he said in summing up. "I suggest you two resolve your differences out here and come back when you've cooled off. But don't you dare be long."

"And what about Caroline?" I fired back. "Would Mum have appreciated her presence?"

"Caroline would have been spending Christmas alone had I not invited her," my father said. "Would you have wanted that?"

"That's not what I meant," I said icily. "What about what Mum would have wanted when she was alive?"

My father reared up to his full height and said with eyes that were liquid fury, "I demand you take that back right now."

"I'm sorry," I croaked, realising I'd gone too far. My father stomped back into the dining room.

Jack and I stood in silence. I lit two cigarettes, giving one to him.

"I shouldn't mention that again, if I was you," he said. "We don't want to ruin Christmas. It's hard enough as it is. I probably shouldn't have gone on at you. We're all tense. Let's drop it, shall we?"

"I think that'd be best."

He took my hand and shook it. "Come on, we'd better go and apologise to everyone else."

The rest of the day went without drama. After lunch we had the presents, then we split into two groups. The young and rebellious in the kitchen, everyone else in the living room. We all drank heavily.

Everyone agreed Jack was out of order. Mel, particularly, was shocked by his behaviour and also apologised for Toby.

"He can be a real tosser," she said in her Aussie accent. "Sometimes he's lovely, then he can be such a div."

Vanessa agreed. "You were right to stand up for yourself," she said. "We all have to live our lives the way we want to."

I kept quiet about what I'd said to Dad.

"Yeah," I agreed. But we all know the truth hurts.

Before I went to bed, I phoned Daisy and left a message on her phone saying how much I loved her and that I needed to speak to her. How much I wanted to speak to her. How much I loved her and missed her...

*****

On Boxing Day, I phoned Daisy again, five times. I wanted to speak to her one last time about the job. Triple-check she was okay with me taking it. I tried again on the twenty-sixth and twenty-seventh. By the twenty-eighth, I couldn't wait any longer. I phoned Peter. He was as warm as usual, delighted to hear from me.

"Have you got something you want to tell me?" he asked, after we'd exchanged pleasantries.

"I want that job," I said. "I want it and I'm going to be damn good at it."

"Excellent. When can you start?"

"As soon as you like."

"You don't have to work notice at the travel agent's?"

"Screw them. They've never done much for me. I'll lose a month's wages but I'm not bothered."

"Okay, fine. I like your balls. I'll tell you what. Why don't you come over to mine New Year's Eve? Bring a few friends with you, girlfriend, whatever. We can celebrate and then the next day we can sort out all the paperwork. That okay with you?"

I told him it was fine.

"We'll look forward to seeing you then."

I put the phone down. A second later, I was hit by a rush of adrenalin. Shit, in a week or so I was going to be driving round in a flash car with a flash job. My career had gone from nought to sixty in the space of, well, a phone call.

I went into the kitchen and broke the good news to my family. Jack had gone back to London, as had Ben, but everyone else was still with us. They all seemed thrilled, especially Vanessa who hugged me tighter than a Koala hugs a eucalyptus. My father even opened a bottle of champagne.

"I'm very proud of you," he said sincerely.

"I'm pretty proud of myself. Cheers."

Chapter Thirty-six

Peter's New Year's Eve party rolled around desperately slowly. It rolled around as slow as a square wheel. I tried to take it easy. You know, not drink too much, get to bed early, get the brain working doing *The Times* crossword, but it wasn't happening. I had to drink loads to sleep. And to drink loads I had to stay up late. The local must have doubled its profits. But it wasn't all wasted time.

One nugget of information I mined in some dark corner of The Duck: badgers are more intelligent than I am. They're more intelligent than us. They're cleverer than humans.

Badgers will not go near the same trap twice. Stuff the cage with as much badger bait as you like but they won't go near it. Not once they've been nipped. Not once they've caught the whiff of danger in their nostrils. Not once they know it's a trap.

I was told this by a rather jovial young man with long hair who works for the Ministry of Agriculture. He told me this as I stood at the bar, ordering up pint six. He loves badgers. He respects them. He adores them. Has he got a girlfriend? No. But he loves something. That's better than nothing.

Talking to this guy, I fell into my most common trap. I ended up staying in the pub far too late and drinking too much. Then I went home and drank some more. Then my father caught me watching an old porn video. Then I burnt a hole in the sofa with my cigarette.

God, I wished I were a badger.

But then again, what I want to know is this. If they're so damn clever, why did I run one over two days ago? Does an intelligent animal lie on a main road gently sunning itself? Does it honestly believe this is a sane place to veg out, take a nap, catch some zzzs? Mmm. Badgers may be bright but they're not infallible.

I'm sure my friend would disagree. He'd say, "Well, it wouldn't get run over twice."

Not true my friend. The poor badger's going to get run over so much, it'll be a tarmac mat. One millimetre high, three-foot by two-foot.

Badger mats. As rare as an amicable phone call to your old boss.

"You're what?" said Kate.

"I'm resigning. As of today."

"You can't do that."

"Yes, I can." It was the 29th December. The end of a year. I could do what the fuck I wanted.

She was unimpressed. They were extremely busy at the Go Away Travel Centre.

"They made you the boss," I said. "You can handle it."

"It's shitty of you not to work your notice."

"I have to take this job right away. The place has hardly done me a load of favours anyway."

"Charming. Yeah, thanks, Guy."

"I'll see you around," I said.

After that phone call, I went back to The Duck and got more drunk. I'd been there since opening. There wasn't much else to do. Daisy wasn't returning my calls and I didn't have work to go to. I was free. And living it up. Well, living down the guilt.

I had a drinking partner in Vanessa. That morning, she and Ben had had another argument and weren't talking.

"Still crap in bed, is he?" I asked her. We were sitting at the bar, the place almost empty.

"No, it's not that."

"So, what's the problem?"

"The problem is he expects me to be chasing around after him in London while I'm on holiday."

"And?"

"And I want to stay down here for a while. Take it easy. Walk a bit, soak up the country air."

"And the country cider," I said, pointing at her half-pint glass.

"Yes. That too."

I scanned the pub briefly. An awful lot of people were drinking cider these days. What was that all about? And there were less smokers too. What was the world coming to?

"Doesn't sound like a major problem to me."

"Well, it is. He can be so clingy."

"He's scared of losing you probably. I would be."

She gave me a kiss on the cheek. "Thanks, Guy."

"Pleasure. Let's have another drink. I've got a favour to ask, actually. Will you come to this New Year party with me?"

Vanessa sipped her cider like it might bite her, gave a little cough and said, charitably, "If you want."

"You can bring Ben."

She gave me a look that indicated she wasn't bothered.

"Yeah. I don't want to go on my own, that's all."

"Need some moral support?"

"Mm. I don't want to go around there looking like nobby-no-mates."

"I can understand that. No, I'd love to come."

"It'll be a good party."

"I'm sure it will. Will he give you the car?"

"I doubt it. He might. Wait and see."

I ordered another pint of Guinness and a cider for Vanessa.

"Cheers," I said. "Here's to a successful New Year."

We fell into silence. I thought back over the year. It had been one of ups and downs, like the flashing LEDs popular on Eighties graphic equalisers. Not altogether good. Not a complete wash-out, either.

Ben ended up coming with us to Peter's party, though there was still tension between him and Vanessa. I was pleased to have him there. I was scared shitless of spending the whole night in Peter's house with Daisy around. I needed a distraction.

"Make sure I don't do anything stupid," I said to them on the drive over. "I mean, we're all going to get drunk but, if I start heading towards her, keep me away. I don't want to blow this."

"You're going to have to be fucking careful for the rest of your life," said Ben. "Talk about putting yourself in a stressful situation."

"I know. Why do you think I ummed and aahed for so long about the job? It'll be cool, though. They say people never notice if their spouse is having an affair."

"No, they don't say that. They say they're the last to know."

"Yeah."

"So if everyone else knows already, you're screwed."

"Give him a break," said Vanessa. "You can be such a pessimist."

"I'm not."

"You are."

I drove on. I didn't want to get involved in their domestics.

The first thing we noticed about Peter's party was that it was the size of Glastonbury (but with no hippy bullshit: the healing fields, scalp massagers, the fire-eaters and bongo beaters, etc.) A marquee the size of a football pitch had been erected in his back garden. Flares had been set up all along the driveway. There were six guys handling the car parking, an entire sixth-form of busty girls running around with glasses of champagne and (unusually) Scotch on the rocks.

"Fuck me," said Ben, as we parked up. "This is mega. Who is this guy, Hugh Heffner?"

"He's my new sponsor. Supplier of my Porsche, payer of my whopping salary, and the person whose wife I'm banging."

"You've got to be insane."

Vanessa tapped me on the shoulder. "That's the last time you say anything like that tonight, mister. Otherwise all of this will disappear, just as fast as it arrived."

She was right. I kept quiet.

Inside, the marquee was buzzing with rich-looking guys and spiffy chicks. A dream world of glamour. There was a jazz band in one corner, in the other some sound technicians were setting up a disco. Down one wall was an enormous buffet. Next to it a bar, not just a table, a bar like you'd find on a beach in the Caribbean. The guy behind it was wearing an Hawaiian shirt and was encouraging guests to indulge in Singapore slings, Long Island ice teas, or a tequila sunrise or two. Next to him, there was a long table full of glasses of wine, champagne and soft drinks. Anything you wanted.

We all picked up a glass of champagne and cruised around a little. There were jugglers, dancers, a magician or two...

"This guy's got some money," said Ben. "Does he have any more vacancies?"

"If he does, I'll let you know. But I won't tell him."

I was trying to be cool, but between you and me, I was feeling overawed. I knew Peter was doing okay, I just hadn't realised he was doing this well. I was getting nervous. To pay for all this he'd need some very good guys working for him. He had me pinned as one of the best of the best. I'd have to work damn hard. But not tonight. Tonight I was going to enjoy myself. Meet a few people, get loaded and party. That's what New Year's Eve is all about.

"Hey Guy," said Vanessa. "There's Daisy."

"Okay, be cool," I said, panicking and not looking; turning

274

the other way in case I gave the game away.

"Where is she?" Ben chipped in. "I want to see what all the fuss is about."

"Don't move. If she wants to come over and talk, she will."

"She looks gorgeous," said Vanessa.

"What's she wearing?"

"It's black and slinky, low-cut, hits the floor. Very Fifties, very elegant. Her hair's brushed back in a wet look, like she's just walked out of the ocean."

"Oh man," said Ben, spotting her. "You're telling me you're sleeping with this woman?"

I didn't reply.

"Shut up," said Vanessa. "Oh wait, she's spotted me. She's coming over."

I turned slowly and was hit by such a dazzling sight I thought I was going to pass out. She looked like an old-school movie star. Totally sexy, total class.

"Hi," she said, kissing Vanessa. "Hi," she said to me, kissing me primly on the cheek. "Hi," she said to Ben. "Who are you?"

"Ben," he replied, and I could see how gob-smacked he was. "Guy's best friend."

"Nice to meet you. So how was everyone's Christmas?"

"Good," I said. I couldn't believe this girl was my 'girlfriend'. She seemed way out of my league standing there in front of me. She seemed out of this world standing there.

"Great. Listen, I have to mingle and schmooze for a while. I'll come and talk to you later."

"Okay," we chorused.

Ben stared at her as she walked away. "You are kidding me. I don't believe you."

"I don't believe me either. But I seem to be developing a certain style, wouldn't you say?"

"Oh my God," said Vanessa, "isn't that a celebrity chef?"

"We've walked into a modern-century *Great Gatsby*," said Ben. "I need another drink."

At the bar, one of the guys from the club came up to us and started talking.

"I hear you're on board, Chamberlain."

"I'm signing-up tomorrow, yeah."

"You won't regret it, my friend. My salary goes up practically every month."

"What exactly do you do for the company?"

"Same as everyone else. Work damn hard. I'll catch up with you guys later. We can talk more then. Whooah. Here's the boss."

And Peter was standing in front of us, looking impeccable in his dinner jacket, a welcoming grin creasing his handsome face.

"Guy," he said, taking my hand and shaking it firmly. "So pleased you could make it. "Are these your guests?"

"This is my sister, Vanessa, and my best friend, Ben, who I went to school with."

"Where's your girlfriend?"

"She couldn't make it."

"Pity. Enjoying yourself?"

"So far we've had fun."

"Excellent. It's not too shabby, is it? Trouble is, I have to keep shaking hands with everyone. I want to talk to you later, Guy, but I'll come and find you. Till then enjoy yourself. And don't worry about getting drunk, we all intend to. Work hard, play hard. That's our policy."

"How very Eighties," Vanessa whispered, as he strode off.

"Hey, the guys in the Eighties didn't do so bad. Come on, let's go and check out the jugglers."

Standing around at Peter's party was a strange experience. The minor celebrities, the beautiful women, the various acts, and Daisy gliding among them looking too glamorous to be the girl I was seeing, made it feel like we were on a film set. On it, but not involved. To handle the alienation, I drank with relentless determination.

Then I spotted someone I knew.

"Ben," I said, pointing. "Look."

He followed my gaze.

"Fuck," he said. "It's the Filipino hooker."

"Filipina," I said. "And she's not a hooker."

"Whatever. Let's go and talk to her."

"She shouldn't be here," I said. "She flew back to the Philippines months ago."

We strode over.

"Hi," I said. It took her a moment to recognise me. She looked drunk, or drugged, and very skinny.

"Hello," she said.

"Why aren't you in Manila?" I asked.

She looked at me with tired eyes.

"I cannot fin job. I hab come back."

"What are you doing here?"

She pointed at a tall, bald man. He was about sixty.

"He gib me money, take care him."

Ben and I looked at each other.

"Oh," we said. "That must be, err...fun."

She rolled her eyes.

"You wan another drink?"

Several hours before the stroke of midnight, Daisy appeared again by my side. She looked even less like my girlfriend now. She looked like the cover of a magazine. She asked if I was enjoying myself.

"I'd be having a better time if it was just you and me in a restaurant somewhere."

"Me too."

We watched the couples dance to the jazz tunes and stood a good distance apart.

"I've got to go in a minute," she said.

"Why?"

"I'm taking the kids up to Norfolk, to Peter's parents. They couldn't make it down this year."

"Why are you going now?"

"It's a good time to go. The roads are clear. I hate all this anyway. It's such bullshit."

"When will I see you again?"

"I'll call you. I've got to go and get changed. Enjoy the party."

I smiled a thin, tired smile. "I'll try," I said. "I'll try."

She kissed me on the cheek and strode off. If Vanessa hadn't caught my arm, I would have followed her.

"It's time you and I had a dance," she said, dragging me towards the floor.

"Where's Ben?"

"He's sitting over there, talking to those girls."

I looked over. "Why's he doing that?"

"He's drunk. Come on, let's move."

Vanessa and I staggered around to several jazz numbers before finding ourselves a table and more champagne. The evening became very hazy then, the fog eventually clearing as an announcement came over the sound system that we should all gather in the garden. There was a minor stampede, the feeling of fresh, icy air and then the countdown.

'Ten, nine, eight....' Everyone was looking up into the darkness. I strained to see Vanessa or Ben. The numbers sounded remote in my head before 'ONE!' An enormous cheer went up and the sky filled with firework flower-beds of light, my ears ringing with what sounded like anti-tank guns, and laughter and more cheers, the crack of champagne bottles going off... and then there was a firm hand on my shoulder.

"Come on," said Peter. "It's time."

I looked into his face. In the light of the fireworks, it looked tired and tense, not the happy face he'd shown me earlier or on our previous meetings. I assumed he'd simply had a bit too much to drink.

He strode away from me and I followed. "Where's your car?" he said over his shoulder. "Which field is it in?"

I pointed to the one we'd parked in. At the gate, Peter asked me for the keys and he gave them to one of the attendants, or bouncers or gate people. The fireworks were still going off, loud and glorious.

"What is it?" he asked.

"It's a Peugeot."

"Colour?"

"Indeterminate, I'm afraid. I think it was black once, before all the dinks and rust got a hold."

"Okay." He scanned the field and spotted it – the only piece of shit there. He then told the burly attendant in the bomber jacket to go and get it. The man strode off purposefully, swinging his torch like a metal detector looking for, er...scrap metal. How apt.

"What are we doing?" I asked.

"We're going to have some fun," said Peter, a wicked glint in his eye. "You and me are going to have some fun. You like fun, don't you? Come on, I know you like fun."

I said I did. I did! But I felt nervous. I'd never seen Peter like this before.

My car arrived almost immediately. The attendant got out and allowed Peter into the driver's seat. I got in the other side.

"These are quite quick, aren't they?" Peter asked.

"Can be."

"Good." He wrenched it into reverse and revved the engine hard. "You don't mind if I drive?"

I blinked.

He backed up fast and did a reverse handbrake turn, spinning us around. Then he sped up the side of the field past the parked cars until we came to a large clearing.

"When I get stressed," said Peter, "I like to do something I enjoy. Do you?"

"I do."

"And I like to drive fast."

He stuck his foot on the accelerator and lifted the clutch. The revs were at seven thousand before he changed up. A hedge came up on us frighteningly fast. He yanked on the handbrake and skidded it around, the back-end breaking out and dragging through the hedge.

"Whooah," I said, laughing (manically), "that was close."

Peter said nothing. He slammed the car back into second, wrestling with the wheel as the car squirmed under torque. At the other end of the field we narrowly missed a stone shed. This was getting out of hand.

"Peter. You're going to wreck my car!"

He slammed on the brakes and selected reverse. In a flash of light from the fireworks, I saw his face. He looked oddly calm. His expression was mean but steady.

He revved the engine again and popped the clutch. We went hurtling backwards, stopping inches from a wall. Both our heads jerked back.

"Peter," I said. "Can we stop now? This is getting dangerous."

He switched the engine off and put his hand into his jacket pocket, bringing out his mobile. "You can come up here now," he said into it and then hung up.

"What's going on?"

"Wait and see."

Soon we saw headlights approaching us across the field. There were two sets. The closest had the inbred look of a tractor, and the low slung set appeared to be a high-powered sports car. The lights came slowly towards us, eventually stopping ten yards away. The tractor was the one I'd seen parked here before. The car – a Porsche. Both drivers stayed in the vehicles, revving the engines.

"There it is," Peter said. "Top speed a hundred-and-forty-eight miles-per-hour. Nought to sixty, I believe, in five-point-eight seconds."

I looked at it. It wasn't brand new but it was in mint condition. Or 'mint' as you, the Chavs, say. You know who you are. And don't give me that look.

"This is the company car we got you," he said, looking right at it.

"Peter, that's fantastic."

"Get out of the car."

I pulled the handle and got out. Peter walked around to my side and led me towards the tractor, until we were halfway between the two vehicles. The tractor was revving hard, smoke billowing from its exhaust into the cold night air, like someone was in the boot smoking a joint the size of a megaphone. Its lights shone straight at us. We had to squint to see.

Peter turned to face me.

"The Porsche was for you," he said. "But not any more. Would you like to know why?"

I stared back at him. My heart was heading south.

He put his hand into his breast pocket and pulled out a mobile phone. An Ericsson, just like the one I had. He scrolled through the messages until he found the one he wanted.

"Listen." He pressed the phone to my ear. It felt extremely cold. It was difficult to hear over the sound of the tractor but I recognised it. It was my voice, drunk, telling Daisy how much I loved her. I didn't move a muscle. Peter eventually removed the handset from my ear.

"Very moving," he said. He was standing perfectly still but I could see the anger bubbling and popping like lava inside him. "Is there anything you want to say?"

I stared at the ground.

"Look at me."

I looked at him. He looked magnificently pissed off. Like the school-master who's just caught you sneaking a drink from his study. But there was something else there. A hurt. A disappointment. He waved the tractor forward. With a massive rev of the engine and a sudden lurch it came, tyres up to my nipple height, covering the distance quickly. Fuck, I thought, I've ended up in the car-crushing scene from *The Italian Job*.

I closed my eyes and waited for the crunch. It didn't come.

The tractor swerved at the last minute. Once I'd opened my eyes, it was already halfway down the field, heading for the gate.

Peter threw me my keys.

"Get out of here," he said, and turned on his heel.

I didn't hesitate. I jumped in, started the car up, and headed off before the tractor driver could change his mind and come back.

Chapter Thirty-seven

Hopes and dreams are all we have. The first day of the New Year and for many days after… I had nothing.

I suppose if there's a lesson to be learnt from my experience, it's this: don't ever imagine you can have it all. You can't.

I wanted to phone Daisy so badly it hurt those first few days. I tried, but I couldn't. She no longer had her mobile and her house in Tetbury (wouldn't you know it) was ex-directory.

I sat next to my phone for almost two weeks, drinking whisky and wondering if she was ever going to phone. I was so drunk most of the time, I began to think I'd dreamt the whole thing.

At the end of January, Ben came down from London. His sole intention: to drag me out of my despair by the ear lobes. The basking in self-pity, like a retiree bobbing in *The Dead Sea*, was no longer permitted.

"Get a fucking grip," were his first words, as he came bowling into my flat, throwing me a can of Grolsch and lunging for the sofa.

"Grolsch?" I asked, looking at his chubby face.

"Time for a change," he said simply. "Time for a life again."

I opened the beer, while Ben told me how many people out there still loved me. How I still wasn't ready to settle down anyway. How the whole experience was doomed from the start.

"Just think. Now you can become a poet or a fucking folk singer. All this torment you've had."

"I can't play the guitar."

"You can't sing either. But now, with all this time on your hands, you could learn. Might as well do something."

I nodded, without much enthusiasm.

"Being morose might be fun for you," Ben sighed, "but it sure is shit on the rest of us. Come back to the planet, man. We miss you."

I stretched my legs out and ran a hand through my hair.

"Tell me what you've been up to," I said eventually.

"Getting on with life," he replied, rather tetchily. "Getting stuff done."

He had a point. But I still wasn't seeing it.

*****

At work again, after a leave of absence (the doctor signed me off with depression. It was the closest the medical dictionary came to heart-fucking-broken), the rise and fall of each day slowly became more bearable.

I concentrated on selling flights. And lots of them. I also took a well-earned rest from the booze. It was refreshing, waking in the morning without having to first poke my nose over the top of the duvet to allow it to sniff out how bad the hangover would be. Even Kate forgave me for letting her down.

"You were sick," she sympathised. "If you hadn't been, I would have chopped you off at the ankles. That is, if you'd dared to walk past the shop."

Being the boss had done nothing to calm her. Neither had remaining valiantly single.

In those first sober evenings of January I decided that, to banish the obsession from my life, I needed to detail every thought I'd had about Daisy. Write them down in a notebook, then close the book forever.

I bought a nice A5 pad from WHSmith and started scribbling. I won't bother telling you exactly what I wrote. You know most of it already. Surprisingly, I didn't mention sex, or her body, that much. It was the essence of her that I'd fallen in love with. And it was that essence, like a strong perfume, or skunk spray, which proved difficult to rub off.

Two A5 pads and a month later, I thought I was nearing completion. It took another two trips to the stationers before I was done, but when I was I felt relief. I laid out all five volumes in my bottom drawer (underneath the porn, for this was far more private, far more intimate) and closed the drawer.

After a week or two, the temptation to read back my thoughts subsided and I finally began to live again. I started reading (and not just *Hello!*), keeping my flat tidy, taking pride in my life. Looking to the future.

*****

One night, towards the beginning of April and the hopeful, hormonal start of spring, like a teenage boy preparing to go to his first dance, I glanced out of my bedroom window. The sunset was like a Seventies kaftan: swirls of pink, orange and red, overlaid with smoky, white clouds. The birds were tuning up for evensong, the road traffic was muted, mollified. Nature was showing off, but it deserved to. It had been a shitty winter of greys, blacks and dark, dark blues. It was time to shine in the season's new, vibrant colours. Amber, topaz, sunburst yellow, sky blue, scarlet and white.

I stood up and looked down at my neighbour's garden. It had grown considerably in recent weeks. The shrubs were stretching up like they'd recently learned yoga and the trees had turned green with envy. All this had happened in the long days when I'd been too preoccupied to notice. The lawn was now ankle-high with grass.

As I pondered this, my neighbour appeared below, hefting a wheelbarrow full of twigs and branches that he'd been pruning off his trees. Making a careful pyramid of paper in the centre of the lawn, he then criss-crossed the wood over it, added a dash of petrol, and flicked a lit match onto it. A lively cocktail.

The paper burst into life like a pipe bomb, the flames roasting, then burning the dark wood, turning it grey and crimson.

My neighbour seemed to have grown over the winter period. He'd shaved his beard. Now he looked approachable and, with a sudden surge of neighbourly goodwill, I opened the window in my bedroom and called down, "Fancy a coffee?"

He looked up, taking a moment to focus on me.

"I mean. We've been neighbours forever…"

"That'd be very nice, young man."

"I'll bring it over to you."

I ducked back inside, put the kettle on in the kitchen, and went for a quick piss. You don't want to get chatting and then have to fuck off because of a full bladder. Might appear rude.

Five minutes later, I was shaking a hand as hard and weathered as a rhino's arse, and looking into a face that crinkled with ease into a picture of good-natured chumminess.

After the initial chat about the bonfire was out of the way, Fred (for that was his name) started to tell me about his job as a gardener at Cirencester Park.

"I thought you looked pretty handy with the hedge clippers," I quipped.

"I like to think I can do my job," his Gloucestershire accent pronouncing the word 'jarb'. "I do work for private gardens, too."

"Oh great," I said. "Maybe you could help my dad out. He lives out in Southrop."

He nodded, scratching at his temple. "I know people out there. What's his name?"

"Amazingly, same as mine. Chamberlain."

Fred raised an eyebrow at this.

"Chamberlain?" he said, poking at the fire with stabbing motions. "I know a Chamberlain over in Tetbury."

"We're all over," I said. "Like a bad case of chicken pox."

Fred nodded pensively. "What was his name now?"

I stared into the fire.

"Hmm...something beginning with 'G'."

"Not Graham?" I joked.

"Yes, Graham."

Well, you can imagine how that news felt. Hit me like a bazooka. I checked details with him for several minutes before concluding it must be my uncle, Dad's Houdini-like brother.

"You'll have to excuse me," I said. "I've got to go and make a call."

I rushed upstairs to my flat to call my father. As I reached for the phone, it started to ring. I snatched it off the receiver.

"Hello!" I almost yelled.

"Hello," said a familiar, incredibly sexy voice.

My heartbeat topped 200. Instantly.

"Oh shit," I replied out-loud.

"Can we talk?" the voice said.

"We can," I gasped.

And then I listened while she said what she needed to say. And at the end of it, I knew that she was right.

I smiled, and replaced the receiver.

It was going to be an amazing summer.

Legend Press

Independent Book Publisher

This book has been published by vibrant publishing company Legend Press. If you enjoyed reading it then you can help make it a major hit. Just follow these three easy steps:

1. Recommend it
Pass it onto a friend to spread word-of-mouth or, if now you've got your hands on this copy you don't want to let it go, just tell your friend to buy their own or maybe get it for them as a gift. Copies are available with special deals and discounts from our own website and from all good bookshops and online outlets.

2. Review it
It's never been easier to write an online review of a book you love and can be done on Amazon, Waterstones.com, WHSmith.co.uk and many more. You could also talk about it or link to it on your own blog or social networking site.

3. Read another of our great titles
We've got a wide range of diverse modern fiction and it's all waiting to be read by fresh-thinking readers like you! Come to us direct at www.legendpress.co.uk to take advantage of our superb discounts. (Plus, if you email info@legendpress.co.uk just after placing your order and quote 'WORD OF MOUTH', we will send another book with your order absolutely free!)

Thank you for being part of our word-of-mouth campaign.

info@legendpress.co.uk
www.legendpress.co.uk